the mud sisters

Edie Claire

Copyright © 2012 by Edie Claire

Cover art by pbj creative studios.

This book is a work of fiction. The names, characters, places, and incidents are products of the writer's imagination or have been used fictitiously and are not to be construed as real. Any resemblance to persons, living or dead, actual events, locales or organizations is entirely coincidental.

All Rights Are Reserved. No part of this book may be used or reproduced in any manner whatsoever without written permission from the author.

Dedication

This novel is dedicated to all my crazy, big-hearted, fun-loving friends in the Mayfield High School classes of the early 1980s, in loving memory of John Edward Elder (December 15, 1962–July 5, 2012), who epitomized the best in all of us.

Chapter One

The atmosphere in the emergency department waiting room hung thick with a volatile mixture of anxiety, boredom, and aggravation. A dozen people huddled in plastic chairs with their coats still on, warding off the icy gust that struck them with each opening of the automatic doors to the parking lot. A small boy ran unchecked from one end of the room to the other, strewing orange cracker crumbs like a jet trail and chortling each time his leaps onto the doormat brought another blast of snow swirling inside. The sound of a television no one was watching droned on like a persistent mosquito, punctuated by the occasional hooting cheer of a studio audience.

From her position in the staff area behind the triage window, Teagan surveyed the crowd with sympathy. Everyone hurried to emergency rooms; yet for any whose condition fell short of dire, time slowed to a crawl once they arrived. She moved up to the window to speak to the little boy just as an elderly woman grasped him by the arm and sat him forcibly down beside her. Several wan faces looked up hopefully toward the new figure behind the glass, eager for any sign that their deliverance had come.

Teagan was sorry to disappoint. But she was not a doctor; she was not even a nurse. She was a social worker, and a rookie one at that. Lighting a fire under the ample rear end of Dr. Sam "Shoot-the-Bull" Sorenson, whose legendary sluggishness was responsible for this particular backlog, was not within her job description.

Which was a shame, because she would have enjoyed it.

"Teagan?"

The charge nurse who had summoned her appeared in the hallway outside the triage room, rolling a clanking piece of medical equipment across the tile floor. Teagan turned from the window and approached her. "*Another* Jane Doe," the older woman said with exasperation, cocking her head in the direction of room number three.

Teagan's eyebrows rose. In the four months she had worked at Northside General, this was the first unidentified female patient she had heard of, much less encountered personally.

"She just got back from radiology," the nurse continued as she moved. "Severe head injury, hypothermia, probably a broken arm. Domestic violence, most likely. She's been alert the last hour or so, but she doesn't know who she is or what's going on, and of course she's got no ID."

The woman's face and voice were expressionless, but her unspoken message was clear: *Some idiot woman got mixed up with some he-man nut job and nearly got herself killed. Now go figure out who she is so registration can get the paperwork moving!*

Teagan knew better than to ascribe the nurse's apparent lack of empathy to unkindness. She had seen the same woman cry bitter tears over an elderly assault victim just yesterday. Facing the continual stream of human tragedy an inner-city ER produced was tough on a caregiver; the tendency to judge, a common defense mechanism. If, by any convolution of logic, the suffering could be considered the patient's own fault… Well, at least it wasn't yours.

Teagan cast a glance at the room in question. "How was she brought in? Was there anyone with her?"

"Nope. She came alone, by ambulance," the nurse answered, opening the door across the hall and whisking the wheeled contraption over its threshold. "Some passerby found her rolled in a blanket and dumped in Riverview Park, unconscious. She's lucky she didn't freeze to death. The police were here and left, but they'll be back again now that she's awake."

"Do you think she's up to talking with me?"

The nurse let out a snort. "Oh, she can talk, all right."

Translation: *Look out. She's hell on wheels.*

The nurse released the door. It clipped the trailing corner of the cart with a bang, then clicked shut.

Teagan clutched her clipboard with its empty patient intake form and let a shy smile escape her lips. She had been at work only half an hour this morning and had already been accosted with two supposed "emergencies," both of which were, in her opinion, trivial administrative issues. The woman in room three, on the other hand, was exactly the kind of challenge for which she had left her job in corporate HR.

Why she found such work stimulating, God only knew. Her husband joked that her passion for the underdog was a compulsion. Pathological or not, one master's degree in social work and over $30,000 shelled out to the University of Pittsburgh later, here she was.

She reached for the handle, rapped her knuckles lightly on the door, and swung it open.

A woman about Teagan's own age lay on the bed, her head and one arm wrapped in gauze, her face blotched and puffy. Her eyelids were closed, but not as if she were sleeping. The woman appeared to be squeezing her lids shut purposefully, like a small child attempting to disappear.

Teagan took a few steps inside the room. "Hello," she began warmly. "My name is Teagan. I'm with hospital social services. I understand that you've had a head injury, and it's left you a little disoriented. I'm sorry."

The eyes remained closed; the reply, sarcastic. "A little disoriented? That's rich. Try completely clueless. Try totally freaked out!"

Teagan's breath caught in her throat. She moved closer. *That voice.*

She knew it. She had heard it before. Husky, yet silky. Inarguably feminine. She took a fresh look at the unmade-up, swollen face on the pillow, and her heart skipped a beat.

Long buried images raced through her brain. Laughter. Sun. Water. Shining circles of gold…

She folded limply, dropping her weight onto the foot of the mattress, her gaze transfixed by the small face on the pillow.

The patient's eyes flew open. "What are you staring at?" she asked irritably, grasping at her blankets. "What am I to you people, some kind of freak show?"

Teagan had seen eyes like that only once in her life. Irises of topaz. Uniformly golden, not nearly dark enough to call brown. The color was rare.

"What *is* your problem?" the patient demanded testily.

There could be no doubt. No matter how long it had been.

Teagan's voice came out a croak.

"*Jamie?*"

Chapter Two

Summer, Indian Lake, Pennsylvania, 1997

Teagan couldn't tell where she was. She knew she had made a mistake, that something bad had happened. She just wasn't sure what.

She couldn't see. Blackness surrounded her. A numbing cold crept into her lean, twelve-year-old body, seeping deeper and deeper toward her rapidly beating heart. Why couldn't she move? Why couldn't she think straight?

Something was missing. Something she needed, something she had to have. Its absence loomed larger and larger, growing until the need itself assaulted her—an insidious, clawing vacuum that sucked painfully deep inside her chest.

Air.

She was underwater.

She was drowning.

Panic seized her, but the rush of adrenaline proved no use. Where was the surface? She had no sense of direction, no sense, even, of her own body. She couldn't feel her limbs. Her chest felt as though it would implode, as if her ribs would at any second collapse inward and crush her thudding heart. The compulsion to act, to *do something*, was fierce—pushing her, driving her, begging her. Yet there was nothing she could do.

Nothing.

She would die.

A sharp pain tore at her scalp, and the contact jogged some dormant part of her brain. All at once she was aware of her arms and legs—they were being squeezed, pulled, tugged. Each sensation was painful, but none could distract from the agony that plagued her chest. Her lungs were flaming, bursting, boiling. A curtain of light accosted her still-closed eyes. Cool air prickled her skin.

She heard a voice.

"Teag! Wake up! If you don't wake up and breathe right now, I swear to God, I'll kill you! Do you hear me? *Wake up!*"

There was water inside her. Flooding her. In her chest, her throat. It rose within her like a tidal wave, and involuntarily she clenched her body into a ball and released the fluid onto the ground in a spasm of gagging and coughing.

The voice swore.

Teagan's eyes opened.

Another girl leaned in close above her, her soft face pale with fright, her ordinarily light-blond hair dripping brown with lake water. "Are you all right?" Jamie asked, her voice cracking with emotion.

Teagan nodded. She coughed some more.

Jamie sat back on the muddy bank with a flop. She dropped her head between her knees, then turned back to Teagan with an accusatory look. "You scared the crap out of me! What *was* that? What were you trying to do?"

Teagan looked into her friend's bizarre golden eyes. When combined with a smile, they could be strikingly beautiful. But when Jamie was angry, their color could be off-putting, almost creepy.

Teagan shivered, though not from fear. She was cold. "It was supposed to be a back flip," she explained, teeth chattering.

"Back flip my ass," Jamie retorted, pushing the drooping straps of her faded, too-large swimsuit back on top of her thin shoulders. She was breathing as heavily as Teagan was, and her voice was still unsteady. "All you did was twist around and slam your back against the edge of the dock. You fell into the water like a rock, and you didn't come up again. Were you *trying* to give me a heart attack?"

Teagan didn't answer. She wasn't used to making mistakes, especially not dangerous ones. This wasn't supposed to happen.

Jamie's eyes turned distant, and her voice dropped. "I couldn't see anything in that water, Teagan. You were at the bottom, just lying there. If I hadn't felt your hair with my feet, I might never have—" her voice broke off.

Teagan tensed. She didn't want to think about it.

"You were limp when I pulled you out," Jamie continued, her tone angry again. "I didn't even know if you were breathing. I just started jerking you around and then you coughed… Like I know how to do mouth-to-mouth! I don't know any of that stuff. You could have *died* just now! Do you know that?"

Teagan's coughs were subsiding, but her lungs still burned. She was dizzy. "I just got the breath knocked out of me for a second," she insisted. "I would have been all right."

Jamie's eyes widened, then narrowed to a glare. "Yeah, you'd have been *fine!*" She stood with a jerk, smacking ineffectually at the mud-smeared seat of her swimsuit. "Whatever. I'm out of here."

Teagan's heart began to race anew. "No!" she pleaded, squelching what was left of her ego. Despite her show of bravado, she was scared witless; she didn't want to be alone. "Don't go. My lungs are on fire and my shoulders are killing me—that really hurt."

Jamie's gaze met hers, and Teagan's face begged silently for understanding. Yes, she had been bragging all summer about the lifesaving course she had aced last spring. Yes, she had probably been really obnoxious about it; and yes, Jamie had every right to be miffed now. But Teagan was *supposed* to be the one doing the saving—not nearly drowning herself trying to show off!

The whole thing was mortifying.

Jamie looked back at her friend's humbled visage, and her expression softened.

Teagan's shoulders slumped with relief. Jamie *did* understand.

They had known each other only since the beginning of the summer. But while most girls their age whiled away their vacation listening to music and giggling about boys, the two of them had quickly discovered a shared thirst for adventure—the desire to explore, to imagine. They had investigated every inch of Indian Lake in Teagan's grandfather's canoe, all the while dreaming up tall tales of jungles, cannibals, and love-struck Polynesian princes. They had other similarities, like being raised by single mothers, but they had spent precious little time dwelling on that.

They had simply been having fun.

Until now.

Jamie turned and knelt on the ground beside Teagan. "Sit up a second," she commanded. "Let me look at your back."

Teagan scooted around in the mud.

Jamie blew out a breath. "You scraped your shoulders up pretty bad. You need about half a box of bandages, and you're filthy besides. You want to go to my house? It's closer."

"No," Teagan said quickly. The Renicks were nice people, but a bit too attentive for her tastes. Jamie's foster mother would probably coat half Teagan's body in iodine and then the foster father would insist on driving her back to her grandparents' house—which would only call more attention to the fact that she had done something monumentally stupid. She would much rather suck it up and slink back home unnoticed. "We can go to my house. I can paddle okay."

"Of *course* you can," Jamie retorted, rolling her eyes. Nevertheless, she crossed to the beached canoe, shoved it into the water, and held it for Teagan to step into. "You'd better not pass out on me once we get on the lake," she warned. "Because I'm not saving your sorry butt again— once a day's enough."

Teagan settled into the front of the boat with a wince. She

was still light headed. Paddling was going to hurt something fierce, but it was better than walking the long way around the shoreline.

"Your back looks awful," Jamie commented shortly, pushing them off into the water.

Teagan didn't answer. She picked up a paddle and started to push, then nearly dropped it. Her shoulders felt as though someone had tried to rip both arms out of their sockets. She pulled her elbow tightly back to her side.

The paddle came out of her hand as Jamie grabbed it and laid it down in the boat. "Just sit still," she commanded, pushing her own paddle expertly into the water. "We'll get there some year."

Teagan stared straight ahead over the lake. It was a haul back to her house. Jamie would be exhausted, doing all the work herself.

She thought you were going to die.

The August sun reflected hot off the water, and the sticky air was devoid of any breeze. Still, Teagan shivered. She had forgotten how recently Jamie had lost her mother, the only family she knew. Had she been thinking of that when Teagan disappeared under the water? Had she been afraid that her new best friend, too, would never come back?

A chill swept down Teagan's spine. The biting coldness cut deep.

"Jamie?" she asked quietly, not turning around.

"Yeah?" came the answer. Terse. Guarded. Still out of breath.

"Thanks."

For several seconds, the only sound Teagan could hear was the lapping of the paddle and the far-off honks of some agitated water fowl. She stole a glance over her shoulder, just long enough to see Jamie's jaws clenched tight, her face red, her eyes brimming with moisture.

Teagan looked straight ahead again.

"You're welcome," Jamie answered.

Chapter Three

The present

Northside General's latest "Jane Doe" stared down at her hands. They looked pale. Her left arm was swathed in gauze; for some reason she couldn't lift it. She picked up the small pocket mirror that had appeared on the mattress next to her and gazed at her reflection. She saw a puffy, tired face with funky yellow eyes and bandages for hair. She laid the mirror back down.

It was a bad dream. There was no other explanation. How else could she be magically transported to a place where she knew no one, not even herself? *She* was real, she was sure of that. It was everything else that was screwed up.

She didn't know where she was supposed to be. She only knew it wasn't here. She wanted to get up and leave, but her body was too weak to walk and she had no idea where to walk *to*.

Why not? What was wrong with her?

Her heart began to pound. She couldn't defend herself here; she wasn't in control. She was as vulnerable as a newborn kitten, and there wasn't a damn thing she could do about it.

Through the narrow window in the door of her room, she could see an endless stream of men and women in cotton uniforms meandering slowly past—talking, scribbling, rolling around various carts, wheelchairs, and poles—all acting as though she didn't exist. What else were they doing that was so important? Why couldn't anyone explain to her what the hell was going on?

The door latch clicked. Someone was coming in. But as the unlocked door began to swing slowly open, Jamie felt more alarm than relief. "Who are you?" she demanded. "What is it you want?"

The female visitor paused in the doorway. She looked as if she were in her mid twenties. Her dark blond hair was pulled into a pony tail, and her clothes were casual—not a uniform. She wasn't magazine-cover pretty, but she had a charismatic, appealing face with high cheekbones, a perky, slightly upturned nose, and large dark eyes. Both her smile and her manner were guileless, and at the sight of her, Jamie relaxed a little.

"My name is Teagan," the woman answered, her tone soothing. "And I don't want anything. I'm just checking back to see if you have any more questions—if there's anything else I can help you with."

Jamie's brow furrowed. The woman seemed to be suggesting they had talked before, which was ludicrous. "Any *more* questions? What are you talking about?"

Teagan smiled knowingly, then stepped closer.

Jamie tensed. The idea that a stranger could know more about her than she herself did was maddening.

"I've been here several times," the woman explained, pulling up a stool. She sat down near Jamie's head, making their eyes level. "But you shouldn't worry about not remembering that. You've had a head injury, and it's affecting your ability to keep things straight. The neurologist says that most of the confusion you're experiencing now should be gone in a matter of hours. Until it is, you have nothing to worry about. You're perfectly safe here. I promise."

Jamie bit at her lower lip. The explanation made a weird sort of sense. Her lip was already sore. "I have a head injury," she repeated.

The stranger nodded. What had she said her name was? Jamie couldn't remember, but the woman's desire to help seemed sincere. Despite her desperately out-of-style sweater and ill-fitting khaki slacks, she had a strength about her—as in whatever she promised, she intended to make happen.

It was a trait Jamie could appreciate.

"You're in Northside General Hospital, in Pittsburgh. You were brought into the emergency department last night, and you're still here. But we'll be moving you to a nicer room up on the floor soon."

A horrific thought dawned. "This isn't… like… a mental hospital, is it?"

To Jamie's surprise, the woman chuckled. It was a melodious chuckle; one that lit up her whole face.

"No, Jamie, it's not a mental hospital. You're as sane as I am. Not that that's such great reassurance!"

Jamie eyed her curiously. The woman was acting, surely, as if they knew one another. But before she could puzzle over the thought, a new one replaced it.

"What did you call me?"

"I called you Jamie. That's your name. Does it seem familiar to you?"

Jamie considered. The name didn't sound wrong, but she wasn't certain it was right, either. "I don't know."

"Don't worry about it," the woman repeated. "As the neurologist explained to me, right now you're dealing with two separate handicaps. You can't pull up memories you've laid down in the past—which is why you can't remember your name or how you got injured. But you're also having trouble making new memories, which is why every time I come in here, you ask me who I am again."

Jamie's eyes narrowed with concentration. She should know the name; she had heard it only seconds ago. But it wasn't there. "What is your name?"

"It's Teagan. Teagan Hansen. I work for the hospital as a social worker."

Jamie felt a sudden wave of disappointment—a disappointment she didn't understand. She looked quickly down at her hands.

She's just doing what she's paid to do.

"What's wrong?" Teagan asked immediately. Her skills of perception were impressive. But Jamie did not respond.

Teagan made a joking guess. "What, you don't like social workers?"

Hell, no, I don't!

The voice rang out so loud and clear in Jamie's otherwise worthless brain that she fought an urge to laugh at the absurdity of it. She did not know her own name, but she knew beyond a shadow of doubt that she hated social workers?

How helpful. Thank you, brain.

Still, she was fairly sure it wasn't Teagan's occupation, per se, that had disappointed her.

Jamie cleared her throat and—perhaps uncharacteristically?—answered the original question with honesty. "It's just that I had the feeling from the way you were talking that maybe you… *knew* me. Before the hospital, I mean."

Teagan was quiet a moment, and Jamie looked up at her. The social worker's face shone with something peculiar—a hopefulness, an excitement. "You thought that maybe we had met before?" Teagan asked. "Do you know where that impression came from?"

Jamie attempted, once again, to concentrate. She tried to remember if she had ever met Teagan—searching her mind for any inkling of the other woman's persona in a stray image, a sound, even an impression. But there was nothing. "It's just that I thought you acted like you knew me," she said dismissively.

She did not understand, much less care to explain, how desperately she had wanted that to be true. She didn't *want* to need anyone. She might be vulnerable at the moment, but that was temporary. She would get it back: her autonomy, her independence, her capableness.

She had to. It was all she had.

Teagan was still smiling at her. But the social worker's soft brown eyes seemed melancholy. "We have met before, Jamie," she said quietly. "That's how I know your name. But it was a long time ago. You might not remember me even if you didn't have a head injury."

Jamie stared back. She could see no reason for the social worker to lie, but the statement lacked candor. Teagan was hiding something.

Of course. Just because they had met didn't mean they were friends, did it? They could have worked together; they could have squabbled over a seat on the bus. Or more likely, over some guy.

You don't have any friends.

Suddenly, sharply, Jamie felt bone tired. "I'm sorry, Teagan. I don't remember anything about you."

The social worker's answering smile was a surprise, even if it did seem forced. "Oh yes, you do. You just said my name! That's the first time since you got here that you've remembered anything for more than about five seconds."

The social worker rose suddenly, then took a step back. "Try not to worry, Jamie. It may not seem like it, but you *are* improving. By this evening, your short-term memory will be in much better shape, even if your past is still a blur."

The words, unexpectedly, struck Jamie like a blow. The present was bad enough, but "the past" bore potential for a whole other realm of horror.

"How did I get hurt?" she blurted, realizing for the first time how little she knew of her true predicament—of the bigger picture outside this hospital room. "What happened to me?"

Teagan's eyes flashed with distress, but her voice remained calm. "I don't really know."

The effort was so lame, it was pitiable. Jamie muttered an expletive under her breath. "You know, for a social worker, you really suck at lying. Now, what happened to me? Was it some kind of accident?"

Teagan hesitated.

"I can tell it's something bad. I'm not stupid!" Jamie insisted. "Just tell me the truth. I have the right to know, don't I?"

Teagan exhaled with a sigh. "I wish I could tell you

exactly what happened, but the truth is, I *don't* know. You were found alone. A passerby noticed that you were hurt and called an ambulance."

"A passerby? Where was I?"

"In Riverview Park. It's a city park not far from here."

Jamie's agitation grew. "Well, what was I doing? Sitting on a bench, sleeping in a car, what?"

"I don't know all the details," Teagan answered. "I just know that you didn't have any identification on you at the time, which is why you don't have any family members or friends here with you yet. But I gave the police your name, and they're working on locating them right now."

Ha! There's no one.

"I'm afraid you have a fractured wrist as well," Teagan continued, seemingly anxious to change the subject. "It needs surgery. You'll probably be scheduled for that tomorrow. By then your head should be much clearer."

Jamie looked down at her bandaged right arm, but could muster little concern for it. If her bones were broken, she must be on some very good painkillers, because she couldn't feel a thing. At least not in her arm.

In her gut, she felt plenty.

The images swirled in her mind in an uneasy pool, gray and smoldering. A head injury. A broken arm. Abandoned in a city park with no ID. It could have been a simple mugging. But the raw feelings raging inside her suggested otherwise.

"Teagan," she said deliberately, confirming the name again.

"Yes?"

"This is a safe place?"

"Very. We have tight security for assault victims. In your case, until we know more about what happened to you, anyone wanting to visit you or even asking for information about you will have to go through the police." Teagan paused, then lowered her voice. "Are you afraid of someone in particular?"

The sense of foreboding in Jamie's mind refused to settle. The more clear her head became, the darker her thoughts turned. She swallowed, but didn't answer the question. Her every instinct was to deny her fear. To hide it, as if the threat that plagued her could smell it like a carnivore.

"No. Nothing in particular."

The last part, at least, was true.

Teagan didn't press. "The police will be back soon to talk to you, but the doctor has explained that you may not be able to answer all their questions. We don't want you to feel pressured."

Lost in thought, Jamie said nothing. Was she afraid of the police, too? No, she didn't seem to be.

She only hated social workers. And perhaps, judges…

"Jamie?" Teagan called from the doorway. "Is there anything else I can do for you now?"

Jamie couldn't look at her. She was tired, and something dangerously close to tears seemed to be pooling up behind her eyes. But tears were not acceptable.

Tears were *never* acceptable.

"I need to get this stupid brain working again," she snapped. "And I need to get the hell out of here. I need to go—."

Home. It was the obvious word to complete her sentence. But somehow, it didn't seem right.

She left the statement hanging. Her eyes closed against the storm.

Teagan's footsteps moved away. The door opened, then softly closed again.

Chapter Four

The sun was just setting, leaving the dimmest glimmer of light to reflect off the still-falling snow, when Teagan pushed the last column of accumulated white stuff down to the foot of her driveway. She was in the process of steering it into the pile around her mailbox when the rumble of a marginal muffler alerted her to the approach of her mother's wood-paneled PT Cruiser.

Teagan moved quickly to the other side of the mailbox. It was only a wooden post, but it was better than nothing.

She watched, jaws clenched, as Sheryl Raye slammed on the Cruiser's brakes well in advance of the driveway, sending the car into a fishtail on the slick coating of fresh flakes that overwhelmed the salt on the road. The car moved in graceful slow motion before coming to rest just short of the mailbox, facing the opposite direction. Sheryl raised a gloved hand from the steering wheel and waved merrily at Teagan as she redirected the car into the drive, then parked at the point closest to the house's front door, blocking the garage.

"Teagan, honey," she called as she hustled out, her coat held tightly around her, "come on inside with me! You must be freezing." Then, without waiting for a response, she jogged up the walk and darted through the front door.

Teagan sighed into her scarf, propped her shovel against the mailbox, and followed. By the time she had shaken the snow off her boots and hung up her wraps to dry, Sheryl had already started tea.

"Do you want regular or herbal?" Sheryl called from the kitchen, her voice a sing-song. "Cinnamon Allspice is perfect for this time of year."

"Regular's fine," Teagan answered, moving into the

dining room and dropping into a chair. "Thanks."

The ancient kitchen was a galley style, separated from the dining room by a doorway on one end and a small serving window midway along the wall. Catching glimpses of her mother buzzing comfortably around inside it filled Teagan with both a sentimental warmth and a tiresome dread. The warmth came from fond childhood memories of one of Sheryl's few exemplary parenting skills — cosseting her daughter with food. The dread came from the obvious reason for the visit, which Teagan had no need to ask. There was only one reason Sheryl ever stopped by a relative's house unannounced.

"So," Teagan began, anxious to get the debriefing process underway. "What's happening?"

Sheryl stopped buzzing and leaned her warmly clad yet perfectly tanned body against the doorway. She was an attractive woman. Never heavy, yet far too curvy to be called thin, she wore her thick, wavy hair long and bleach-blond, in contrast to her large, dark eyes. The most recent in a dynasty of artificial breasts, in concert with Sheryl's own natural vivaciousness, completed a picture that oozed sex appeal. As a child, Teagan had thought her mother beautiful. As a teenager, she had thought her cheap. As an adult, she simply thought of her as Sheryl. With only a sixteen-year difference in their ages, Sheryl, now forty-two, had always been more of a sister to Teagan than a mother.

"It's over," Sheryl announced. "I thought maybe Stephen and I really had something, but I guess I was wrong."

Teagan nodded solemnly. "He went back to the ex wife, then?"

Sheryl confirmed the tragedy with her signature expression — the pending cry. She was an expert at forming tears that were visible to an observer, yet never actually spilled forth to smear her mascara.

"I'm sorry, Mom," Teagan offered, projecting as much sympathy as she could muster. "But I'm sure it's for the best. You'll find someone else soon enough."

Teagan was, indeed, quite sure of it. For as long as she could remember, her mother's life had been a quest for the perfect man—the perfect husband who would sweep her off her feet and whisk her away into the sunset. But though Sheryl had been swept and whisked many times, she never seemed to stay where she was put. When she married for the first time her daughter was only six, but even at that tender age Teagan had no expectation of permanency. She had accepted that first stepfather, and later his two successors, with the same cheerful nonchalance as she would an ice cream sundae. It would be fun while it lasted, but there was no point getting attached.

Sheryl withdrew her tears with a nod. "So, where's that gorgeous husband of yours?"

Teagan suppressed a smile. Her mother always brought the conversation around to Eric eventually.

"And why were you shoveling the driveway?" Sheryl continued. "Isn't that supposed to be the man's job?"

Teagan looked at her watch. "Eric will be home any minute. As for the driveway, don't be sexist. I needed the exercise." Remembering the reason for her burst of nervous energy, her gaze returned to her mother. Teagan didn't ordinarily discuss hospital business outside the hospital, but her own reunion with Jamie seemed a personal matter. "You'll never guess who was brought into the ER last night. This morning I—"

Sheryl's face paled. "Not Derrin!"

Teagan blinked. It took several seconds for her to recall the man in question—an erstwhile flame of Sheryl's deposed for repeated DUI convictions. "No," she answered coolly. "A friend of mine from ages ago. Remember that girl I met at the lake that I liked so much? She was a foster child of the Renicks—the family who used to own that big gray house on the peninsula across from Grandma and Grandpa's place. Her name was Jamie."

The tea kettle whistled. Sheryl poured the steaming water as she considered. "You mean that summer I was in

California?"

Teagan nodded. Carl, the memorable bisexual painter her mother had married during her brief artistic period, had invited both Sheryl and Teagan to spend that particular summer in San Diego, enjoying a long honeymoon with his four Lhasa Apsos in a beach condo owned by his "best friend" Stan. The lure of a West Coast vacation had been strong, but Teagan, not blind to the red flags, had opted instead for Indian Lake, where she could frolic under the caring, yet not particularly watchful eye of her grandparents. Sheryl had followed in mid August, separation papers in hand.

"Yes," Teagan answered. "I was really disappointed when we lost touch. When I saw her again, I couldn't believe it."

"Did she remember you?" Sheryl asked with feigned interest as she set Teagan's cup of tea down on the table, then returned to lean against the doorway. She bounced her own teabag up and down in her cup, as if to hurry the process along.

"No. But she doesn't remember anything at the moment. She has a concussion." Teagan's tone turned grim. "I don't know where she's been all this time, but I have a feeling her story isn't pretty. Her injuries were no accident."

Sheryl stopped dunking. She turned and faced her daughter with widened eyes. "She's not that woman from the park, is she? The one that somebody beat up and left in the snow?"

Teagan straightened in her chair. "Where did you hear that?"

"On the news! They said a jogger found her. It freaked me out—I used to walk through there all the time when we lived in the city. What do you think happened to her?"

Teagan sighed. The hospital hadn't released any information about Jamie to the media, but police scanners could be easily monitored. The unfortunate result of such publicity was that whoever had hurt Jamie would now know that she had been found and taken to Northside General. They would also know that she was still alive.

"My guess," Teagan answered tentatively, "would be domestic violence. It didn't seem like a random attack."

Sheryl's lips pursed. "No, I suppose not—if some stranger jumped out at her in the park, she wouldn't have been found wrapped up in a blanket, would she? Sounds more like she was dumped there. Is she going to be all right?"

Teagan winced at her mother's casual use of the word "dumped." The unofficial consensus at the nurse's station had been just that—that Jamie had not been assaulted at the park, but had been brought there and left for dead. Radiology speculated that the break in her arm had come after she was unconscious; the nature of it suggested an arm that was bent at an odd angle and struck something hard, quite likely with her weight falling on top of it.

Teagan suppressed a shudder. The temperature had been below freezing. Jamie had lost a fair amount of blood and could easily have died. Her only luck had come in being found and transported to the hospital so quickly. "Yes," Teagan answered, "she should be fine."

Physically, anyway. The last, unspoken words left a bitter taste in Teagan's mouth. She rose and picked up her tea.

The front door opened and closed, and a swirling blast of cold air made its way from the hall into the kitchen. The old house was drafty, but Teagan couldn't complain. Eric's Arizona-bound grandparents had given it to them as a wedding gift, which had eased their heavy student-debt woes considerably. Every time she looked at the avocado-green toilet in the half bath, she forced herself to remember that.

Sheryl straightened instantly, all trace of interest in the conversation gone. "There he is," she said warmly, setting her cup on the table. "My favorite son-in-law. How are you?"

"Just fine," came the smooth, familiar baritone. "How are

you, Sheryl?"

Teagan watched as her mother enfolded her husband in an effusive, slightly-too-lengthy hug. Teagan took a sip of tea, half smiling behind her cup. She could hardly blame her mother for admiring Eric, as she was thoroughly besotted herself. Cold and wind-blown, his Scandinavian good looks and cherry-red hair gave him even more of a "Viking-marauder" look than usual, a mirage which—though completely inconsistent with his personality—never failed to appeal to women like Sheryl. What had first attracted Teagan, conversely, was his smile, which betrayed both good humor and a tender heart. From the moment he had first fixed it on her, she had been lost.

Not that she didn't appreciate the rest of the package. Sheryl might fit an entire matrimonial arc inside of ninety days, but for Teagan, the sixth month of marriage was still honeymoon.

Eric returned his mother-in-law's embrace with reserve, sliding his eyes over to Teagan with a pained look. She chuckled and rose.

"I'm wretched, thank you," Sheryl responded, stepping back with obvious reluctance. "But I'll get over it. I always do, don't I?"

Eric smiled charitably. "Always." He sidled past his mother-in-law and greeted his wife with a kiss.

It was not the kiss that Teagan would have received had her mother not been in the room. But despite both its brevity and the cold that clung to Eric's wind-whipped face, it warmed Teagan to the bone.

Marriage was good. Growing up with Sheryl would have left most daughters skeptical of the institution, but for the ultra competitive Teagan, her mother's repeated failures had only increased her determination that she, like her grandparents, would do the marriage thing right.

Step one, clearly, was finding good material.

Eric released his bride only halfway, keeping one arm possessively—or defensively—around her waist as he turned back toward Sheryl. Teagan wasn't the least concerned with her mother's flirtation, knowing full well that Sheryl, for all her apparent lack of depth, would never hurt her only daughter. Sheryl's failure to apply the brakes on her naturally seductive behavior was, ironically, a direct result of the women's mutual understanding of this fact.

But it bugged the hell out of Eric. "So, Sheryl," he began, his tone slightly stiffer than it would be with a friend. "How's business? Sold any mansions lately?"

Sheryl harrumphed with disgust. "In this weather? No. All the agents starve in January. But I've got a little put away. In two weeks, I'm off to the Bahamas."

She sat down at the table and began to describe the vacation in detail, and as Teagan pretended to listen, Eric drifted out of the conversation and searched the kitchen. "What's for dinner?" he asked Teagan when Sheryl had finished.

She eyed him wryly. "Whatever you're fixing. It's your night."

He frowned. "Pizza?"

Teagan shook her head. "We agreed no more than twice a week, remember?"

He breathed out with a sigh. "All right then, Hamburger Helper it is." His eyes turned to Sheryl, and only Teagan noticed the twitching in his jaw muscles as he asked politely, "Would you like to join us? There'll be plenty."

"Oh, I'd love to, but I have a showing in a half hour," Sheryl said with genuine regret. "I just wanted to check in with my baby girl, first." She took a sip of tea, looking thoughtful. "But tomorrow night would be perfect! How about that? I'll make dessert."

Teagan and Eric exchanged a rapid glance, searching their brains for a legitimate excuse to decline. His eyes told her he had come up empty. So, unfortunately, had she. She loved her mother, but Friday night was date night.

"Well, actually, Mom—" she began.

"That'll be fine," Eric interrupted, his voice amiable. "We

haven't had one of your gourmet desserts in a while now, have we? Why don't you surprise us — try a new recipe?"

Sheryl beamed. She dipped her chin and replied coquettishly. "Anything for you, kid." She then started in mid flirt, spilling a drop from her tea cup onto the table. She sprang up and made a grab for her coat, which she had thrown over a chair. "Oh! I almost forgot. I brought some decorating articles for you, Teagan. The ones on restoring colonials. I left them in the car — I'll go get them."

Sheryl hurried out, and Teagan turned to her husband. "You didn't have to do that," she said appreciatively. "But thanks."

"No problem. I know how she gets when she's lonely. Better dinner with us than drinks at some singles bar, right? Besides, you said you have to work Saturday anyway." His gaze turned intent. "Just *don't* leave me alone with her."

Teagan offered a mock salute. "I'll protect you with my life. Promise."

Eric put down the box of Hamburger Helper he was holding and pulled her into his arms, but just as she was really beginning to enjoy herself, the front door opened again.

Eric rumbled a low growl in her ear. "Teagan," he whispered. "Do you love me?"

"Desperately."

"Then find that woman another boyfriend. *Soon.*"

Teagan stared at the clock on her nightstand. It was 2:56 AM. She itched to turn onto her other side, but Eric's arm was around her waist, and she didn't want to wake him again.

Given the preceding pleasantness, she knew she should be sleeping like a baby. But instead she had been tossing and turning, unable to rid herself of the mental image of Jamie, unconscious and bleeding, being rolled up in a blanket and dumped out of a car.

What could have happened to her? What series of events could possibly have transpired, between that long-ago summer and now, to bring Jamie to such a place?

Both girls had grown up with disadvantages, true. Neither had ever had money to spare, and both had been forced to move frequently, enduring the repeated trauma of being "the new kid." But they had also had loving, if not perfect, mothers; and there was no question they had smarts. They had mused about becoming businesswomen, lawyers, entrepreneurs. Had Jamie ever been adopted, or had she spent the rest of her teenage years floundering in foster care?

Eric stirred. He withdrew his arm and turned over onto his back, and Teagan turned with him and settled in again, her head nestled in the warm, smooth curve of his shoulder.

Somebody beat Jamie up, she speculated, her teeth clenching at the thought. But could it really have been a boyfriend? Or a husband?

Teagan's professional training told her yes, absolutely. But her gut instinct said no.

She knew full well that victims of domestic violence could be found at every level of the socioeconomic ladder, and that they were not all meek, simpering women who lacked self-esteem. Still, she had a difficult time picturing the Jamie she knew falling into the typical abuser's trap. That girl had been fiercely independent. Proud. Street wise. She was not one to take any kind of mistreatment without a fight.

How could smart, savvy Jamie get involved with a person capable of such callousness? Whoever had abandoned her in the bitter cold must have known that she could die—must almost certainly have intended it. Unless, perhaps, they believed when they left her that she was already dead. An accidental blow to the head could have rendered Jamie unconscious; a faint pulse could be missed. But even if her injuries were an accident, what excuse could anyone have had for dumping her body in the snow and walking away?

There was no excuse.

It was *murder*.

Eric shifted position again, and Teagan drew back to prop herself up with an elbow.

She was never going to sleep. Not until she came up with a reasonable plan of action. She might as well get on with it.

She stroked her husband gently on the cheek. "Are you asleep?" she whispered.

"Yes," he answered, eyes closed.

"I need to ask you something. About Jamie." She had given him a rundown of the situation over dinner, including a recap of her "long-lost friend from the lake" story, which he had already heard and, touchingly, claimed to remember. When it came to stories of his own childhood, Eric wasn't much of a talker. But he didn't seem to mind listening to hers.

His response now, however, was a grumble.

"Medically, she'll be ready for discharge in a day or two," Teagan began. "But even if the police do figure out where she's been living, it may not be safe for her to go back there. And if they can't find out anything… if no family or friends come forward and she still can't remember either where she lives or who assaulted her, the hospital will have no choice but to discharge her to a women's shelter."

She paused. Eric remained motionless. "The problem is that shelters aren't equipped to deal with clients with memory deficits. They can't make her stay if she decides to leave, and she's got to have help—for her own safety. That's why, if it's all right with you, I'd like to offer her the garage apartment. Just for a few days, until her head clears. She'll be safe there. And besides… it would be good to spend some time with her again."

Eric's eyes opened. He studied his wife between blinks. "Are you sure that's what you want? You're not just feeling guilty because she saved your life that time?"

Teagan tensed. Of all her babbled tidbits of childhood lore, why did he have to remember that one? *Saved your life* sounded so melodramatic. She certainly hadn't put it that way.

"It has nothing to do with that," she said shortly. "I just want to help her. I don't intend to make a habit of dragging my work home with me, but she was a good friend once, and I'm worried that, as independent as she is, she'll—"

Eric's eyes closed again, and he raised a finger to Teagan's lips. "It's fine. Whatever you want to do." After a moment he added, hopefully, "Can she cook?"

Teagan grinned. So far, the only downside to setting up house as a married couple was that they were equally inept in the kitchen. Neither could fry ground beef without burning it, and both had, unfortunately, hoped to solve the problem by marrying a chef.

"I don't know," she chuckled. "I'll ask her." She bent and kissed him softly on the lips, then settled into his shoulder again. "Thank you."

He responded with another grumble.

Teagan closed her eyes. Her mind was more at ease now, and a pleasant heaviness began to creep over her. She was so comfortable. No feeling in the world was better than sleeping close to the man she loved. Warm. Happy. Secure.

Knowing how many people spent their entire lives without experiencing such contentment, she sometimes felt as if her own situation were too good to be true—as if she might wake up tomorrow and discover that meeting and marrying Eric had all been nothing but a wonderfully pleasant dream.

Chapter Five

Jamie stared into the hand mirror. The turban of gauze was gone now, revealing short, naturally blond hair in desperate need of a wash. But she knew better than to touch her head, which had brought itself to her attention with a screaming fury around four o'clock in the morning when her happy pills had worn off. Her arm also ached abominably, leaving her only too content to be put under anesthesia soon.

She had been staring at herself for almost an hour, trying to make sense of the disjointed images now dancing before her eyes. First fleeting, then more concrete; all strangely antiquated. She didn't know the woman in the mirror, at least not by sight. The images in her head were those of a child.

She could remember her mother. Blond and pretty, but pathetically thin. Smoking like a chimney. Working like a dog. What was her name? Jamie wasn't sure. But to her daughter, she had been the whole world. A single young mother, striking out on her own. She had worked in childcare centers until Jamie was old enough to go to school; then she had turned to waiting tables, clerking, medical assisting. Once Jamie had a clear picture of her mother in mind, the uniforms had followed, one after another, as if she were watching a career-day fashion show. How many jobs? How many moves? How many friends had Jamie made, only to lose them again?

She could see their hatchback car, packed to the brim for another change of venue. Her three beloved Barbie dolls, complete with horse and car, in a bag at her feet. Julie Bear. Alice the Tiger. Her mother had always made sure Jamie had her things about her, safe, something to hang onto amidst the chaos that was their ordinary life.

She had not been an unhappy child. The abnormal was her normal; each hardship, another adventure. That she could remember it so was a tribute to her mother. The mother who had been hers and hers alone, who had always loved her, always been there for her.

Until she died.

Jamie felt a twinge in her middle, an uncomfortable burning.

She could remember the funeral, too.

She had stood by her mother's casket, silent and unmoving. The graveside service was short; the adornments, nonexistent. The absence of flowers had bothered her, and she had made the minister wait while she scoured the carefully groomed hillside, collected a handful of renegade dandelions, and strewed them over the flat wooden lid. Before the talking had even ended, the yellow blossoms had wilted in the sun.

Only a handful of people had been present. The minister and maybe four or five others. Two in particular she would never forget.

Her mother's parents. The grandparents she had never met before—or at least couldn't remember meeting. Jamie's mother had not gotten along with them, had always said that she and Jamie were better off without them. Jamie had wondered why. But her questions were never answered.

The woman who introduced herself at the funeral as Jamie's grandmother was in her fifties or so, her short hair dyed an unnatural shade of auburn. She wore thick glasses and had a lumpy mole on her neck, neither of which would have bothered Jamie if the introduction had been accompanied by a smile. The man with her was older and potbellied, with white hair, red cheeks, and bright blue eyes. He hadn't smiled either.

"You look lovely, Jamie," the woman had said, not meeting her eyes. "Your mother would be proud. She would do anything for you, you know that."

Jamie had no response. The words seemed

complimentary on their face but had come out sounding like a reproof.

The man laid a hand on top of Jamie's head, tousling her hair. But he, also, avoided looking into her eyes. "I hope they find you a good place," he said stiffly. "I'm sorry we can't—" he broke off with discomfort. "But you know, we're getting old. It's just too hard, now." He looked away altogether, talking more to himself than to her. "They'll find you a place."

The couple did not linger after the ceremony. Without another word to Jamie, they had gotten into a car and driven away.

She had not understood, then. But she could remember quite plainly the moment, several days later, when she finally did.

"Your grandparents aren't able to take you, Jamie," caseworker number one had told her gently. Number one had been a middle-aged, heavyset African American woman whose eyeglass frames were patched along their bridge with duct tape. She had been kind enough.

But kind wasn't enough.

"They love you very much, but they just can't raise another child right now," she explained with a smile. "So we're going to see if we can't find you a new family. All right?"

Jamie had gotten it, then. She had understood that it was, in fact, the cryptic circumstances surrounding her own birth which had caused the rift between her mother and her grandparents. Whether the couple had ever loved their own daughter, she didn't know. But they did not, nor would they ever, love her.

They sure as hell didn't want to raise her.

Nor, apparently, did her biological father—a specter about whom she knew exactly nothing. When she was very young, she was told she didn't have a father. Once she learned enough about the mechanics of the process to question that claim, her mother had switched to a convoluted tale about an anonymous sperm donor. But Jamie, who could easily calculate that her mother had become pregnant while still a teenager, had never been naive enough to believe that one. All she could assume was that the man had either been married, a criminal, or both. She had taken some comfort in believing that he wasn't a rapist—because, after all, her grandparents couldn't possibly have blamed their daughter for that, could they?

Looking back now, Jamie wasn't so sure. They had known that their twelve-year-old granddaughter was both alone in the world and innocent of her mother's supposed wrongdoing. Yet they had washed their hands of her anyway.

She looked into the mirror again and realized that her hand was shaking. Her golden eyes were red-rimmed.

Another image. Standing outside a door, listening. A man's voice, soft, but serious. "She seems like a nice enough girl. But I can't take those eyes. They give me the willies. There's something just not right about her. Let's keep looking, okay?"

Jamie laid down the mirror. She didn't know where that memory had come from; she couldn't place it. But the theme had been the same.

No one had wanted her. Her and her damned yellow eyes.

A knock on the door sounded. She looked up, heart pounding.

A woman stood smiling at her: the friendly, potentially useful social worker she had spoken with yesterday.

"Hello," Jamie said hoarsely. Her voice sounded close to tears, and she struggled to correct it. "It's Teagan, right?"

"That's right," the woman answered, stepping over and sitting on the stool again. "How are you feeling this morning? They tell me you're doing much better. No more disorientation, no more confusion."

Jamie let out a bitter chuckle. "I wouldn't go that far. I remember what happened yesterday, and some things from my childhood are coming back." There was no question of going into detail, with Teagan or anyone else. Internalizing her emotional battles was as involuntary as breathing. "But every fifteen minutes someone asks me what my name is, and I still can't answer. You said you knew it, though. What is it? Jamie what?"

Teagan paused briefly, as if trying to decide whether to share a cheat sheet. "When I knew you, your name was Jamie Knight."

"Knight?" Jamie's eyes narrowed for a moment, then she shook her head. "That's not right. It's Jamie something, but not Knight."

Teagan frowned. "I suppose your name might have changed if you were adopted. Or you could have gotten married."

As if!

"I'm not married," Jamie said shortly. How she could be so sure, she didn't know. But she was.

The social worker's eyes met hers, studying her. The scrutiny made Jamie suddenly uncomfortable, and she looked away.

"The neurologist said that it's perfectly normal for sensory memories to come back first, with factual details, like names, taking a little longer. He also said that the first memories to resurface are often a person's earliest ones, from childhood."

"You don't say," Jamie responded, keeping her voice level even as her heart, for unknown reasons, began beating like a jackhammer.

The social worker's presence had become oddly disturbing. Jamie could feel Teagan's gaze like a laser, even as she herself stared at the wall, at nothing. There had been something in the other woman's eyes just now... something strangely compelling. What was it? And why, when Jamie wanted so desperately to know the answer, could she not bring herself to take another look?

"Jamie? Is something wrong?"

Who are you?

"Keep talking," Jamie blurted, still not able to face her. "Say something else!"

The order made no sense, even to Jamie. Yet after only the briefest of pauses, Teagan answered in a voice nothing like her usual, professional tone.

"I keep telling you, I *like* my hair in a ponytail! I don't care if it makes my ears look bigger. And this hat is *not* disgusting. It's an antique, a relic. It's *art!*"

The words broke through the darkness of Jamie's memory like a wrecking ball, opening it to a beam of bright summer sun.

Her head snapped toward the sound. But the image that met her eyes was no social worker. It was a snarky, bossy, know-it-all preteen with her hair skinned tight off her forehead and hidden behind a baseball cap so hideously frayed, discolored, and stained it looked like it had been peeled off the bottom of a garbage truck by a Rottweiler.

The girl herself was chewing gum, the pink wad dancing around in her mouth as she prattled on about...

About everything. The gym showers at her old school. The fishing gear in her grandfather's storage shed. Spree versus SweeTarts. The wonderful living world of pond scum. The right way to do the butterfly stroke. Why all prisoners should be rehabilitated. Her mother's awesome cherry cupcakes. The unfairness of standardized tests. How puppies are born. The shallowness of people who fussed over their appearance and the moral superiority of those who didn't care. The stain on the right side of the cap's brim—well, that was barbecue sauce. Or maybe it was ketchup...

Words caught in Jamie's throat. A hundred things to say had tumbled forward together, massing into one huge knot of emotion. As she struggled, the image of the girl before her turned, ever so gradually, back into that of the twenty-something woman who now sat beside her bed, leaning forward slightly in eagerness, waiting for the words that seemed forever in coming.

Jamie swallowed.

"God, that hat was gross."

Teagan dissolved into peals of laughter, nearly falling sideways off her stool before catching onto the seat and planting both feet on the floor. "Was not!" she retorted when she could breathe.

"Oh, it *so* was," Jamie said with certainty, sitting up. She could not remember everything; she still wasn't sure why, where, or how she had known Teagan. She only knew that she did—and that the memory was flooding her with a unfamiliar warmth, a thrill that was almost dizzying.

"I still have it, you know," Teagan bragged.

Jamie shook her head with a smile. "Where... I mean when..." She paused a moment as the images filled in. "We used to paddle a canoe around, didn't we? On some big lake..."

"Indian Lake," Teagan supplied. "My grandparents used to have a cabin there."

"And that was—"

"Almost fifteen years ago," Teagan finished. "When we were twelve."

Fifteen years. Jamie's otherwise damaged brain performed the calculation swiftly. "So, I'm twenty-seven now."

"Almost," Teagan answered. "Your birthday's in April."

Mom died in April.

Jamie fought back at the sadness that gnawed at her. She couldn't think about that now. Her mother was gone, but Teagan wasn't. Teagan was right here.

"What happened after that?" Jamie blurted, her mind racing ahead of her words. Surely there was more between them than just one summer. Their connection was deep. She could feel it. "Why do I only see you as a kid?"

Teagan's genuine smile faltered; slipped into something artificial. "We were only together the one summer. Then I went back to live with my mom." She looked as if she were going to say something else, then stopped.

"Really?" Jamie questioned. She didn't disbelieve it, but she could see that, once again, Teagan was hiding something. "Tell me more about the summer, then. What else did we do?"

Even as she asked the question, the images continued to appear—scattered, disconnected visions of water and sun. "I can picture you in a swimsuit," she narrated, not waiting for Teagan's answer. "There was a tree that leaned out over the water. We used to jump off it!"

Teagan grinned. "That was the 'jungle' swimming hole. We had a couple favorite spots. We would paddle around and then stop and swim. You'd never been in a canoe before that summer, but pretty soon you were doing the steering. You had a real knack for it."

Jamie looked into Teagan's face again, thinking hard. But despite the plethora of images and feelings the other woman evoked, no coherent story line materialized. "Tell me something specific that happened," Jamie begged. "Something I can try and bring back."

Teagan considered. "Well, there was the time we came up on a water snake, and you were so fascinated by it you made us paddle beside it halfway across the lake. But then we both leaned out over the side at the same time, and the canoe tipped. You about screamed your head off when you realized it was wriggling around in the water a couple inches from your face."

Jamie shuddered. She had no desire to remember *that*. "I hate snakes!" she said with a grimace.

Teagan snorted. "Tell me about it. Every time after that I wanted to annoy you, all I had to do was yell 'snake' and you'd start throwing things at me."

Jamie smirked. She could remember none of what Teagan was saying, but the "throwing things" part sounded true to form. "Did we tip over often?"

"Only about a hundred times."

"Whose fault?"

"Yours. Always."

"Liar."

Teagan narrowed her eyes suspiciously. "Do you remember that, or are you just guessing?"

Jamie smirked again. "I'm just guessing. But as I already told you, you suck at lying. Now, try another story on me."

Teagan appeared to think a moment, and Jamie watched as something resembling mischief flashed behind her eyes. But instead her tone turned serious.

"There was one thing I'm sure you'll remember. There was, well, a kind of an accident. You tried to do a back flip off the dock, but your shoulders hit the edge of it on the way down and you got the breath knocked out of you. You were under the water for a while before I found you — you'd taken in a couple of lungs full of lake water already. Once I got you out, you coughed it all up, and you were fine. But it was scary."

Jamie stared. The story seemed incredible.

"Do you remember any of that?" Teagan asked.

Jamie shook her head with frustration. Shouldn't nearly drowning leave some sort of impression? Yet she was not afraid of water. She was fairly certain she could swim well.

"I did a back flip?" she asked.

Teagan nodded.

"Funny," Jamie continued. "I don't see myself as the daredevil type. Not with stupid stunts and things like that."

"Think about it," Teagan urged. "I'm sure it will come back to you."

Was I different back then?

Jamie picked up the mirror that lay on the mattress beside her and, for the hundredth time that day, studied her reflection. The more she looked at herself, the more ire rose within her; and despite her excitement at having remembered Teagan, this view of herself had the same, aggravating effect.

"These damned eyes!" she said bitterly, tossing the mirror aside again. "They're not right!"

Teagan stared at her in surprise. "Your eyes are beautiful!

What do you mean they're not right?"

"I mean I fixed them. They're not supposed to be yellow anymore."

Teagan looked confused.

Unaccountably, Jamie's face flushed with heat as tears welled up behind her lids. She fought the impulse with a vengeance. Why on earth was she crying over her eye color? How stupid was that?

But it wasn't just her eyes. There were things she knew, yet didn't know—things hovering just outside the reach of her feeble brain. Sensing them there, yet knowing they were unattainable, was maddening. The problem with her eyes was just the tip of the iceberg; they weren't *supposed* to be yellow, no matter what the mirror showed. It was like being told you were only six when you knew full well you were ten.

"Maybe you got contacts," Teagan suggested. "Colored contacts. Does that sound like something you might have done?"

The bizarre warmth that associated itself with Teagan swelled up in Jamie like sunshine, quelling her tears on the instant. "Yes!" she practically shouted. "Hell yes, I would! And I did! I know I did. So where are they?"

Teagan's face clouded, as if she were remembering something unpleasant. "Your personal effects were put into a bag," she explained. "But it was just clothing. You didn't have a purse with you. If you were wearing contacts when you came in, I'm sure they were removed—and probably thrown away. But I can check your record and see if there's a note about it."

"I want some others," Jamie demanded. "Can I get them here?"

Teagan's expression showed a concern that was clearly readable. *Why the hurry?*

Jamie wasn't able to explain herself. All she knew was that every time she looked in the mirror, everything about her felt wrong. She felt naked, exposed. She wanted to look like the person she *felt* she was.

Before Teagan could answer, a throng of uniformed people opened the door without knocking and entered the room, stretcher in tow. "It's time to get you ready for surgery," a woman in blue scrubs announced, pulling the stretcher closer.

Teagan rose and moved out of the way. "I'll look into it," she replied, sounding like a social worker again. "But try not to worry about it right now. Just concentrate on getting better. This surgery will be over in a snap, and before you know it, you'll be up and walking out of here."

The newfound warmth inside of Jamie began to cool.

She's getting paid, you know. It's her job.

Another image. Another time. Another woman who claimed to care. *You won't be here long; this is just a temporary placement. The time will be over in a snap, and before you know it, you'll be adopted and in your very own "forever home." Okay?*

Peachy.

But it was a lie. They were always lies. Delivered with a cheerful smile.

"Jamie," Teagan asked, sounding as if she were having to repeat herself. "Are you all right? I'll be back to see you after the surgery."

The crew had moved her onto the stretcher; a woman with colorful rainforest frogs on her smock was inserting the plastic cannula of a syringe into the port on Jamie's IV line.

Teagan tried again, "Are you —"

Jamie's eyes closed. "Peachy," she muttered with a shiver. The stretcher was cold. "Just peachy."

Chapter Six

"We can't come up with jack on that name. She thought of any other possibilities?"

Teagan slumped in her chair, but she could only slump so far before her knees hit the desk. The social services "office" was a windowless closet just outside the ER; the news coming over the phone from the city homicide detective was unexpectedly bad. "*Nothing* on a Jamie Knight? But how is that possible? Did you look in Somerset County?"

"We checked all the standard databases, statewide and national, with that age and history, and I'm telling you, the woman doesn't exist. No birth certificate, no social security number, no school records, nothing. You've got the wrong name."

"Maybe the spelling—"

"We ran every conceivable alternative spelling, too."

Teagan let out a breath. Thirty-six hours had passed since the assault was first reported to the police. The detective on the other end of the line had been helpful enough, and Jamie's case was rightly being treated as an attempted homicide, rather than a simple assault. But this news proved a serious setback. Teagan had assumed that once the police had Jamie's name, it would be easy to locate a relative, neighbor, or coworker who could finger the appropriate suspect. She had even hoped that the threat to Jamie might be removed before she was discharged from the hospital.

"How much does she remember now?" the detective asked.

"She's remembered some things from her childhood, but that's all," Teagan answered. "No names yet. The neurologist says that's all normal; he thinks she's got a good shot at getting nearly everything back within the next four or five days. But he also said she may never remember the last couple hours before the injury."

"They often don't," the detective agreed, "but if this is a domestic situation, she should still be able to give us our suspect. I'll try to talk to her myself later today or tomorrow. In the meantime, if she gives you anything: a last name, a significant other, even part of an address—call this number."

Teagan agreed that she would and hung up. Lost in thought, she spun her chair back and forth like a pendulum until a smarting sensation in her knee informed her that she'd been ramming it against the file cabinet. She was positive that "Knight" was the name Jamie had told her. Why on earth would a twelve-year-old girl lie about her surname?

She stopped fidgeting and got up. Jamie should have recovered from the effects of the anesthesia by now. It was time for another talk.

Teagan walked to the elevator and pushed the up button. How else could she find out Jamie's legal name? The Renicks had left Indian Lake over a decade ago. Knowing Jamie's first name, one set of foster parents, and her month and year of birth, Teagan or the detective could probably wrangle the information out of the county Children and Youth Services department eventually. But that process could take weeks, even months.

Teagan rode the hospital elevator to the fifth floor and headed toward Jamie's room with her feet dragging. She wished she had some positive news to share. But not only had the police failed to discover any potential friends or family of Jamie's, not a single soul had contacted the authorities about a missing woman matching her description.

Teagan knocked softly on the door and pushed the lever.

"Yeah, wait a minute," Jamie's voice answered with irritation, and Teagan paused with the door open an inch. Footsteps and the sound of rustling fabric met her ears. "Yeah, okay."

Teagan swung the door open just wide enough to admit herself, then closed it behind her. Jamie was standing by the bed, one hospital gown covering her front and tied in the back, another slung over half her body in a failed attempt to cover the flipside. She could not get her arms through the holes, and with a cast on one arm and an IV line trailing out of the other, it was no wonder.

Teagan crossed to one of the cabinets and pulled out a white gown decorated with blue and green squares. "Here," she said, swiftly preparing and handing it over. "Try this one. It has snaps instead of arm holes. I did the one arm already; just slip it over the cast and then you can snap the other one around the IV."

With any other patient, Teagan would have helped by snapping on the gown herself. Any other patient would have rung for a nurse in the first place. But Jamie wasn't like most patients. When it came to doing things herself, she was as obstinate as a two year old. It was a quirk Teagan remembered well, because they shared it.

"Thanks," Jamie offered, following directions. It took her several minutes, but at last she had the snaps fastened and some semblance of a decent garment in place. She dropped back onto the bed, looking exhausted.

Teagan surveyed her with an irrepressible twinge of jealousy. Even sporting dirty hair and a frumpy hospital gown, Jamie was the kind of woman who could draw second looks from any heterosexual male past puberty. Anyone who knew the girl could have predicted she would grow up pretty, but Jamie's evolution had exceeded all expectations. As preteens the two had been of equal height, but while Teagan had turned out half a head taller, Jamie had emerged the better proportioned. Her figure—already enviable by the age of twelve—had matured to a natural perfection even Sheryl's plastic surgeon couldn't duplicate.

"I feel like crap," Jamie snapped. "They won't let me take a shower yet."

Teagan grinned. "Still obsessed with your appearance, I

see." She dropped into the thinly padded recliner that was the only other piece of furniture in the room.

Jamie grinned back. "Some people try *not* to gross out the general public." Her expression turned suddenly antsy, and she sat up. "I want out of here, Teag," she commanded. "They can't make me stay here any longer, can they? I can walk out whenever I want. Right?"

Teagan let out a breath. Jamie had always been both smart and practical. Much more practical than Teagan herself. But in this case she was denying reality.

"I just talked to the police," Teagan began, deciding not to sugarcoat her message. "You were right; Knight isn't your name. So they still haven't been able to identify you. Nor has anyone come forward to file a missing persons report."

Jamie's eyes swam with a flood of unreadable emotions, and Teagan's heart ached as she searched for something—anything—uplifting to add. But for all intents and purposes, Jamie remained a "Jane Doe," which meant that she was homeless, penniless, unemployed, and uninsured.

The first problem Teagan hoped to remedy, at least temporarily. The last was proving more difficult. Jamie's fracture had been stabilized. Her rebound from the blood loss and hypothermia had been amazingly quick, and her memory deficits alone—serious as they were—didn't justify further treatment as an inpatient. Homeless or not, whole or not, Jamie would be discharged first thing in the morning.

"If you were to leave," Teagan asked quietly, "where would you go?"

Jamie's cheeks slowly reddened. Her gaze moved to the floor.

"It's my job as your social worker to make sure you're released to a safe situation," Teagan said after a moment. "Ordinarily, for an assault victim, that would be a women's shelter."

Jamie's chin jerked up. "I am *not* going to any shelter. Nobody is going to make me stay anywhere I don't want to be!" Her eyes blazed with determination, but her voice betrayed the cry of a former foster child, still smarting over her own powerlessness.

Teagan squelched a sympathetic sigh and walked to the window. Its view of the north side of the city — all concrete, brick, and dirty snow — was bleak. The women's shelter would be bleak, too. There was no way Jamie would stay there.

"Then where would you like to go?" she continued. "It would only be for a few days. The neurologist seemed pretty sure that's all it would take — until you remember enough for us to get you home, I mean."

When no answer came, Teagan stole a glance over her shoulder. Jamie was looking at the floor again. Her limbs had begun to tremble.

Teagan steeled herself and pressed on. "Well, you can't live on the streets in the middle of winter. We have an apartment over our garage that's empty, but as your social worker I'm not sure it would be kosher for me to offer it. You might look into one of the charities that helps —"

"You have an apartment?" Jamie interrupted.

Still facing away, Teagan allowed herself a smile. She might be a poor liar, but she wasn't bad at more subtle manipulation. Jamie wouldn't want her charity any more than anyone else's. She had to proceed carefully. "Yes, but that would be against the rules," she lamented.

"So who's going to know?" Jamie argued.

Teagan hesitated, laying on the fake reluctance a bit thicker. But when she turned to see Jamie's face reddened with embarrassment, she realized she had gone too far.

"I guess you've already done enough for me, haven't you?" Jamie conceded. "Seeing as how you saved my life that time —"

Jamie's voice broke off. She looked toward where Teagan stood at the window, and her golden eyes widened.

She was remembering something again.

In one motion Jamie drew in a breath, puffed out her chest, and grabbed at the box of tissues that sat on her nightstand. In the next second the same tissue box came speeding through the air aimed directly at Teagan's ducking head, missing her by a good twelve inches but striking the window blinds with an impressive *thwack.*

"You wench!" Jamie shouted playfully. "I pulled *your* butt out of that stinking lake! How dare you take the credit?"

Teagan removed the hands that shielded her face. "No need to get testy about it," she responded smugly. "And *you* said I was a lousy liar. Ha!"

"You couldn't stand it!" Jamie continued, her face alive with delight. "You absolutely *hated* that anyone had to save you, particularly a girlie-girl like me. You were *so* arrogant!"

"Was not," Teagan argued. "It wasn't that big a deal."

"It was when *you* were pretending to be the hero!" Jamie replied.

Teagan felt an urge to change the subject. "So I owe you, okay? Are you happy? What am I supposed to do about it?"

Jamie studied her thoughtfully. "You said 'we' earlier. As in 'we have an apartment.' Who's we?"

Teagan smiled and dropped back into her chair. "My husband Eric and me. It used to be his grandparents' house. Now it's ours."

Jamie's eyebrows rose. "You have a husband?"

"Yes, I have a husband! You didn't think any man in his right mind would ever marry me, did you?"

"I didn't think that," Jamie said quickly.

But that was exactly what she did think. Under other circumstances, Teagan might have been offended. All she could think now was how much fun it was going to be to introduce Jamie to Eric.

Her inner devil frolicked. "He may not look like much, but he's mine," she said defensively. "He's a corporate attorney. Works in employment law."

"That's nice," Jamie said, all interest gone.

"The apartment isn't part of the house; it's over the garage, which is a separate building. Eric's grandparents used to rent it out to college students. We haven't wanted to mess with that, so we've just let it sit. Cleaning it up now would be a real pain—"

"Look," Jamie interrupted, "is it available or not? I don't care what kind of shape it's in as long as it's heated. Where else am I going to go? I saved your life once; can't you at least let me crash at your place for a couple days?"

Hook, line, and sinker!

Teagan couldn't resist. Her eyes narrowed. "Are you messy?"

"Not as messy as you!"

"Touché."

"I have handwriting a person can actually *read*, too."

Teagan paused and looked up. Had she missed something?

"You wrote me a letter once," Jamie explained, her voice quiet. "After that summer. I was just remembering it."

Unexpectedly, Teagan's eyes grew moist. They had promised each other they would write. They had sworn it—sworn it in mud. It was the way they swore everything. Teagan had dutifully kept her promise. Jamie had never responded.

"I loved getting that letter, even though I could barely read the thing," Jamie continued. "I kept it under my pillow. I was going to write you back, but—" Her voice became strained. "Before I got around to it, I lost it. For a while it seemed like I was changing foster homes every couple months. It was chaos; every place had lots of kids. I remember when I realized I'd lost your address." She paused briefly. "I was really upset."

Teagan blinked back tears. Failing to hear from Jamie after they parted that summer had hurt. It had hurt her far more than she had ever admitted—to anyone. She had sent her first letter right away, to the Renicks, but by the time she tried again with a second one, Jamie had moved on. Resending the letter in care of social services had obviously not worked either, and no wonder, if Teagan had the wrong surname. Yet in all the scenarios Teagan had run through her adolescent head explaining why her best friend had dumped her, she had never considered the possibility of a lost address. Not until she became an adult herself, and understood what the life of a foster child was like, had she been able to reassure herself with that explanation.

With an effort, Teagan shrugged off the old wound's pang. "Well then," she said cheerfully, "since you're the one who broke the letter oath, I won't feel so guilty about the apartment smelling like rotten pizza."

For a moment, Jamie smiled. Then a shadow crossed her face. "But wait—didn't you say I can't go to your house as long as you're my social worker?"

Teagan hesitated. It *was* a bit unorthodox, but technically speaking, Jamie would cease to be Teagan's charge as soon as she was released from the hospital. She only brought it up as part of the ploy—to let Jamie know about the apartment without seeming overanxious to offer it.

Jamie's smile returned. "No matter. I can just say what I've always wanted to say to every fake, lazy, lying social worker who's ever gotten assigned to me."

Teagan tried not to bristle. "And what's that?"

Jamie grinned. "Your ass is fired!"

Chapter Seven

Jamie climbed up the slatted wooden steps a few hours later, clutching the railing with her good hand. Teagan walked close behind her.

"If you get light-headed at all, just stop," Teagan suggested. "You've got to be weak as a kitten still."

Teagan's voice had an edge to it, but Jamie knew that her friend's simmering ire was directed elsewhere. What had—and was still—infuriating Teagan was how the hospital had used her own competence as an employee against her, booting Jamie's uninsured butt out the door the second the social worker had unveiled her cleverly crafted discharge plan.

For her part, Jamie was thrilled.

"I'm sorry about these steps," Teagan apologized. "I wasn't planning on making you tackle them until you'd had another night's rest and were feeling stronger."

Jamie put extra effort into climbing the remainder. They were a little slippery, having been buried—until five minutes ago—under several inches of snow. But the main problem was that, to Jamie's quivering leg muscles, they appeared to extend several hundred feet into the air.

She was exhausted and more than a little dizzy, but she couldn't bear the thought of looking weak. "Oh, I'm all right," she assured, struggling to catch her breath. "Don't worry about me. Having an apartment all to myself sounds like sheer bliss right now. I'd run a marathon to get to it if I had to."

Reaching the landing at last, she turned around and threw Teagan a playful grin. "Any place where no one wakes me up at three AM to ask me if I remember my name is heaven. So if you were planning on doing that yourself,

I'm warning you—from now on I'm keeping a blunt instrument under my pillow."

Teagan laughed. "No worries there." She mounted the landing, pulled a ring of keys from her pocket, and inserted one in the door lock.

Jamie turned aside to sneak a few more deep breaths, cursing her feebleness. She was sure that she had been healthy before, always able to rely on her own strengths, mental and physical. Having both impaired now was beyond disturbing—it was maddening.

She leaned heavily on the railing, ostensibly to take in the view, but mainly to rest her limbs. They were somewhere in the suburbs north of Pittsburgh, in a countrified residential area hosting a hodgepodge of old and brand new houses. Teagan's home was an unpretentious wooden two-story, with a small and ancient-looking front section deepened by what had probably been a long series of modest additions. The separate garage and apartment building was much newer, with aluminum siding and a modular appearance. Most impressive to Jamie was the yard behind, an empty area of undisturbed snow large enough to be called a field. Large, flat spaces in Pittsburgh were hard to come by, and the sight struck her as novel. She drank in the peaceful expanse with a sense of awe, recalling how well she and nature had become acquainted that summer on Indian Lake. She had a feeling they'd been strangers ever since.

"Here it is," Teagan announced, holding open the apartment door. "Sorry it isn't ready yet. I was going to do everything tonight..."

As Teagan launched into another tirade against her employer, Jamie stepped inside and looked around with a smile. From her hostess's cautions, she had expected to see piles of dirty dishes and discarded pizza boxes. But the room, though simply furnished and without any sense of style, appeared both tidy and comfortable. It was a studio apartment, with a small kitchen by the door, a bathroom tucked to the side, and a great room with a double bed and couch. Large windows adorned every wall. There were no linens on the bed, and the room was cold. But it was also refreshingly bright, and the air was free of must, instead smelling faintly of fresh paint.

Teagan stepped over to adjust the thermostat, and within seconds, the whoosh of a furnace kicked in. "Don't worry about the heat," she offered, her voice chipper again. "This place really cooks up fast. Eric's grandfather insulated it like it was in the arctic. He used to spend half the winter in the workshop downstairs because it was warmer than the house."

Jamie walked toward the bed. She was so tired she could easily collapse flat onto the bare mattress, but she settled for sitting on its edge. "It looks perfect," she exclaimed. "Calm and peaceful. Just what I need. Thank you." Her hands were cold. She tried to stuff them into the pockets of the shaggy coat she was wearing, but her cast made that only half possible.

"When I get the sheets and blankets, I'll bring you some decent clothes, too," Teagan offered.

There had been no clothes in Jamie's hospital room. When she asked about whatever she had been wearing when she arrived, she was told that none of it was in any condition to be worn again. Whether that meant it was torn, covered with blood stains, or simply in bad taste, Jamie didn't know. The only reason she wasn't naked now was because Teagan kept a bin of clothes in her office for use by homeless patients. The best it had to offer today had been a baggy pair of sweatpants, a scratchy button-down sweater, and a man's coat that looked like it had been donated *by* a homeless person. Black plastic boots, on loan from a friend of Teagan's in security, topped off the ensemble, and though Jamie appreciated the effort, the ill-fitting duds, on top of nearly forty-eight hours with no shower or shampoo, made her feel beyond hideous.

Teagan, bless her, seemed to know that.

"Here's what we'll do," the social worker began with her

typical, take-charge attitude. "First, I'll bring up some towels and a plastic wrap to cover up that cast. Then as soon as it heats up in here, you can take a shower. I'll bring a hair dryer and some makeup and some clothes of mine that might fit, and I'll get the bed made up. Then when you're ready, you can come to the house and have dinner with us." She paused, her lips twisting ruefully. "And don't worry about imposing, because my mother already did that. If I have to cook for three, one extra is no problem, believe me."

Something warmly humorous passed through Jamie's brain, and she felt herself smiling. She could see herself and her own mother cuddled up on a couch together, watching a movie. A funny movie about mothers and daughters. When she thought of Teagan's mother, she thought of that movie — and of a dark-haired actress whose name she couldn't remember.

"*Mermaids*," she announced, feeling a jolt of pleasure that her stymied brain had finally produced the name of something, even if it was something as useless as a movie title. "You said that was your favorite movie, because that mother was just like yours."

Teagan's eyes widened, then she laughed out loud. "Wow. Of all the things to remember! Yes, I adored that movie. Winona Ryder was my hero for years. The Cher character *was* my mother. Except for one minor difference, of course… Mrs. Flax liked to attract men, but wouldn't marry them. My mother's into both." She sat down on the mattress next to Jamie. "You'll get to meet her tonight. She remembers how much I used to talk about you. I think you even met each other at the end of that summer. Can you remember her?"

Jamie concentrated. She pictured a shapely blond woman in bright, expensive-looking clothing, standing on the deck at Teagan's grandparents' cabin. Jamie had found her fascinating— sophisticated and worldly. She had been surprised that Teagan, in contrast, could be such a tomboy.

"Yes, I did meet her," Jamie answered.

"Well, she's a character," Teagan continued. "And you'll love Eric. He's a great guy."

Jamie smiled politely. She was happy that Teagan seemed content, but since she couldn't look at the woman without seeing the ball-cap wearing, gum-chewing girl, she had a hard time picturing what sort of man she could have ended up with. Teagan had such a dominating personality—her husband would have to be a recessive type. Some quiet, meek intellectual, no doubt. A.k.a., a nerd.

Jamie felt slightly guilty at the analysis. After all, Teagan herself was hardly boring—she was smart, creative, enthusiastic, wicked brave, and generally fun to be around. But men didn't go for that sort of thing. They wanted super-sexy, low-maintenance women, not winning personalities. "I'm glad you're happy," she said offhandedly, wondering where her attitudes about men and relationships were coming from, given that she couldn't consciously remember a thing past puberty.

Her brain seemed to be teasing her.

"Jamie," Teagan asked, her voice cautious. "Are you sure you can't remember a man? Can you at least feel whether there was someone, a boyfriend, even a male friend you were close to? It could be really important for your safety. Do you understand?"

Jamie blew out a breath, then closed her eyes. Of course she understood. She wasn't deaf; she had overheard countless people in the hospital describing her to each other as "a domestic," and they hadn't meant a housekeeper. She also wasn't stupid; if the police thought she had been assaulted by a random stranger, she wouldn't have been asked a hundred times if she could remember the last significant other she had been involved with. Nor would Teagan have hustled her out of the hospital via the staff entrance with the hood of her coat pulled up and a security guard standing by the car door.

Didn't they think she would remember if she could?

She was tired. Tired of being frustrated, tired of trying to remember all the important bits and pieces to which her brain refused her access. Her memories were like screwed up DVDs — some skipping randomly forward and backward, others pixelating in mid scene, most all with the audio garbled. She couldn't even control which show was playing. But one thing was for sure. Everything onscreen so far had been strictly G-rated.

Was there someone? Anyone?

She breathed in slowly, and for a moment tried only to feel rather than remember. She searched for a male presence. She searched for any sense of fun and excitement.

There was nothing.

How could there be nothing?

Jamie opened her eyes. "I really don't think there is anybody," she said shortly. "I'm sure there have been men in my past — I sure as hell *hope* there have been. But I don't think there's anyone now. At least not one that means anything to me. I think I would know if there were."

Teagan looked back at her thoughtfully. "Yes, I guess you would."

Jamie felt an odd ripple of emotion. Sitting here shoulder to shoulder with Teagan, talking and sharing as they had so often done as girls — it was as if the intervening years had never existed. They were not girls anymore; they had both changed in any number of ways. But when Jamie looked at Teagan, grown woman or not, the friend she remembered was still there. Ageless. Invariable. Her essence shining from her soft brown eyes like a flame.

I've missed you, Teag.

Jamie swallowed and looked away.

Teagan slapped her hands on her knees and rose with a bounce. "Okay then — I won't bug you about your memory any more tonight. You're perfectly safe here, and for now, that's all that matters. You just relax for a couple minutes, and I'll go get everything from the house. It's getting warmer now, at least."

Jamie nodded mutely in agreement. The heater did work

fast. Her eyes absently followed Teagan across the room and toward the door. Her gaze came to rest on the refrigerator.

Blue and gold.

A bumper sticker, plastered diagonally across the freezer compartment, struck her brain like a lightning flash.

"Teagan!" she said excitedly, bouncing sideways on the mattress to get a better view.

Teagan stopped and whirled around. "What?"

Jamie pointed to the image of a snarling panther. "Pitt!" she exclaimed. "The University of Pittsburgh. I went there!"

Teagan looked at the sticker, then back at Jamie. "Really?"

"I've seen that thing a thousand times!" she insisted. "I can remember wanting to go there for so long..." Jamie's heart pounded in her chest as somewhere in her brain, a floodgate opened.

"It's like I can remember wanting to go to college but not being able to," she explained. "Like I didn't have the money. For years and years. I worked instead—I would do anything to make it happen, and then finally, FINALLY, I remember that I did. I can just barely see myself sitting in classes, schlepping books around. That part of it is really vague, but I know I'm not making it up. I really did go to college!"

Teagan smiled. "Of course you did. It's all coming back to you gradually, just like the neurologist said it would. By morning, maybe you'll have some idea what you actually studied."

Jamie felt like laughing. Nothing about her situation was funny, but the sudden rush of information had most definitely raised her spirits. "I went to college," she repeated proudly. "See there? I wasn't a total loser."

Teagan's smile faded. She walked closer. "You were never a loser. You're a very intelligent and determined person—of course you went to college. I just can't believe we went to the *same* college." She sat down on the mattress again. "I went two years to Pitt Johnstown before coming to the main campus in Oakland, but I finished up my business degree there, and then a couple years later I went back part time to get my MSW. We were probably on campus at the same time at one point or other."

Jamie's eyebrows rose. Being at the same school should have seemed a happy coincidence, but instead the possibility saddened her. Pitt was a huge inner-city university teeming with people; for the two of them to run into each other by accident, much less recognize each other out of context, was hardly a given. Yet when she imagined herself walking down a bustling Oakland street, passing by an equally absorbed Teagan, neither the wiser to what was happening, the thought hit her gut like a bomb. The idea that they could have come so close to reuniting before was far more aggravating than it was amusing.

"Do you remember high school, then?" Teagan questioned. "Where you graduated from?"

Jamie thought a moment. "I think I went to a couple different high schools. Those years are all a blur still. I remember the summer at Indian Lake really well now — but after that, not so much. It was a bunch of different families, a bunch of different schools. I don't remember any of them the way I remember wanting to go to Pitt." She paused. "I think what I remember the clearest is what I was the most excited about."

Like having you for a friend.

Jamie's eyes moistened, and she blinked.

"I don't think I was a very happy person during those years," she said quickly, struggling to fight yet another unbidden surge of emotion. Surely, in healthier times, she wasn't so maudlin! "Mainly because I can't remember any important faces. I mean — I remember *your* mother. Don't you think that if I was adopted, I would remember mine?"

Teagan didn't answer.

Jamie continued. "I was in a bunch of different foster homes. I can halfway remember lots of people, but none of them really meant much to me. I don't remember a high school graduation ceremony... maybe I didn't go. Who knows? What I do remember is how good it felt to be *out* of high school. And I can picture myself working… fast food, I guess."

The stream of images had come to a halt. But the jumble of emotions they evoked held Jamie in a fog.

"Sorry," she mumbled after a moment, realizing that Teagan was still with her, watching her. "I don't think I've remembered anything that would be useful to the police. The spot where my last name should be is still a blank. I've been trying hard to remember it, and my mother's first name, since yesterday, but whatever I'm doing just isn't working. I'm probably only making it worse. But I do know that I went to Pitt. For whatever that's worth."

Teagan rose from the bed. "You're doing great," she assured, her voice upbeat. "Maybe you shouldn't try so hard. In fact, I think I'll take my own advice and stop pushing you. It's coming fast enough. Just think, only this morning you could barely remember what happened when you were twelve! I say two days, tops, and we'll be taking you back to your mansion in Sewickley Heights and finding the keys to your Jag. Right now, I need to get back to the house and get you some clothes." She crossed to the door and opened it, then leaned back in. "By the way… if you really do have a mansion in Sewickley, you'd better believe I'll be borrowing yours."

She let herself out and pounded down the wooden staircase.

Jamie grinned after her. Teagan always was a trip.

Her smile faded as she wondered whether she had any other girlfriends out there. Women who knew her, cared about what happened to her.

If she did, they had yet to miss her.

She stood up slowly, then crossed to the window. Snow was falling again. An icy wind tumbled the light, white flakes in a frenzy, crashing them against the glass at every conceivable angle. Yet even next to the window, the apartment's heater rallied a pleasant cloud of warmth.

She had been cold before. Cold with no recourse. Huddled under ragged blankets, wearing layers of street clothes to bed, glaring with disdain at the cheap, digital alarm clock that she knew would rouse her before dawn…

Jamie shivered.

She shook her head and turned from the window with a jerk. Some things, she didn't *want* to remember.

She stood, staring at nothing, pondering the strange hollowness that had begun to grow inside her. A dark mass of… nothingness. The more she remembered, the more it seemed to swell; the deeper it seemed to ache.

Perhaps it came from missing someone who had been important to her. But if that were so, why could she not remember the person? She was beginning to fear that her first instincts — the sinking feeling of loneliness she had experienced from her first waking moments in the ER — had been shouting the truth straight in her ear.

Nobody out there gave a damn about her.

Chapter Eight

Jamie finished applying her mascara, priding herself on a reasonably steady hand. The shower had been wonderful, as had the shampoo. She was hungry, and still plenty weak, but being clean and wearing decent clothes again had boosted her spirits. Having makeup available had been the icing on the cake, and even though the sight of her mutant eye color still bothered her, she looked good enough to hold her chin up.

Teagan had told her to wait in the apartment, that she would come back to get her as soon as dinner was underway. But Jamie was impatient. She carefully slipped the coat her hostess had provided over her cast, opened the door, and started down the stairs.

The wind blew in her face, and she grimaced against the cold. She kept her eyes peeled on the wooden steps before her, but her mind was playing another disc. City streets. Walking people. Coats, hats, backpacks. A panhandler. The high-pitched squeal and hiss of bus brakes. The scent of exhaust. Coldness. Constant, bone chilling coldness.

Enough already, she mumbled to herself, holding tightly onto the rail with her good hand. When she reached the bottom she paused to look out over the snow-covered field, reveling once more in the vast span of clean, natural space. *You're not starving in the city now*, she informed herself. If she was going to remember something, she could remember something else. Something a little more cheerful.

She dipped her chin against the wind and hustled to Teagan's back porch, where she found the screen door open. She crossed the porch and rapped on the inside door with numb knuckles, but no one answered. Looking through the window, she realized she was outside a laundry room, and that with the wind, probably no one could hear her. Without hesitation she tried the knob, found that door also open, and entered.

She stamped her feet on the mat and loosened her coat. It was warm in the house, though not nearly as warm as in the apartment. An aroma of roast chicken filled the air, and Jamie could hear women's voices in the distance, laughing. She felt herself smile, even as her stomach rumbled. Something about the scene made her think of Thanksgiving. Not hers, though. Somebody else's.

"Hello?" she called out, walking toward the sound. "Teagan?"

She had expected the laundry room to lead to the kitchen, but it did not. A narrow hallway instead routed her through a small parlor used as an office. She glimpsed a couch and end table in the room beyond and kept going. As she stepped into a large, warmly lit living room, a man appeared suddenly at her side—having risen, apparently, from a recliner by the doorway.

"Hello," he said pleasantly, extending a hand. "You must be Jamie."

Jamie turned. She lifted her gaze to meet his.

Red hair. Striking blue-gray eyes. A smile with straight, white teeth.

Her knees felt suddenly wobbly. "Yes," she said, surprised to hear herself stammer. "Hello."

The curve of the jaw. The height. The shoulders. It was all so predictable. So familiar.

"Jamie!" came a voice from beyond him. It was Teagan's. "You made it down on your own, I see. And you've obviously met Eric. Fabulous. You hungry?"

Jamie forced her gaze back to Teagan. "Starving," she answered.

"Well, we'll eat in just a minute," Teagan continued, heading back out of the room already. "My mom's just finishing the salad. Take your coat off and have a seat. Eric can fill you in on the menu."

Teagan was gone as quickly as she had come.

Jamie's eyes returned to Eric. The smile he had greeted her with so cordially only seconds ago had disappeared from his face. The hand he had offered was back at his side. He stood still as a statue, watching her.

Her pulse quickened. She averted her gaze and began to shrug off her coat. As it slipped from her shoulders Eric stepped forward to help her, easing the armhole back over her cast and laying the coat neatly over a chair. But he said nothing.

"So," she offered finally, her voice still tenuous. "What's for dinner?"

She felt awkward. Ridiculous. Like a middle-school girl at her first dance. Surely she was reading too much into his reaction—or lack thereof. She didn't really know the man. Her damaged brain was simply playing tricks on her.

His guarded eyes gave no clue to his thoughts. "Chicken," he answered at last. His own voice faltered slightly, and Jamie's pulse rate increased another notch. But then he seemed to collect himself, offering another smile. "Rotisserie style, from Giant Eagle. And potatoes from a box." The fact that he was able to restore his rich, confident baritone so quickly should have made Jamie feel better. Rather, every word he spoke sent a tremor down her spine.

You know that voice.

"I hope you weren't expecting anything fancy," he continued. "Nobody around here can cook—we live on the prepackaged and the microwaveable. But Sheryl does make great desserts."

"I'm sure it will be wonderful." Jamie allowed her eyes to study him a moment, yearning to place his significance. He was handsome enough for any woman to stare at, but the sight of him intrigued her at another, deeper level as well. Her eyes saw the man before her, but her brain saw something more. An overlay of memory, hovering. He was...

Her mind turned cartwheels.

He was naked.

Mayday!

She whirled away from him, attaching her gaze firmly to the fireplace mantel. It had a clock on it. The clock had roman numerals…

Hang the clock! What the hell is wrong with you?

"Jamie?" Eric's voice came from behind her. Soft, worried. Its timbre filled her with a flush of heat. "Is something wrong?"

She spun back around and straightened. Nothing was wrong. She was losing her ever-loving mind, but nothing was wrong. It was perfectly normal to walk into a friend's living room and picture her husband buck naked.

In the shower. Out of the shower. His arms coming around her…

Holy hell.

"I'm fine," she chirped. "Really. I just get a little dizzy now and then. From the concussion, I guess."

"Oh," came the reply. A conversationalist, the man was not. Or maybe he found it unnerving to be stuck entertaining a woman with a mental disorder.

He didn't know her. If he did, he would have said something. She was losing it. This was all in her mind. Maybe he was the first decent-looking man she'd seen in a while. Maybe she was such a nymphomaniac that even forty-eight hours of deprivation was beyond her tolerance.

Teagan walked into the room with a smile and slid up to her husband's side. His arm went around her, and she reached up and kissed him on the cheek. "Dinner's on," she said cheerfully.

Teagan passed the dish of au gratin potatoes around the table for the third time. They weren't very good, since she had taken the stovetop shortcut, but they weren't awful either. Yet Eric had only picked at his, and Jamie, who had claimed she was starving, had hardly eaten a bite of anything including the chicken, which actually *was* good.

Teagan watched gratefully as her mother, always the social butterfly, pulled their guest into conversation with ease. Sheryl had enough experience chatting with strangers to find common ground with a trapper from Tibet—engaging Jamie in a dialogue about Indian Lake was child's play. But despite what Teagan had hoped would be a relaxed setting, Jamie seemed uptight. Perhaps a family dinner was too much, too soon.

Nor was Eric helping. He was acting both reserved and tense—nothing like his usual good natured, outgoing self. She had been expecting him to make Jamie feel comfortable, but his attitude was anything but welcoming. They hadn't had a minute alone since he got home, and she began to wonder if something had gone wrong at work, and he was waiting to tell her about it until they could speak in private.

"So, Jamie," Sheryl twittered, taking an additional, albeit miniscule, serving of potatoes. Sheryl always dieted between boyfriends, no matter what her weight. "Teagan tells me you're putting together more of your past every minute. What are you up to now? College?"

Teagan stiffened. She had told Sheryl specifically not to put her houseguest on the spot about her recovery.

But Jamie answered promptly, her voice no more strained than it had been for the other questions. "I think I went to Pitt. But I probably worked a few years first. I remember walking to class and studying something, but it's still all very vague."

Eric rose from his chair. He picked up his plate of barely touched food and carried it to the kitchen, and he didn't reappear until the women were done eating. Then he picked up their empty plates and carried them away as well, as silently as a butler. Teagan's stomach twisted with discomfort. She knew her husband well enough to know when he was torn up about something; and since most of life's minor annoyances rolled off his back with ease, that prospect alone was enough to trouble her. But she also couldn't help but resent the timing. She had envisioned he and Jamie hitting it off fabulously—in fact, she had been counting on it. She wanted Jamie back in her life again; she wanted them all to get along. But between Sheryl's probing and Eric's brooding, Jamie was probably wishing she'd stayed in her room.

As soon as Eric had finished toting the last possible dish back to the kitchen, Sheryl stood up with a bounce. "All right, kids," she announced. "Tonight's dessert is a real masterpiece, if I do say so myself. Eric and Jamie, you sit tight. Teagan, you come with me. I may need some help on this one."

Teagan watched as Eric, smiling tolerantly, slipped back into his chair. Heartened slightly, she rose and joined her mother. "We'll be right back," she said with as much pleasantness as she could muster. But the situation seemed grim. Jamie and Eric had hardly exchanged a glance since the meal began, and at the moment, both seemed inordinately interested in the tablecloth.

"Don't keep us waiting too long," Eric responded, his voice artificially cheerful. "If dessert is up to Sheryl's usual standard, I may have to come in after it." Teagan tried to catch her husband's eye as he spoke, but he wouldn't look at her, either. His attention had turned to the salt shaker.

She turned and followed her mother into the kitchen.

Jamie stared at the empty chair across the table from her. Eric was seated to her right. Her heart beat so loudly she was sure he could hear it. But if he did, he gave no indication. In fact, he said nothing at all.

She raised her chin and turned her head, forcing herself to look at him again. She had to settle this. She had to know whether she was imagining things. Or not.

His profile was beguiling. Maddening. The thick, wavy short hair. The set of his shoulders, his arms. Teagan had said he was a lawyer.

A table, glasses clinking. Jamie could see the other room as clear as crystal. Her feet hurt. She was waiting tables. Picking up glasses, picking up tips. The lighting was dim; the air smelled of cigarettes and beer. Mostly, it smelled of men. Attractive, available, educated men.

She tried to picture the faces around the table in that other room, make out their masculine voices. But all she saw in her head were the glasses. The trays. The greenbacks. The occasional quarter.

The image left her. The man at her side still didn't look at her, but gazed straight ahead. His jaw muscles were clenched. He looked miserable.

Another wave of heat flushed Jamie's cheeks. She forced herself to speak. Loudly. Clearly.

"Eric?"

"Yes." The answer was immediate, deadpan.

"Do you know me?"

His next reply took a few seconds in coming. But his voice was just as flat.

"Yes."

Jamie drew in a breath with a shudder. Her damned hands were shaking again. "And *how* do you know me?" she asked, her voice back to a stammer.

He stood up and took a step away from the table. He ran his hands over his face, expelling a heavy breath. "What do you remember?"

She remained in her chair. "Just that you look familiar to me," she answered, lying a little. "You seem to remind me of a restaurant."

He lowered his hands. This time his blue-gray eyes pierced right through her, opening up a door in her brain like a battering ram. She could see him standing close to her, his face bending toward hers. Her arms were around his neck. She could feel his lips, his hands…

The next word out of her mouth wasn't fit for mixed company. She shot up out of her own chair and paced behind it. "Dammit!" she whispered harshly, staring at him.

"You *more* than know me, don't you?"

He shot an anxious glance toward the kitchen serving window, but Sheryl had closed its shutters. Sounds from the dining room could still be heard through the doorway, if the women in the kitchen had been listening. But they were not; they were talking animatedly to each other.

Eric's voice dropped to a whisper. "We dated for a while, yes. But it was a long time ago. I—" he broke off. "I wasn't sure if you'd remember me."

"Well, I do," she whispered back, her voice still harsh. "*Dammit!*" she repeated.

His eyes hardened. "Like I said, it was a long time ago." Then he studied her, puzzled. "Why are you so angry?"

Jamie closed her eyes. She was angry. Very angry. She wasn't sure of the reason. Maybe because yet another person had more knowledge about her own life than she did. Maybe because she had been angry with him back then, and she felt it still, even though she couldn't recall the circumstances.

Or maybe because the one and only thing that actually meant something to her in the *present*—Teagan's friendship—had in one fell swoop been cut off at the knees. And all because of some stupid-ass roll in the hay she didn't even have the pleasure of fully remembering!

What were the odds? It wasn't fair. It *wasn't.*

"You *cannot* tell her about this," Jamie ordered, her tone as adamant as a whisper could be. "Please, Eric. I'm begging you. Just let it rest. I barely remember you, anyway. Really."

He looked at her with surprise. His own whisper was equally firm. "I'm not going to lie to her, Jamie."

"You don't have to," she protested. "Just don't say anything. What does it matter, anyway? The two of you are happy, right?"

"If it doesn't matter," he answered, "then there's no need to keep it a secret."

"There is a need!" Jamie hissed. Her eyes were misting again. "Teagan is my only friend in the world right now.

And if she knows, it will ruin everything between us!"

He shook his head. "She's not like that. What happened between you and me happened years before Teagan and I even met. She'll understand—"

"No, she won't!" A tear escaped one eye, and Jamie swiped at it viciously. "Don't be stupid. No woman can stand to think about the man she loves being with—" She cut off her own speech. How the hell did she know all this? She rubbed at her face with her good hand and collected herself as best she could. "Things would never be the same between Teagan and me. *Never.* Please, you've got to believe me."

He turned his face to the side. He blew out a breath. Was he wavering?

"She doesn't have to know," Jamie reiterated. "I don't know whether you ever cared about me or not, but if you do care about her, please don't hurt her. Just forget it ever happened." She surprised herself with a sound that seemed half chuckle, half sob. "I've done my part at the forgetting, haven't I?"

He looked back at her. Then, for the first time since he had introduced himself, he offered a genuine smile. "I did care about you, Jamie," he said softly.

"Specialty of the house!" Sheryl screamed. "Flaming cherries jubilee!"

Jamie looked toward the doorway as Teagan and her mother made their grand entrance with the fiery dishes. Jamie scanned their faces frantically. Had they seen anything that looked suspicious? Could they tell she'd been crying? Teagan was so blasted perceptive—would one glance at the two of them tell her everything?

Jamie watched as Teagan looked from her to Eric, then back. Teagan's smile remained perfectly pleasant. But her brown eyes swam with angst.

Chapter Nine

"I'm telling you, honey—if you don't listen to anything else I say all year, you'd better listen to this. That woman is trouble. Do *not* trust her with him."

"Mom," Teagan said impatiently, pulling her coat tighter against the relentless wind. "Stop it. I don't know why Jamie was acting so strange tonight—maybe she was overwhelmed. But I'm not going to get paranoid about it. The woman needs help and I intend to help her. As for Eric, something's obviously bothering him too, but that's another issue."

Sheryl lifted one perfectly plucked eyebrow. "Is it?"

Teagan growled under her breath. She had never had any confidence in her mother's opinions when it came to relationships, and at the moment, she was in an even less receptive mood than usual. Jamie had picked at her dessert as if it were poison, then excused herself to her apartment, claiming exhaustion. Sheryl had chosen the same moment to leave, though Teagan suspected that her offer to accompany them both to the garage was a ruse to get Teagan alone again. "Enough, Mom," Teagan said firmly. "I can manage. Thanks for coming over, and for bringing dessert—"

"That's another thing," Sheryl proceeded, pointing with a gloved finger. "When have you ever known your husband not to wolf down one of my creations? You saw the way they were looking at each other when we came back in the room. I'm telling you—that woman tried something. She made a pass."

Teagan stepped backward toward the house. "Goodbye, Mom. I'll talk to you later."

Sheryl opened her mouth to say something, but evidently thought better of it. She popped open the door of her PT cruiser with a sigh. "We *will* talk later," she agreed. "I'll call you tomorrow."

"Goodbye," Teagan repeated, turning back toward her front door in earnest. If listening to another person voice her own darkest concerns wasn't bad enough, she was freezing her tail off. She jogged up the front steps, yanked open the door, and moved into the warmth of her living room in double time.

Eric appeared in the doorway. She had barely managed to remove her coat before his arms were around her.

She held on to him with equal earnestness, though she was aware, even as the strong feel of him buoyed her spirits, that he had sought the embrace for his own comfort as much as hers. The thought of why chilled her insides.

When at last he released her, she stepped back to face him. "All right," she commanded. "Tell me. What's been bothering you all night?"

He had kept hold of one of her hands. At the question, he picked up the other one. His eyes brewed with two emotions she had no desire to see: dread and guilt. A tremor threatened to rock her shoulders, but she refused to give in to it. Whatever was wrong, it couldn't be that bad. She would not let her mother's passion for drama override her own common sense.

"Come and sit down," he urged.

Teagan shook her head. "Just tell me."

Eric paused and took a breath. He swung his arms a bit, pulling hers with them. Then he faced her squarely and began. "It's Jamie. Tonight wasn't the first time I've met her. I know her from somewhere else."

Teagan's heart began to thump with excitement. Such an announcement was hardly what she expected. This was good news. "You do? From where? Do you know where she's living now?"

Eric shook his head. "Sorry. No. I don't think I know anything helpful; I haven't seen her in years."

Teagan was disappointed, but her intrigue remained

high. She waited for Eric to say more, and when he didn't, she squeezed his hands with impatience, prompting him. "Well? What do you know about her? Where did you meet?"

He didn't say anything else. He seemed like he might for a moment, but the words never made it to his lips. He simply stood, looking at her with an expression that, in one horrible instant, brought her racing heart to a standstill.

He didn't need to say the words. She could read the message loud and clear.

She dropped his hands. She turned her head to the side and focused on the couch. The cold that had been gnawing away at her gut all evening exploded into a full blown ache, complete with a heaviness that made her want to flop down on the couch like a rag doll.

But she didn't. Instead she straightened her shoulders and cleared her throat. She forced her eyes back to his. "I see," she said quietly. "Which one was she?"

When it came to past relationships, they had long ago decided to clear the decks, sparing the other any unpleasant surprises. She had asked him point blank about the other women he'd been with, and he had told her. The list had been mercifully short, and she had been grateful. Particularly since her own list had been nonexistent.

He answered with a steady voice. "The waitress at Vermelli's."

Teagan sucked in a breath. She stepped away from him and sat down on the couch. *The waitress at Vermelli's.* The incredibly sexy, flirtatious blonde who had picked him out of a crowd of adoring freshman law students and promptly become a fixture in his apartment. *A short-lived affair,* he had claimed. *The feelings weren't strong either way.*

Not an emotional relationship, she had interpreted. Which meant it had been a purely physical thing.

Her stomach roiled.

Eric dropped down beside her. "I'm sorry, Teagan," he said softly. "I know this is the last thing you wanted to hear.

But—"

"Why didn't you tell me earlier?" she snapped. "I told you her name was Jamie. I told you about her eyes! How could you not know?"

Eric bristled at the accusation, but his voice remained calm. "I never even thought about it. There are lots of Jamies in the world. And when I knew her, she had blue eyes."

Teagan stared at him incredulously, but her skepticism soon gave way to the more rational thinking she prided herself on. What reason could he possibly have for lying about the exact point at which he had recognized Jamie? He didn't have to tell her any of this.

"She wore colored contacts," Teagan muttered. "Evidently you didn't notice."

Eric, wisely, didn't comment.

Teagan's limbs itched to move. She stood up again and began to pace. "Does she remember you?" she asked.

Eric rose as well, but remained by the couch. "She said I looked familiar, and that I reminded her of a restaurant. She seemed to know we'd been involved, but I'm not sure what else she remembers."

"And that's what the two of you were talking about when we came back in with the dessert?"

"Yes."

Teagan blew out a breath. She paced a few more times, saying nothing.

"I wasn't sure whether I should tell you," he admitted. "I don't want this to ruin whatever friendship there is between the two of you. And it shouldn't. What happened between Jamie and me was over with years before you and I even met. It's ancient history."

Teagan stopped and stared. "Why *did* you tell me?"

Eric seemed taken aback. "Because," he stammered, "the woman is right here under our noses, and I know you. You would have realized something was up. You suspected as much at dinner already, and I didn't want you to think there was something between us *now*. Besides," his tone dropped lower. "I know how I would feel if our roles were reversed. I would hate like hell to hear it, but if you had been involved with someone I knew, someone I had to face on a daily basis, I would *want* to know that. And I'd be furious with you if you kept it from me."

The heat of anger that had been pulsing through Teagan's veins, filling her head with images too horrifying to acknowledge, began slowly to abate. What was she so upset about? It had all happened years ago, hadn't it? She had known about the waitress at Vermelli's all along and been fine with it. Why should putting a real face on the abstract character make a difference?

Eric was devoted to *her*. Had he not shown as much, just now, by being honest with her? She loved him for that. Hang the rest of it.

Teagan closed the distance between them in two strides and wrapped her arms tightly around his neck. "I'm sorry. I've got no business being angry with you. The whole thing just messes with my head a little, that's all."

He returned her embrace, ending it with a kiss. "I understand. Don't apologize. It's not anyone's fault. It's just damned bad luck."

Teagan wiped her eyes. Not that she was crying. She never cried.

She took a deep breath and straightened her spine. This was okay. Everything would be fine. She had known that something big was bothering him—were there not plenty of worse things he could have told her?

"Maybe it's not all bad luck," she said, attempting to add some pluck to her still unsteady voice. "You may be just the link to Jamie that the police need to solve her case. You knew her your first year of law school, so that's been what— five, six years ago?"

That's it, woman. Stick to business.

He nodded. "But back then she was living in some dive basement apartment with four other people. There's no way she'd still be living there now, especially if, as she says, she went to college."

"But you know her last name," Teagan insisted. "Don't you?"

He started. "Of course. Jamie Meadows."

Teagan forced a smile. "See there? That's more than the detective or I have managed to come up with so far. Meadows should be the name on her birth certificate, then, unless she was adopted." She looked back at her husband. The ache in her middle still nagged. "Or unless, when you met her, she had been married before."

Eric's eyes widened. The thought seemed to strike him as preposterous. "Um… no," he said cryptically. "I doubt that."

What does that mean?

Teagan wanted to ask. But she didn't. She wanted to ask many things. A part of her wanted a play-by-play account of every single second that had ever transpired between her husband and Jamie; another part of her couldn't bear to think of them together at all. For the moment, the latter part won out.

She launched herself back into his arms again, relishing the comfort she always found there, even now. She would *not* act like some insecure, jealous idiot. She was Teagan Raye Hansen, and there wasn't a damn insecure thing about her. She would handle this nightmare with aplomb, just like she handled everything else.

She knew she had no reason to worry. Eric loved her. They were blissfully happy together. Maybe other women had no faith in their marriages, but she wasn't other women.

And she would prove it.

She released him, reluctantly, and forced another smile. It was obvious, really, what she needed to do. A relatively simple way both to show confidence in her marriage and to get Jamie out of danger and — of sudden importance — out of the garage apartment, as quickly as possible.

Just do it.

Teagan cleared her throat. "You know I have to work tomorrow," she reminded. "I really can't get out of that;

there's no one to cover for me."

"I remember," he answered. "I was thinking I would go into the office, too. It's quiet on Saturdays, at least. Maybe I can get caught up."

She took his hands in her own. "I was kind of hoping you could do me a favor."

His eyebrows rose. "What's that?"

"Jamie really shouldn't be alone all day. I was going to ask you to check on her anyway, but now I'm thinking—"

"You want me to *babysit* her?" Eric interrupted sharply.

Teagan grinned. He made the prospect sound horrifying, which pleased her. "I know it's an awkward thing to ask, but the reality is that you're in a unique position to help her get her memory back quicker."

He dropped her hands and took a step back. "Teagan," he said roughly, "I'd be perfectly happy if Jamie never remembers that particular block of time, and I suspect she would be too. She wasn't a happy person back then. Why push it? Why not let her remember what she wants to remember, on her own time?"

Teagan felt a rush of heat within her. Selfishly, she appreciated his resistance. She relished it more than she could say. But he didn't understand what was at stake.

She caught his hands again and pulled him closer. "Jamie doesn't *have* time. She doesn't know this herself yet, but somebody tried to kill her, Eric. They bashed her in the head, rolled her bleeding body up in a bedspread, dumped her in the snow, and left her to die. Jamie may not remember him, but *he* remembers *her*. For all we know, he's out looking for her right now, waiting for the chance to take another crack at her!"

Eric's jaw muscles clenched. "I understand that she came out of a dangerous situation. But she's safe here, as long as no one knows where she is. I don't see how rehashing a bunch of stuff that happened five years ago is going to help anybody."

"It wouldn't," Teagan agreed quickly. *And please don't try it.* "But think about it—until she *saw* you, she couldn't remember that period of time at all. If anything can speed up her recovery, it's putting her in touch with the right catalysts—sights, sounds, even smells can trigger memories. Now that we know she went to Pitt, we might be able to kick start her brain into remembering something more current. If she was working her way through school, she might not have graduated until recently."

Eric breathed out heavily. "So is that what you want me to do? Drive her around Oakland? See if anything looks familiar?"

Teagan smiled. "Yes. That's all. Show her the classroom buildings, the apartments. She may remember places she's lived in once she sees them. Or a landlord might remember her. If you could locate even one friend that she's kept in touch with, that friend might be able to give the police a suspect's name days before Jamie herself could remember it."

Eric's expression remained doubtful. "I don't know, Teagan. It's not that I mind spending a couple hours on a Saturday driving around my alma mater. I don't. And I'd be happy to help any friend of yours, you know that. But..."

His voice trailed off uncertainly.

"But what?" she prompted.

"I don't think it's a good idea. I think it's going to bother you more than you think it will—and I don't want to be responsible for that."

Teagan's heart melted anew. She moved closer. "It's not going to bother me," she insisted. "I trust you. It doesn't matter whether I trust her or not." *Which is good,* she thought ruefully, *because I don't.* "I can't very well abandon a good friend just because of one unfortunate coincidence. Not when I'm all she's got."

Eric looked at his wife for a long moment. Then he pulled her to him and kissed her thoroughly. "You're amazing, you know that?" he said when at last he drew back. "I appreciate your trusting me. Thank you."

Teagan smiled. "You don't think I'm crazy?"

He laughed out loud. "A woman who intentionally sends her husband off alone with an ex, all because of some pathological compulsion to champion the less fortunate? Of course I think you're crazy. But I knew that when I married you."

Teagan moved her face closer to his. "Lucky for me, I have other qualities that make up for it."

"Indeed you do."

Their next kiss did not end quickly. The anxiety of the evening, having reached its unpleasant crescendo, at last began to dissipate, and Teagan felt herself falling gratefully into the warm, comfortable state of mind with which marriage to Eric had spoiled her. She was in the midst of this happy state—and deciding to let the dirty dishes wait until morning—when the repellent image intruded into her brain, sharp and ferocious.

Eric with Jamie. Kissing her, just like he was kissing Teagan. Holding her. Caressing her...

No.

Teagan clutched her husband closer. She would not let what happened in the past get to her, because it didn't matter. Jamie was out in the apartment now. Alone. It was Teagan who held the cards; Teagan who held the man.

And Teagan who was going to keep him.

Chapter Ten

Jamie's covers were tight. Way too tight. She tugged at them in one direction while attempting to shift her body the other. Nothing happened. Her hands grappled blindly for an end. She couldn't see one, couldn't feel one. The covers were all around her, her head, her feet, constraining her. Smothering her.

Her pulse began to thud within her ears. She cried out, but the sound was muffled; it seemed to go nowhere. She wiggled and pushed frantically against the heavy material that bound her, but nothing seemed to help. She was locked in a cocoon of cloth, the air too thick and pungent to breathe. All around her was a rumbling noise; a constant, droning vibration. She couldn't see. Was she in her bed at all? Where was she? What was happening?

In an instant she was screaming and fighting against the cloth, desperate to reach the surface, the outside, some semblance of freedom. But the more she fought, the more she could feel her reserves dwindle. Her muscles ached. Her brain seemed fuzzy. She realized she had stopped struggling, and she tried to start again. But she couldn't. Her arms were limp. She couldn't move. She could barely even think.

She was dying.

"No!"

Jamie pulled herself upright in the bed, heavy gasps of breath rocking her chest. She stared at the ancient television set that rested mutely opposite her on an unpainted chest of drawers. The room was dim, but streaks of winter sun peeked around the blinds, heralding the morning. The apartment was calm. Quiet. Ordinary.

Safe.

That's right. She was at Teagan's house.

Jamie reached down and pulled the blankets from her legs. She was hot. She had been sweating like a pig.

What the hell was that all about?

She didn't often have nightmares. The ones she did remember having were lame vignettes about being late for something or having her teeth fall out. Waking up in a sweat was hardly her M.O. — at least not when she had gone to bed alone.

She bit her lip tentatively. She felt different this morning. Her very manner of thinking seemed to have graduated to a more mature and sensual mode. Twenty-four hours ago, she wouldn't have had such a thought. Her brain was indeed getting its act together — at a steady, if still not sufficiently rapid, pace.

By the time she drifted off the night before, she could recall most of high school with chronological clarity, but the years afterward still consisted of random flashes. Already this morning, without any urging, her first months of legal adulthood had fallen magically into place. She could smell the grease in the burger joint's fryer as if she were behind the counter now, pressing picture buttons on the cash register and pushing plastic lids onto paper cups. She could see a guy with blond curls hauling a bag of fries out of the freezer and dumping them in the vat, his feet sliding along the greasy floor as he sang country music off key. He was cute and uncomplicated. He had been her first.

What was his name?

Damned if she knew.

She swung her feet onto the floor and stood up, but her legs were unsteady. She swore and sat back down.

Not even bittersweet memories of what's-his-face could erase the funk such a claustrophobic nightmare had left her in. Why would she dream such a thing? She could believe it was her imagination's way of telling her that she was caught up in her covers, except that she hadn't been. The blankets were still tucked along two sides of the bed; she couldn't possibly have done much thrashing. So why?

She didn't know. Under ordinary circumstances, she might not care. But there was a difference this time. This dream had seemed real.

She took a deep breath and stood again.

Well, it wasn't real. Get over it.

If her legs were still shaky, she pretended they weren't. She crossed to the small bathroom and treated herself to another long shower. The process went slowly one-handed, but she managed, still conscious of how good it felt to be out of the hospital and doing things for herself again. When her hair was blown dry, she fingered critically through the selection of zip-up hoodies and fleece jackets stacked on the dresser. Clearly, Teagan had been looking for things that Jamie could get on easily over her cast, which was fine. But Teagan's fashion sense had improved only marginally since the days of the baseball cap. While the shirts fit Jamie's generous form somewhat reasonably, Teagan's own slim torso must absolutely swim in them, and the baggy sweats were far too big for either woman. How could a mind as sharp as Teagan's be so clueless in such a critical area? Being thin and muscular was Teagan's best asset, why not showcase it?

Never fear, she thought with a smirk, *Jamie is here!*

She could and would get Teagan looking better. It was, after all, the least she could do.

With some difficulty, Jamie managed to squirm one-handedly into the provided plain-Jane underwear (which appeared never to have been worn before) and stretchy sports bra (which stretched so much Teagan would probably never wear it again). She then shrugged on the least objectionable of the fleece tops and sweatpants and moved to the mirror to fix her face.

Jamie smiled. Aside from the yellow eyes, she didn't look half bad this morning. She couldn't do much with her hair because her scalp still hurt around the staples, but it looked windblown and clean and was still perfectly, naturally blond. She was grateful the hospital hadn't shaved her bald. Guys liked her hair.

Joshua. Was that his name? Or maybe it was Jason.

The nightmare butted against her conscious brain, nagging at her to dwell on it. But she was determined not to. As she applied her makeup she focused on the fast-food job instead, trying to match her sensory memories with the concrete words and numbers that should go hand in hand. But her efforts were fruitless. She could remember that her erstwhile paramour had a moon-shaped scar on his abdomen, the result of a motorcycle accident. She could remember that he was allergic to shellfish, that he played bass guitar, and that he owned a pair of cowboy boots made of rattlesnake skin. But she could not remember his name.

Her stomach rumbled. Despite the day's unsettling start, she was famished. Surely Teagan had some food in the house. She only wished she'd eaten more at dinner…

A dark cloud penetrated her thoughts. *Eric.*

She had forgotten.

She moved back to the bed and sank down on it. The nightmare hadn't been a complete waste after all, had it? It had at least displaced her other one.

Damn. What had happened between Teagan and her husband last night after Jamie returned to the apartment? She had been too tired to worry about it then, too exhausted to contemplate her options. Had Eric told Teagan that he and Jamie were lovers?

She glanced at the digital clock on the microwave. It was almost ten o'clock. Teagan had said she would drop by before she left for work. Surely she must be gone by now. She hadn't stopped in after all.

She probably never will again.

Jamie rose from the bed, her empty stomach feeling heavy. Maybe Eric hadn't told his wife anything. Maybe Teagan had simply decided to let Jamie sleep. She was considerate about things like that; she was a good friend.

You mean she used to be.

Jamie ignored the internal pessimism. She slipped on her coat and headed for the door. She was not going to give up on Teagan, no matter how bad things looked. Maybe she had done that in the past—let friendships slip away—but it wasn't going to happen this time. She wouldn't let it.

The voice of one of her more annoying foster siblings popped mercilessly into her head. *Don't you have ANY friends?*

Of course I do! Jamie had retorted. *I have a best friend. Her name is Teagan, and we're really more like sisters than friends. I spend every summer with her family at Indian Lake. Her parents are rich, and they let us go sailing, and waterskiing, and...*

Jamie paused at the door, her hand on the knob. Teagan had no idea for how long—and to what extent—she had been Jamie's rock. Letters or no letters, Jamie had clung to their friendship like a child to a teddy bear, from house to house, family to family, disappointment after disappointment. Her mother might be dead, but Teagan, near or far, in contact or out of it, was still alive—and that meant there was hope. As long as Teagan was still out there, Jamie knew that there was at least one person in the whole, stinking, rotten cold world who really, honest to God, loved her.

Some days, it had been the only thing that got her through.

And no damned guy was going to mess it up now.

Jamie braced herself for the cold and pushed open the door. It would be okay. Eric had no reason to say anything about her. Why would he? And even if he did, a little white lie could still fix it... he could just say they had dated, and leave it at that. She could explain to Teagan that whatever happened with Eric was a long time ago, and that she didn't even remember it...

Jamie stopped short on the landing.

But she would remember soon, wouldn't she? And if her sensory recall proved as astute as it did with the fry cook, she was in for one hell of a slideshow.

She shook herself and started down the stairs. Teagan could *not* know. She just couldn't. If Eric was stupid enough to tell her, he was too stupid a man for Jamie to have become involved with in the first place.

She chuckled ruefully, her breath forming a visible vapor on the cold morning air.

Not even she believed that one.

"Are you sure about the name this time?" the detective asked, his tone openly skeptical.

Ordinarily, such rudeness wouldn't make a dent in Teagan's well-worn psychological armor. But this morning, she was in no mood.

"No, I'm not sure," she snapped into the telephone receiver. "So if you have anything more certain, please feel free to use it. I'm giving you the name she used five and half years ago. As of last night, she hadn't remembered anything more recent than that."

The detective cleared his throat. "So she still has no memory of the events leading up to the attack."

"None."

"But earlier things are coming back?"

"Steadily."

There was a pause on the line, and Teagan felt suddenly contrite. It was unlike her to be such a shrew; not only was it unprofessional, but she knew it would get her nowhere. What was she thinking?

"It's only a matter of time," she continued, modulating her tone. "At the rate she's going, I think she'll remember everything by tomorrow or Monday. But at least we know now that she was enrolled at Pitt under the name Jamie Meadows. Surely that can speed things up? I mean, every day that passes, this guy's trail is going to get colder, right?"

"Right," the detective murmured. It sounded like he was typing on a keyboard.

"Have you come up with anything else about the attack?"

Teagan pressed. "Has anyone reported her missing yet? Any potential witnesses?"

The clicking stopped. "Still no missing person reports that match. As for witnesses, we're not going to get any new ones stepping forward unless we involve the media — start circulating her picture and asking the public for help. We've been holding off on that because you said you knew her. But if this name's a bust too — if she's one of these people who's constantly screwing around with aliases — we may not have a choice. We can't wait much longer, not if we want to nail this guy. Memories fade. Witnesses move on."

Teagan's brow furrowed. "But couldn't publicizing her situation feed information to the attacker about her condition, maybe even her whereabouts? Not to mention the amnesia thing making her vulnerable to any nutcase who wants to claim she's his sister or his cousin?"

"That's the risk we take, yes."

Teagan closed her eyes, and dark images taunted her. Jamie's face blue with cold. Blood from her lacerated head seeping into the snow. Her attacker watching the afternoon news, seeing a picture of her on the television monitor. Touching his beefy finger to the screen, tracing the line of her cheekbone with a fingernail...

"Let's hold off on the publicity," Teagan said. "I'm sure we'll have an address to go with that name soon. She'll remember everything herself in twenty-four hours. Maybe less."

"Let's hope so."

Teagan hung up the phone. Acid churned in her stomach.

She had committed to helping Jamie get safely back where she belonged, and she was going to do that, no matter what. Her social work training had taught her the importance of relating to people without being judgmental — and she had not paid tens of thousands of dollars in tuition for nothing. Whether Jamie was her client, her friend, or both, the woman was in desperate, critical need, and Teagan's concern for her wellbeing was sincere.

The fact that she felt an overwhelming urge to dump Jamie's picture-perfect ass at the nearest women's shelter was immaterial.

She could hardly be blamed, could she? The woman had slept with her husband. Jamie might not remember much about that, but Eric sure as hell would.

Teagan stared at the phone. She wanted to call home, but she knew she shouldn't. She had not only assured Eric that everything was okay, she had gone to great lengths to demonstrate it.

And everything *was* okay, really. What was the big deal with two people who used to date spending a couple of daylight hours together? Whatever Jamie and Eric had shared once upon a time was unquestionably over. Had they not broken up on their own, years before Teagan came into the picture?

Although just *who* had broken up with *whom*, Teagan didn't know.

Her desk phone rang, and her hand swooped down at it like a lifeline. She was eager to keep busy. The last thing she wanted was to be alone with her thoughts.

Chapter Eleven

Jamie rapped tentatively on Teagan's back door with her good hand. Her injured arm had begun to ache again, but she hesitated to take more pain killers. The previous dose had made her loopy, and the last thing she needed was an additional mental handicap. What she really needed was confirmation that Teagan was still in the dark about her husband's prenuptial activities. Once that was settled, she could enjoy a good breakfast.

There was no response. As Jamie was lifting her arm to knock again, she saw Eric through the window, approaching in his own good time. She withdrew the hand and stepped back. The memory assaulted her with a rush.

What are you doing? He had asked her with a grin. He was younger, slimmer.

She had stood at the door smiling back, a duffel thrown over her shoulder. *What does it look like?* she had teased, brushing past him front to front, pressing her chest against his on the way. *I'm moving in with you.*

Eric opened the door. Jamie blinked, attempting to stuff the past back wherever it had come from—and quickly. The Eric she saw before her now was a little older and a little heavier, but the added pounds were no liability. His face and figure were merely fuller, more mature. He didn't look like a kid anymore. He looked like a man.

"Good morning," he said evenly. Coolly.

"Good morning," she returned carefully, every muscle in her body tense. She wasn't used to making nice and being polite; she wasn't use to giving a flip what other people thought of her. But she could not afford any missteps. It was too important that she stay on Eric's good side.

"Are you hungry?" he offered, stepping back for her to

enter.

"Very." She walked in, giving him such a wide berth on the way that her backside scraped against the dryer. She swallowed. "Is Teagan here?"

"No," he answered tonelessly, leading her through the office and into the kitchen via a swinging door she had failed to notice the night before. The layout of the additions was strange, indeed. "She left for work hours ago."

Jamie's heartbeat quickened. "Oh."

Eric kept his back to her as he puttered in the cabinets. "What are you hungry for? We've got a couple kinds of breakfast bars, plus toast and bagels. There's cereal, too, but it's on the stale side, I'm afraid. Or I could scramble some eggs."

A mental flash showed Jamie the younger Eric—holding a spatula and a crusty iron pan, fighting to scrape the last shards of tough, over-browned eggs onto a grimy plate.

She couldn't help herself. She chuckled. "Um, I think I'll pass on the eggs. Thanks."

Eric looked back at her, but his gray-blue eyes were devoid of mirth. There seemed to be a question in them. Did she remember?

Jamie averted her gaze. She didn't want him to know what she was thinking. "Breakfast bars would be great," she said with forced cheerfulness. "But don't feel like you have to wait on me. I can scavenge up my own glass of milk. I'll make myself a cup of coffee, too, if you have it."

He turned from her without comment, placing several boxes of breakfast bars on the counter along with an empty glass. As she settled onto a stool, he went ahead and poured her some milk, then put the tea kettle on the stove. "All we have is instant coffee," he said stiffly. "Is that all right?"

"Perfect," she answered. Instant had been her usual, at least as far as she could recall.

"Sugar, no cream?"

Jamie's eyebrows lifted. He wasn't guessing.

She fidgeted on her stool, not looking at him. "That's

right."

When he said nothing else, she released a heavy breath. Could this encounter possibly be any more awkward?

Left with nothing else to do, Eric retrieved his own coffee cup and leaned against the far counter. Jamie selected several bars and began to nibble. Both sat in silence as a hot blue flame danced under the tea kettle.

"So," Jamie said finally, the silence fraying her nerves even more than the talking had, "I was hoping to see Teagan this morning before she left. Was she—" she broke off, unsure how to ask the elephant of a question that stood between them. She didn't ordinarily have trouble coming to the point, but these were hardly ordinary circumstances. "Was she all right?"

Eric watched her, his face showing nothing besides the cool wall of distance he seemed determined to keep between them. "She was fine," he answered. Then, as if remembering something he was embarrassed to have forgotten, he started and pulled a folded piece of paper from underneath a magnet on the refrigerator door. "She left you a note. Here. Sorry about that."

Jamie took the paper from his hand and unfolded it, resting her wrists on the counter to steady them.

> Jamie,
>
> Sorry to take off, but I hated to wake you—you do need the sleep. Help yourself to anything you want for breakfast; Eric will make sure you get lunch. I'll be back mid-afternoon sometime.
>
> Teagan

Jamie read the nearly illegible scrawled lines, then reread them. She breathed deeply, then read them again. No "dear" at the beginning; no "love" at the end. But this was just a note, not a letter. Besides, Teagan wasn't the effusive type. What mattered more was the implication in the middle.

Teagan obviously expected her husband to treat Jamie to lunch. Didn't that alone give her the answer she was looking for?

Jamie let out her breath with a gush, folded the letter, and laid it on the countertop. Her cheeks felt hot; her body warmer. Teagan didn't know. Everything would be fine.

She looked back up at Eric with a genuine smile. "So, you got drafted to entertain me," she said good-naturedly. "Sorry about that. It's really not necessary. I assure you, I'm quite used to fending for myself. Lunch included."

For an instant, her announcement seemed only to heighten the coolness in his eyes. But just as quickly, he smiled back at her. It was as forced a smile as her previous ones, but it was there. "I don't mind helping you out," he said unconvincingly. "You can only do so much with one good arm. Besides, Teagan has given us a mission."

Jamie's eyes widened. "Oh?"

The tea kettle whistled. Eric poured the water into a mug bearing the curious message: "I [Heart] Antiques Roadshow," added some sugar and a spoon, and handed it over. "She wants me to take you to Oakland and drive you around. See if you remember any of the classroom buildings or someplace you might have lived."

Jamie stirred her coffee slowly. The driving-around-Oakland thing sounded like a good idea, given that the sooner she remembered everything, the sooner she could regain control of her life. But being back on the Pitt campus with Eric... there were just too many things that could go wrong with that. Things she didn't want to think about. "I see," she answered. "That was thoughtful of her. But you don't have to take me. I can catch the bus."

They both knew she had no intention of taking the bus. Weekend service from the suburbs to the university was nonexistent, not to mention that the temperature was below freezing and she was too weak to walk any distance.

Eric did not dignify the suggestion with a response. "We can leave whenever you want. Traffic shouldn't be bad on a

Saturday." He glanced at his watch, then straightened. "I thought I might do some work in the garage for a while. You finish breakfast and let me know when you're ready to go. Okay?"

Jamie looked up at him. He was determined to play the chauffeur, determined to fulfill Teagan's request. Perhaps he was also trying to prove something. "All right," she responded tonelessly. "Thank you." Perhaps it would be good for her to remember more about what had happened between the two of them, along with everything else. She couldn't help but wonder why they had broken up. And whether there was anything she could do now to defuse the aggravation her proximity seemed to be causing him.

And vice versa.

The ten-year-old boy stared at Teagan with puffy eyes. He was small for his age, and even though the standard ER stretcher bed proved too narrow for many patients, his skeletal frame seemed lost within it.

"I wasn't trying to kill myself! I wasn't! Why won't no one believe me?"

"I believe you," Teagan answered easily. Oddly enough, she did. Emotionally disturbed children used all manner of methods to attempt suicide, most of which were too ill-conceived to be effective. But slashing one's palm in a shallow X didn't seem the act of a child who truly wanted to bleed to death.

"You did hurt yourself, though," she continued smoothly. "Why did you want to do that?"

He stared down at his sutured and bandaged hand. "It didn't hurt that much. Can I just go home now?"

Teagan considered. The typical self-destructive, attention-seeking "cutter" carried enough baggage to fill a freighter. She was reluctant to draw conclusions prematurely, but this boy didn't seem to fit that mold. He had no history of acting out, he answered questions about his family with the same slightly bored tone as would most emotionally healthy fourth graders, and his parents seemed not only concerned, but genuinely bewildered.

Perhaps some sort of club initiation? She had seen and heard of stranger things.

"What does the mark mean?" she asked. "Why didn't you make a T, or a V?"

The boy looked at her as if she was crazy. "It don't matter what you make," he argued. "It just got to bleed."

"Why does it have to bleed?"

"So it'll work!" he replied, exasperated.

Teagan tried again. "But what does the blood *do* exactly?"

"It seals it!" The boy seemed suddenly self-conscious. He lowered his voice. "You know… the brotherhood."

Images raced through Teagan's head in a whirlwind. She heard her own voice, youthful and bossy. She saw her hands digging along the shore of the lake, scooping up fistfuls of dripping mud.

We don't have to be blood sisters. That's not hygienic. But we can be MUD sisters!

Jamie's voice now, giddy and carefree. *Ew! You are SO gross, Teagan. Why does it have to be mud?*

Well, we have to have something, don't we? To seal it. Your blood is supposed to mingle, but mud can mingle, too. And besides, it rhymes. Then we'll be real sisters. You in, or not? Here, you take this pile. She had picked up a huge blob of mud and carried it to where Jamie sat on the bank. She then dropped it at the other girl's feet, where it promptly splashed all over both of them. Jamie squealed with annoyance, but wound up laughing.

You're crazy, you know that? But fine. I'm in. We'll be mud sisters. "Sisters of the Mud."

Not like nun sisters, though, Teagan had qualified. She wanted to get married someday.

No way! Jamie agreed. She never wanted to get married.

We'll be just like real sisters, Teagan had continued, her voice more serious. *Just like if we had the same parents and everything. You can't break that bond, not matter how far apart you wind up living. It's for life.*

Jamie's voice was equally solemn. *A sister's always a sister. No matter what.*

Teagan had put a scoop of mud in her right palm and held it up in the air. Jamie, wrinkling her nose, had done the same. Their hands had met with a slap, spattering mud everywhere, raining down brown splotches till they both looked like liver-spotted Dalmatians. But they did their best to withhold their giggles.

I hereby declare us official Sisters of the Mud!

Sisters of the Mud! Jamie had echoed.

It was as far as they had gotten. The ceremony had ended with peals of laughter and, as Teagan recalled, a race to the swimming hole.

"Hey, Lady?"

Teagan snapped out her reverie.

"It's not like a gang or anything, I swear!" the boy explained quickly. "It's nothing bad. But my dad, he gets real hyper about stuff like that. I don't want him to get mad at me, you know?"

Teagan swallowed. The kid would need a little more sounding out on this one. She would have to talk to his parents, as well. But he could be telling the truth. Not all childhood clubs had gang violence on their agendas.

Sometimes, a kid just needed something, or someone, to belong to.

No matter what.

Chapter Twelve

Jamie sat stiffly in the passenger seat of Eric's Civic, wishing he owned a slightly roomier car. They were too close for comfort. He was an attractive specimen, and though the conk on the head might have screwed up her brain for a while, it hadn't touched her hormones. Flirtation seemed to be her primary method of dealing with men, and given how incredibly off limits Eric was, even the most innocent elements of her repertoire seemed inappropriate. She was determined to watch herself, for all their sakes. But self-restraint was not her forte.

"So," she began casually, making another attempt to break the tension. Eric was being friendly enough, but he still spoke as though he were being taxed by the word. She was certain he hadn't always been so laconic—if he had been, she wouldn't remember his laughter. "Tell me. Where was I when you first met me?"

He didn't answer right away, and Jamie's jaws clenched. He was doing it again—the awkward pause, the stalling. Could the man never think on his feet? Be spontaneous?

"I'm not sure how much I should tell you," he answered at last, his voice thoughtful. "I don't want things I say to influence your memories—it might mess them up. Why don't you tell me what you think you remember, and then maybe I can confirm some things?"

"Fine," Jamie replied, not bothering to hide her exasperation. The grownup Eric might be good looking, but so far he was proving an unexpected bore. What had she been thinking back then? How had she gone from fry munching, guitar-strumming Jerry to him?

Jerry. She sat up with a smile.

Hot damn. It was coming back.

"We're in Oakland now," Eric announced as they drove past Magee Hospital and into the university's congested main corridor. "I'll just circle around. You tell me if you want to stop anywhere."

Jamie looked out the windows and attempted to concentrate. She couldn't say what looked familiar, because it all did. If she had been asked to picture the Pitt campus before they left home, she might have struggled, but now it seemed as familiar as the back of her hand. Of course she had been here. She had spent ages here.

"Anything?" Eric asked, turning off on a side street. Brick row houses, virtually all converted into apartments, rose up on either side.

"Everything," she responded. "I've seen it all before. But I remember it from on foot. I don't think I had a car."

Eric turned to face her. "Did you ever get a license?"

Jamie considered. "It seems like I can drive. In fact, I know I can. But I don't remember getting a license, no." Her brow furrowed. How could she recall the mechanics of how to drive, but not the learning process? All she could remember was that she had been desperate to get a license from the day she turned sixteen, but back then, no one had been willing to teach her.

"My plan was to get a car as soon as I started working," she continued, the facts flowing from her brain as she voiced them. "But I couldn't afford one. I couldn't even find one to practice on."

"I let you drive mine."

Jamie turned her head to look at him. She couldn't remember that. "You did?"

He nodded. For a moment she thought he might smile, but then he caught himself. "You told me you had a learner's permit, but I never saw it. I always suspected you were making it up."

Jamie raised an eyebrow. "So why did you let me drive your car?"

Another grin threatened to escape, but he fought it back.

He seemed every bit as determined as she was to play the stoic. But in that moment she realized that his motivation was different from her own. He wasn't so much worried about the impression he was making on her as he was determined *not* to enjoy himself in her company. Jamie could admire his husbandly loyalty, but she wasn't in the habit of spending her time with robotic, humorless men, and she had no desire to start now. Not when she was fairly certain that Eric could be a lot of fun—if he wanted to be. They were both being ridiculous. They just needed to relax.

"Look, Eric," she began, careful to keep her tone light, despite the gravity of her words. "I don't know what I was like when we were together, but I promise you, I have no interest in making any trouble for you and Teagan. You don't have to be so careful with me—it's not like I'm going to throw myself at you. I'm sure I have any number of *much* better-looking guys already lined up and waiting for my return. So, drop the cold fish thing, okay? I'm dealing with enough tension."

She watched his face carefully, unable to predict his reaction. She was hoping he would smile. But his deep, explosive chuckle startled her.

"What?" she demanded, grinning. "What's so amusing?"

"You are," he answered, his voice lighter. "You haven't changed a bit, you know that?"

Her grin faded a little. "No, I don't know that. I was kind of hoping I had."

Eric continued to smile. "I'm not insulting you, Jamie. And I haven't meant to be rude. But you're right. Teagan took the news well—I shouldn't underestimate her."

The blood drained from Jamie's face. Her stomach churned. *"What?"* she sputtered, disbelieving. "You *told* her?"

Eric had the gall to appear surprised. "Of course I told her," he answered. "I told you I would."

"But—" Jamie's retort curbed itself as her mind skipped ahead. So Teagan knew. She had known when she wrote the note this morning.

Was she nuts?

"She *knows*," Jamie asked heavily, "and she still asked you to drive me around today?"

Eric's smile bordered on smug. "I told you she wouldn't hold it against you. Teagan is a truly remarkable person." He paused, and his voice dropped. "That's why I love her. In case you're wondering."

Jamie was wondering about a lot of things. She knew that Teagan had cared deeply about her once, and she seemed to care still. But one fun summer fourteen years ago was hardly an adequate basis on which to trust another female when it came to a man. Jamie was pretty sure no woman had ever trusted her with a man, and from what she remembered, they had good reason not to. So what kind of game was Teagan playing, throwing her and Eric together like this?

"What exactly did she say?" Jamie asked. "How much does she know?"

"She knows we lived together for a couple months," Eric answered. "She knew about it already, she just didn't know until last night that the woman I'd told her about was you. She was shocked at first, just like you and I were—it *is* a pretty unbelievable coincidence. But she was able to put it all in perspective."

Jamie sank back into her seat and stared out the window, her feeble mind still spinning. She wished she could believe Eric's rosy assessment of Teagan's reaction, but her skeptical side ran deep. What women said and what they were feeling were often two different things. There was no way in hell that Teagan wasn't bothered by the thought of Jamie's having slept with her husband—no matter how long ago it had happened. Any sane woman's first reaction would be to toss Jamie's butt out onto the street. But Teagan had played it magnanimous. Not only had she kept Jamie around, she had insisted that Eric spend time with her. Alone.

Why? More row houses rolled by outside Jamie's

window, but as she pondered the question, a very different scene played before her eyes.

I bet I can do a back flip.

The twelve-year-old Jamie had rolled her eyes. *Yeah, right! Just go already.*

Did you know I was the best tumbler in my gym class last year? The skinny girl in the ball cap had bragged. *I really was. The teacher said so. If I had the money for real gymnastics lessons, I bet I could make it to the Olympics.*

Jamie hadn't answered. She had merely planted her hands on her hips and glared until Teagan had finally taken her turn off the dock. Teagan had tossed her hat onto the wooden planks, walked to the edge, and turned to face Jamie. Then she had jumped into the air, twisted…

An unexpected chill swept down Jamie's spine. The seconds that followed had been among the most frightening in her life. Yesterday she had been able to recall pulling Teagan from the lake, but she hadn't remembered the horror of watching her friend's body strike the dock, crumple, and drop into the water. Jamie had screamed. She had stared into the murky depths. Waiting, watching. Hoping. Teagan hadn't come up.

"Jamie?" Eric's deep voice interrupted her reverie. "Take a close look at this street, okay? This is the second time we've been down it, but I'm not sure you were paying attention."

Jamie straightened. She hadn't been paying attention. But she was beginning to understand. Teagan's apparent show of faith shouldn't surprise her. What might be odd behavior for a typical woman was completely in character for the gum-chewing back flipper of Indian Lake. *You don't worry me,* Teagan's bold actions proclaimed, *because I know he's mine.*

Jamie shook her head with a smile. Teagan might not brag out loud anymore, but she still had Chutzpah with a capital C, and sheer gall was something Jamie could appreciate in a woman. It was no wonder she'd always liked

Teagan. This thing with Eric could be prickly, true, but it wasn't insurmountable. She wouldn't let it be.

Her gaze, which had been skipping idly along the pavement outside, came to a sudden, crashing halt. A basement window, glass block and nondescript, had leapt from the building before her and positioned itself front and center in her brain. The sight of it washed all thoughts of Teagan from her mind.

"Eric," she said with a croak, "I know that place."

The car slowed down. She didn't need to tell him which place. He steered the car over to an empty spot of curb a half block down and parked. "Do you want to get out and walk around?" he asked.

His voice had changed again. It was gentle now, concerned. Jamie would think it was sexy if she were thinking that way, but she wasn't. Instead, she felt cold inside. Hopeless. She knew the feelings had something to do with the window. She wasn't sure she wanted to know why.

"Just tell me," she blurted. "Why do I remember that place?"

"Probably because you hated it so much," he answered. "You were living there when I met you. You said it was all you could afford."

Jamie slumped down into her seat and closed her eyes. She didn't want to see the window again. She didn't need to. The images were already in her head. Three other girls and a guy, two tiny bedrooms. Mattresses on the floor. One bathroom with a tub—no shower head. Living underground like moles, getting natural light only from the two glass-block windows in the bedrooms and the illegally barred, long-since broken one in the kitchen. She didn't have to live there; not if she was happy to wait tables forever. But she wasn't. She wanted more.

More took money. Money she'd worked her butt off to save. Money she'd nearly sacrificed her sanity for.

"I hated that place," she reiterated, more to herself than to Eric. "It was always so dark inside. And so cold. The space heaters kept tripping the breaker. At night, we'd turn the fridge off so we could keep them on."

Grim memories poured into her brain. Working, always working. Two part-time jobs, sometimes three. Never any full-time spots. Never any benefits. She hadn't cared where she lived because she was so rarely there. She had no belongings to steal. Just a slowly but steadily growing bank account that became an obsession. She wanted out. She wanted to make it. She was *going* to make it.

"You told me that it was the second apartment you'd lived in since you graduated from high school," Eric offered. "Do you remember the first? I would drive you by it too, but I don't know where it is."

"It doesn't matter," Jamie answered, both her voice and her mood dismal. "I remember it well enough." She had left her last foster placement in what she believed to be a blaze of glory—heady with the thrill of at last gaining both her majority and her freedom. She had secured a decent apartment in the "happening" university area of town and taken on two part-time jobs she believed would pay the rent.

She had been wrong. Each month of even the most basic living expenses had driven her deeper into a financial hole, and since she was already wearing nothing but uniforms and subsisting on greasy fast-food leftovers, the only place to cut corners had been her rent. She had wriggled out of her lease early and vowed to find the absolute cheapest digs available—at least until she could land a full-time job. But at eighteen years of age, with no experience, no connections, and no family support system, she had found that task much more difficult than expected.

"I was naive," she explained simply, not wanting to share all the sordid details of her past. For all she knew, she already had. "It took me a while to realize that being willing to work hard wasn't enough to earn myself a decent living. My first apartment was way too expensive; that dump back there was probably less than I could afford. But after the first year or so of working my tail off, I knew that I wanted to go to college, and I was desperate to save as much money as I could."

Eric made no response, and she turned to look at him. He had removed his seatbelt and was leaning comfortably against the inside of the driver's door, studying her. His expression was kind, almost admiring. "You were the most headstrong, determined woman I'd ever met," he said with a smile. "And believe me, in law school, I met plenty. I was really glad to hear that you made it to college. I never doubted that you would someday."

Jamie blinked. Watching him speak, allowing their eyes to meet, affected her memory like a strong wind — rattling thin windows and blowing open stuck-tight doors. He had been a breath of fresh air then too, hadn't he? So much more intelligent than the other guys she had dated. She was used to being the smart one; after a while she had believed all men were stupid. But Eric had been a surprise. Other men challenged her patience; he had challenged her intellect.

She could remember being with him — talking, laughing. She could see the two of them walking long distances around the campus, and yes — she could remember a car now, too. They had gone to the Carnegie Natural History Museum and stared at stuffed animals and dinosaur bones. They'd taken in a flick at the Omnimax theater. It had been spring. She could remember seeing all the flowers outside when they walked past the Phipps Conservatory. He hadn't much money to spare, either, but they had always found something interesting to do. She had enjoyed his company. She had enjoyed it very much.

"It's coming back to me now," she said, suddenly mindful of her long silence. The new images were plentiful, but they were still unfocused. She wanted to remember everything, and she wanted to remember it in order. "So tell me," she urged again. "Exactly when and where did we meet?"

His response wasn't immediate, but this time he did decide to answer. "Not quite six years ago, during my first year of law school. You had just started working at a restaurant where a lot of the law students used to go for drinks."

Jamie, who had sunk down in her seat to where her knees rested on the dash, sat up abruptly. "I remembered that place last night!" she said proudly. "Dim lighting, smoky. I was always toting around those big, thick mugs of draft—those suckers were *so* heavy. But I liked working there—it was better pay with all the tips, and I liked the people."

She looked back at Eric. "That's where I finally got my first full-time job, wasn't it?"

He shook his head slowly. "I'm not sure. You were working towards it when I knew you—you were certain that a spot would open up and that you would be next in line. But I never heard what happened after we broke up."

"I did go full time," Jamie answered with confidence. She suddenly knew that fact beyond question, even as the other event she strove to remember stayed outside her grasp. "I worked at that restaurant for years. But I don't remember breaking up with you. What happened exactly?"

Eric's eyes locked with hers for only a second. They were searching, almost sad. Then he moved to face forward again, reaching for his seat belt. "Sorry," he said stubbornly. "You're going to have to remember that for yourself." He smiled a little. "I suspect your version will be different anyway."

Jamie's brow furrowed as he shifted the car into gear and started to pull back out onto the road. "Well," she responded shortly. "I suppose it hardly matters. What I really need to remember is who I am now, right?"

"Exactly," he agreed.

Jamie felt her face flush with heat, and her aggravation aggravated her. Who did he think he was, anyway? He had been fun, but it wasn't as though he had been the love of her life. She was quite certain she'd never had one of those. If Eric had meant something to her back then, surely she would feel more for him now. She felt physical attraction, maybe even a reluctant fondness, but that was all.

So why was he being so secretive? Was it possible, perhaps, that she had meant something more to him? A smile spread slowly across her face, even as a pang of guilt nagged at her conscience. *I bet he was in love with me.* If so, it was no wonder the whole situation was so awkward for him—no wonder he didn't want to discuss their breakup. The more it had hurt him, the less he would want to dwell on it. Even now.

So what had happened? What had she done to him? Were her own actions responsible for the fleeting undercurrent of resentment she had sensed in him last night?

She bit her still-sore lip. She could remember their relationship as nothing but pleasant, and yet clearly, she had thrown it away. Thrown away a chance with a smart, handsome guy whom any idiot could see was destined for success.

What the hell had she been thinking?

She wanted to remember. Whether it mattered to her recovery or not, she wanted to know.

"Eric," she said with authority. "I want to go back to that restaurant. Will you take me there?"

She watched as the muscles of his jaw clenched, then unclenched. He breathed out heavily.

"Sure," he said, his voice noticeably tighter. "Whatever you think will help."

Chapter Thirteen

Teagan's office phone rang. She was on her way back out to the ER and debating leaving it to voicemail when she had a sudden premonition that the caller might be Eric. She wanted to hear his voice.

"Social services. Teagan Hansen."

"Hey, honey."

Teagan's shoulders fell. The voice was not Eric's. It was two octaves higher.

"Hey, Mom. What's up? I'm kind of busy at the moment. Can I call you back later?"

"*No*," the voice said emphatically. "You may not. This is important. Are you sitting down?"

Teagan closed her eyes and breathed out slowly. The last thing she needed at the moment was a dose of her mother's theatrics. Despite her best intentions at concentrating on work, she found her nerves fraying further by the hour. She wondered where Jamie and Eric were now, and what Jamie was remembering. Would she concentrate on recalling what mattered to getting her life back, or would Eric's presence derail her thoughts in the worst possible direction?

"What is it, Mom?" she asked impatiently.

Sheryl cleared her throat. "I went by your house this morning. You know, to check up on Jamie. I didn't think it was such a good idea to leave her there alone with Eric all day, even if she was up in the apartment. And just *guess* what I found?"

"They weren't home."

"They weren't—" Sheryl broke off. "You knew that? Well, where did they go? You didn't send them off *together*, did you?"

Teagan put her free hand to her temple. "Look, Mom. It's

fine. All those weird vibes you picked up on last night were nothing. It's just that Jamie and Eric thought they recognized each other, and they did. She used to wait tables at one of his law student hangouts."

Sheryl remained silent for a while. Teagan envisioned her mother's eyes widening, her jaw dropping slowly down...

Finally, the question came. "Well, how well did they know each other?"

Teagan's teeth clenched. She had always been a firm believer in plain, unvarnished truth as the ultimate problem solver. Unfortunately, her devotion to the cause had rendered her a lousy liar.

"As well as anybody gets to know a waitress, I guess," she answered, cringing at the double-entendre. "In any event, I thought she might get her memory back quicker if he drove her around Oakland this morning. Maybe she still lives there... who knows?"

Sheryl allowed another long silence. Teagan's whole body fidgeted as she itched to get off the phone and back to work. Why couldn't her mother be in the midst of her own romantic problems now? Had not whole weeks gone by in the past when Sheryl had forgotten she even had a daughter?

The timing was too cruel.

"Teagan, honey," the dreaded voice returned, fraught with sympathy, dripping with tragedy. "You've *got* to stop being so trusting. I adore Eric, you know I do, but the fact is—he's a man. And as for that houseguest of yours, you take my word on it—she's a home wrecker. I can smell her kind a mile away, and this one reeks to high heaven. If she hasn't made a play for him yet, you'd better believe she will—"

"Mom—" Teagan interrupted.

"Don't 'Mom' me," Sheryl interrupted back. "I know exactly what I'm talking about, and we both know it. I'm telling you, if they really did know each other from before, she's going to use that to get to him. She'll tell him she *needs* him to help her remember, that he's *all* that links her to her past, that he's the *only person* who can make her feel whole again. My God, the possibilities are endless! Eric is in serious trouble."

"My husband is not an idiot!" Teagan said firmly, her patience gone. Her face was hot, her hands sweating. Why did Sheryl have to be so blasted good at making her daughter's imagined fears seem real? And she didn't even know the worst of it. "He's not going to fall for some stupid helpless act. As for Jamie, I'm committed to helping her get back on her feet, and I'm not going to throw her out just because she's a flirt. What would that say about me and my faith in my marriage? You worry too much. I'll call you later. Goodbye, Mom."

"Teagan Nicole! You—"

Teagan pretended not to hear anything more as she dropped the phone into its cradle. *A man.* Her mother needed a man. Where could she get one? The classifieds? She'd call some likely fellow, set something up…

The phone rang again. Teagan stared at it warily. Could Sheryl hit redial that fast? Probably. And yet…

Her hand reached out and picked up the phone. She was so rattled she forgot to answer it professionally. "Hello?"

"Hey there."

A warm wave of relief swept through her body. She sank down onto her desk. "Eric," she replied softly. "How are you? What's going on?"

The background noise seemed loud, and his cell phone kept cutting in and out. But every note of his calm, familiar voice soothed Teagan like a salve. "We're in Oakland now, on our way to Vermelli's. Jamie remembered one of the apartments she used to live in, but not much about school yet. I'm sure she will soon, though. How's everything with you?"

Teagan let out a breath and smiled. "Fine. Saturdays are always busy. I'd rather be home, though."

A rap on the door startled her. She looked through the

narrow window pane. It was one of the ER charge nurses, gesturing sharply, holding up two fingers. Teagan was needed in room two. Now.

"I'm sorry, Eric," she responded, her regret genuine. "I can't talk now—they need me. Tell Jamie good luck, and… thank you. For doing this."

His voice softened. "No problem. I love you."

A hot, burning pressure assaulted Teagan's eyes. She shut her lids tightly.

"I love you, too."

She dropped the phone into its cradle for a second time and made a grab for a tissue from the box on her desk.

She blew her nose and got back to work.

***

"It won't open for another twenty minutes," Eric explained, looking from the sign on the door to his watch. "You want to go across the street to the bagel shop? We can get some coffee and wait there."

Jamie withdrew her hand from the ornate metal handle reluctantly. The green painted front door of Vermelli's had spurred little memory in itself, since she had always used the staff entrance in the alley. But looking through the windows beneath the awnings into the dim restaurant had made her heartbeat quicken. She recognized every booth, every dark-green vinyl table cloth, every artificial plant. Going inside would be like walking back in time, and it was a walk she was anxious to take.

But the door had been locked tight. They stood now on the sidewalk outside, pulling their coats tighter around them. A biting wind bounced between the traffic and the pavement, whipping street litter around their ankles.

Cold. Always so cold…

"Sure," Jamie responded eagerly, moving toward the nearest crosswalk. "Let's get coffee."

They hustled into the tiny restaurant, stood in line for two regular javas, and settled into a table near the window. Jamie sipped at the hot coffee with a mixture of pleasure and angst. Eric had paid for both cups. He had to, because she didn't have a dime. Considering everything else he was doing for her, one might not think that accepting a couple dollars' worth of coffee should be a sensitive point. But for Jamie, it was.

"I'll pay you back," she repeated, stone faced.

Eric rolled his eyes. "Will you knock it off? I'd have thought you would have outgrown that obsession by now."

Jamie stiffened. "Obsession?"

He chuckled good naturedly. "You have to be the only female I've ever met who absolutely refused to let anyone buy anything for her. *Ever.* Being able to take care of yourself was always a point of pride with you."

Jamie's lips drew into a smile. "Right. I was pretty firm about that, wasn't I?"

Eric smirked. "You could say that."

An image of Jamie's mother floated peacefully into her head, warming her thoughts as the hot coffee warmed her body. *You gotta take care of yourself in this life, kiddo,* her mother had said tenderly as she plopped two marshmallows into a cup of instant hot chocolate—Jamie's favorite. *You can't count on anybody else to do it for you. And you won't need to. Because I can tell already, sweetheart—you've got what it takes.*

A voice interrupted her reverie. "Hey there, Jamie."

Jamie looked up, startled. A woman about her own age stood above her, holding a plastic tray. She was wearing a work apron from the coffee shop and had been bussing tables around them before she stepped up. She was plump, but not unattractive, with brown hair and eyes and dimpled cheeks. She looked familiar. Sort of. "Haven't seen you around in ages," the woman continued, unsmiling. Her words were pleasant, but her tone was reserved. "What have you been up to?"

Jamie studied the other woman's face, searching for some

clue to explain not only who she was, but the reason for her not-so-subtle coolness. Jamie had seen her before, but where? No circumstances, much less a name, were forthcoming. There were a hundred questions Jamie wanted to ask the woman, but the words wouldn't come. She sat, tongue-tied, having no idea where to begin.

When the silence turned awkward, Eric came to her rescue. "Jamie had a head injury a couple days ago," he explained. "She's still having some trouble with names and faces, so don't take it personally if she doesn't remember you." He extended his hand. "I'm Eric Hansen, another old friend. She didn't remember me either at first."

The woman's dark eyes moved from Jamie to Eric. She shook his hand awkwardly, then returned her attention to Jamie. "A head injury?" she repeated with skepticism.

Jamie bristled. She was getting the disturbing feeling that this woman not only disliked her, but was disinclined to believe a word she said. With an effort, she kept her own voice as pleasant as possible. "Yes. I'm sorry I don't remember your name. But you do look familiar to me. If you could tell me your name and where you know me from, I would appreciate it. It might help me put things together again."

The woman looked back at Eric, as if weighing the odds that he were in on whatever bizarre scam Jamie might be playing. Whether it was his lawyerly presence or his apple-pie smile that swayed her, Jamie didn't know, but after several seconds of consideration, the woman glanced back at the restaurant counter, pulled up a chair, and sat down.

"My name's Kirsten," she said, studying Jamie curiously. "We worked together at Vermelli's for a while—before you left. We never heard from you again. You said you'd keep in touch with everybody, but you didn't."

Jamie felt a dull pressure in her stomach. The woman's eyes weren't hostile, but they were hardly glowing with affection. Had Jamie known her well? Had she done something to offend her?

Jamie couldn't remember. But when she looked into Kirsten's face, her feelings about the other woman, ironically, were nothing but positive. She seemed, even, to respect her.

"When did all this happen?" Jamie asked, not sure how to ask the rest of it.

Kirsten shrugged. "Oh, I don't know. Four, five years ago now. I worked there another year after you left, and then I got a full-time factory job with Heinz. But they laid me off last summer, so here I am, back in Oakland, wiping down tables again."

Silence descended. Jamie didn't know what to say. She tried to picture Kirsten in a Vermelli's apron, and the image came easily. She could picture her joking around with Jamie and the other girls. But the memories ended there. If Jamie had liked her so much, why hadn't they kept in touch?

The pressure in Jamie's stomach increased. She knew why, didn't she? Because that's the way it always was. She made friends easily, but nothing ever lasted. When it was time to move on, she moved on, and she didn't bother looking back. Getting attached to people only made you hurt more. It was a lesson all foster kids learned, but the smart ones learned it sooner.

"Do you remember where Jamie was living when you met her?" Eric asked. His tone was casual, but judging from the intensity in his eyes, Jamie believed he was almost as anxious for the information as she was.

Kirsten considered, then shook her head. "Sorry, don't remember." She looked back at Jamie. "I only ever saw you at Vermelli's. You didn't go out with the rest of us much."

"Do you know of any other friends she might have kept in touch with?" Eric pressed. "The problem is, she doesn't remember where she was living before the accident. It's important we figure that out as soon as we can, so finding a recent friend or coworker could really help."

Kirsten's dark eyes widened. "Oh, I didn't realize. No, I don't know of anyone like that." She seemed suddenly embarrassed. "I mean, Jamie might have had other friends, but I'm sure she didn't keep up with anyone else at Vermelli's. Not after the way she left..."

The sentence died on Kirsten's lips, and Jamie's face burned. Once again, someone else knew more about her business than she did. And in this case, it was obviously something embarrassing. "So what happened?" she demanded, no longer bothering to watch her tone. "What exactly did I do? Did I get fired? Did I shoot somebody? Did I do a strip tease on the bar? What?"

Kirsten's chubby jowls twitched a little, as if she were considering a grin. But she decided against it. "You really don't remember?"

Jamie's internal temperature skyrocketed. "*Tell* me!"

Kirsten shrugged. "Okay, fine. You got fired."

"For what?"

Kirsten hesitated only a second. "You and one of the other girls had a knock down, drag out fight in the kitchen. Nobody got hurt, but you ruined a lot of food, and you were yelling so loud that everybody in the restaurant overheard it. You both got fired."

Jamie swallowed. She seemed to know the likely cause of such a confrontation, even though she couldn't remember that particular one. Two things would be givens. One: the fight was over a guy. Two: she hadn't started it.

"Let me guess," she responded in a deadpan. "This woman was interested in some guy who was interested in me, and she thought it was all my fault. Am I right?"

The lines of Kirsten's face hardened. "They were engaged. But after you started coming on to him, he broke it off with her."

Eric scooted his chair back and rose. "I think I'll get some more coffee," he announced, making haste toward the counter.

Jamie sighed. She didn't want to believe Kirsten's account, but she knew it was probably true. She liked to flirt. She was good at it. Men responded without fail, and the supply of attentive ones was endless. Flirting not only brought in good tips, it livened up her otherwise humdrum existence. Men were easier to get to know, more fun while they were around, and less hassle to dump than were women friends. They lived for the moment; they shook things off. They liked to keep things light—and temporary. In other words, they met her needs perfectly.

Could she help it if some men liked her a little too much?

"I don't remember any of that," Jamie explained. "But I do remember working at Vermelli's—that's why we're here waiting for it to open. I want to go in and see what looks familiar." A thought inspired her. "Do you know if anybody who worked there when we did is still there?"

Kirsten shook her head. "No, everybody's gone. The owner's the same, but he wouldn't be any help to you—he never had anything to do with the wait staff. He just dealt with the managers, and you know how those guys come and go."

Neither woman spoke for a moment, and Jamie realized that Kirsten was studying her again. "I like your contacts," Kirsten said finally. "That color is really interesting. But your blue eyes were always so pretty, I don't know why you'd want to change."

Jamie had no chance to answer. Kirsten glanced over her shoulder, and upon seeing Eric pick up his refill and head toward the table, she leaned in toward Jamie conspiratorially. "Come on," she cajoled, her eyes flashing with mischief. "Did you really lose your memory? Or is all this for *his* benefit?"

Jamie's face grew hot with indignation. Lying to a man was one thing, but scheming to trap him was another. As if she ever had to work that hard for sex!

"This is not a joke," she retorted, her voice sober. "What, you think this cast is a fake, too? The truth is, somebody hit me over the head and left me with no ID."

Kirsten's eyes widened, and for several seconds she sat still—almost as if in shock. Eric returned to the table and sat down again.

"Oh, my God!" Kirsten exclaimed. "You're not that woman they found in the park on the Northside, are you? Beat up and rolled in a blanket?"

An icy chill pervaded Jamie's chest. Her limbs turned numb. *Rolled in a blanket.* She knew she had been found unconscious in the park, but the detective had never said anything about a blanket. Neither had Teagan. Kirsten must be thinking of something else. Despite what everyone at the hospital seemed to think, Jamie was sure she'd been jumped by a mugger. Some strung-out kid wanting drug money, probably. It was the only thing that made sense.

No mugger would wrap her in a blanket.

A cool sweat erupted on her skin as this morning's nightmare rushed back at her. She had felt confined, restrained. There had been cloth around her. She couldn't breathe. There had been that strange vibration, that droning noise...

"Jamie?" Eric's concerned voice cut only partway through the din. "Are you all right? What's the matter?"

"Oh, my God," Kirsten repeated with a squeak. "That *was* her, wasn't it? Didn't she know?"

"Jamie?" Eric reached over and put a hand on her arm.

Jamie's mind returned to the present. She flinched and drew back. "Sorry," she said weakly, not looking at either of them. "I just got distracted." She moved her gaze out the window and across the street, her pulse racing. "Vermelli's is probably open, now. Let's go, Eric."

She stood up.

"I'm sorry if I said something I shouldn't have," Kirsten apologized, rising. Her concern seemed genuine, and for a second, Jamie felt an impulse to reassure the other woman. But she couldn't. There was no reassurance in her.

"It was good to see you again, Jamie," Kirsten continued. "I hope everything works out for you."

"Yeah, thanks," Jamie offered in a half whisper, shrugging on her coat as she headed for the door.

Beat up. Rolled up.

You're suffering from hypothermia…

The nightmare played on. Vibrations. A droning noise.

She reached the door of the bagel shop and stopped, her head resting against the glass. The room was spinning. She knew what her brain was trying to tell her. She just didn't want to hear it.

It wasn't a nightmare, Jamie. It was real.

She had been wrapped up in a blanket. Wrapped up tight, head to toe. She had been found at the park, but she hadn't been attacked there, had she? She had been taken there. Driven in a car.

Stuffed in the trunk.

"Jamie!" Eric said firmly, turning her to face him. "Look at me. Are you feeling all right?"

She tried to back away from him, but the closed door stopped her. All she could do was stand there, blinking at him.

"I'm fine," she lied.

She was familiar with indifference; she was familiar with dislike. She was used to people, particularly women, getting angry at her.

This was different.

Someone hates you, Jamie.

"Do you still want to go to Vermelli's?" Eric asked quietly. "We don't have to if you'd rather not."

Jamie looked back at him. She saw a sudden flash of his younger self— shirtless, shaving in front of a mirror. He had a great body. She had enjoyed being with him immensely…

She averted her eyes. How she could possibly think about sex, even as her every limb shivered with horror? Was it the only way she'd ever known to escape?

"I want to go," she answered sharply, pivoting away from him to push the door open. "I want to find out what happened. *Now.*"

The door didn't move. Like an idiot, she was pushing on the wrong end. Eric reached out a long arm and gave the door a shove. She had to shuffle close by him to exit, and the touch of his body aggravated her very marrow.

Slut.

She burst through the half-open door and headed for the crosswalk, not waiting for Eric to follow.

Somebody hates you, Jamie.

She heaved in great gulps of the freezing cold air. Her heart pounded against her ribs.

Hates you enough to kill.

Chapter Fourteen

Teagan slumped down in her desk chair, letting her head fall backwards over the seatback. There was a water stain on the ceiling. Actually, there were several.

She had been running like a madwoman for hours, unable to get back to her office, even for a second. Now at last, she had found a couple minutes to breathe and check her messages.

The results were disappointing. Two messages from Sheryl, which she had skipped and saved, knowing full well she would never open them again. A half dozen from inside the hospital. None from the police, who should certainly have a home address for Jamie by now, if not a complete employment history. Nothing from Eric.

She could call him on his cell phone, of course.

But then he would think she was worried.

The ceiling square directly above her head was off kilter by a good inch. She averted her eyes, knowing that if she stared at it one second longer she would itch to climb up on her desk and fix it, and she was not getting paid to inhale asbestos. What she was getting paid to do was clean out the social service department's overflowing inbox, and she had best stop brooding and get to it.

She allowed herself a sigh. Paperwork was her least favorite part of the job, and it showed. At least three days' worth of mail and memos packed the clear plastic bin, with the most recent delivery escaping over the side rail and fanning onto the desk like a deck of cards. She picked up the escapees one by one, separating internal documents into one stack and postal deliveries into another. She began with the latter, which required less thought. Junk mail. Conference notice. Community action flier. Get well card. Get well card.

Get well card.

She thumbed through the latter without enthusiasm. People often sent cards to the hospital for patients who were already discharged, and at Northside General, it fell to social services to either forward them or return to sender. Priority wise, the task was bottom of the barrel, and Teagan was about to drop the envelopes into her catch-up bin when the address on the last one caught her eye. She released the other two and pulled it in for a closer look.

"The Woman Found in the Park"
c/o Northside General Hospital

Teagan drew in a quick breath, but then shook her head and released it. The card was no cause for concern. Jamie's plight had been broadcast on every local news station; it was not unusual for "famous" patients to receive well wishes from strangers. Her first name had not been mentioned; how else was the sender supposed to address the envelope?

Teagan moved to slip the card into her bag with the intention of giving it to Jamie when she got home. But her hand stopped in midair.

What if it *wasn't* from a stranger?

She studied the nearly square envelope, bending it slightly. It felt like a standard, ninety-nine cent greeting card. She held it up to the light, tilting it, pressing down on the surface. The front was covered with flowers.

It's nothing.

Teagan's teeth gritted. She knew she had no business opening Jamie's mail, even if it was addressed so impersonally. But something about this correspondence bothered her.

There was no return address. The postmark was from downtown Pittsburgh, which was meaningless. Few people lived within that zip code, but any person passing through downtown could have dropped it in any box.

It was the perfect choice for anonymity.

Teagan's pulse quickened. The card could be important.

It could be evidence. Maybe she shouldn't show it to Jamie at all. Maybe she should take it straight to the police…

Screw the police, she thought angrily. Why would they care about a card that was probably from some kindly grandmother, when they were too busy to run a simple address check? Wouldn't it make more sense to find out what she was dealing with first?

She flipped the envelope over. Her fingers ripped open the flap and pulled out the card. A bouquet of daisies graced its cover. The heading read "Fondest Wishes for Your Recovery." Without further debate she opened the card and looked inside.

> I don't know who to say "dear" to, because I don't know your name. But I heard about what happened to you, and I just want you to know that my thoughts and prayers are with you. I have never had injuries such as yours, but I was hospitalized at Northside General for quite some time when I broke my hip last winter, and I know from experience —

Teagan relaxed. It was nothing. A legitimate get well card from a legitimately concerned citizen. Or perhaps just a lonely one. In any event, it was nothing to worry about. Perhaps Jamie would enjoy it.

She folded the card closed, planning to stuff it back in its envelope, but then she hesitated. The handwriting seemed odd. It was unsteady, as one might expect from an older person. But it was printed rather than in cursive, and the letters seemed stilted. It looked like a man's handwriting.

Teagan opened the card again. Men did break their hips, and some probably did send get-well cards to strangers. But not as often as women did.

She glanced down at the signature. "Yours Truly, Alice."

Teagan's eyes narrowed. Her gaze returned to the top of the long paragraph of scrawl, and this time she read through to the end.

...I know from experience that it's not pleasant to be in the hospital for any length of time, especially when you don't have your loved ones around you. I hope your family is with you now. I don't have any family and that made my illness very hard for me. You see, I was diagnosed with glaucoma and cataracts, and I've had surgery a couple times for a narrowed urethra listen to me, please. this is all a misunderstanding. What happened was an accident. I know you'll remember soon, and when you do, Please, please call me before you talk to anyone else. We can work this out. I'll make it worth your while. I promise. Then when I got out of surgery for that, I started having trouble with my heel and needed foot surgery. So you see, I know what it's like to have a lot of health problems and feel alone. So I thought maybe this card, even though it's from a stranger, might help. God bless you, my dear.

Teagan's face flushed with heat. "You bastard!" she cried out loud. "You think you're so damned smart!"

She dropped the card onto her desktop as if it were on fire. *Accident, my ass!* It was him. The man who had left Jamie to die. He knew he was in danger of exposure and he wanted to buy Jamie off... or worse. If she made that call, would he ask to meet her someplace? Someplace deserted, perhaps?

"So sorry!" Teagan sputtered with venom. "But Jamie's not that stupid. And neither am I."

Her hand reached out. She picked up the phone.

It took several seconds for Jamie's eyes to adjust to the light—or lack thereof—on the inside of the solid wooden door of Vermelli's Restaurant. Only the landing on which she now stood was at street level; the rest of the space was underground. She placed an unsteady hand on the wrought-iron railing and felt her way down the plush carpeted staircase, half feeling as if she were walking in a dream.

The aroma was as familiar to her as any scent could be.

Coffee. Alcohol. Grease. A hint of cooked meat. The navy blue and hunter green checked carpet beneath her feet was worn in all the same places. The metal light fixtures hanging from the walls were just as dusty, and their funnels of thick red glass still subdued what little light was shed by the cheap bulbs within. She had tried to slip in a hundred watt once, by the cash register, so she could read the stupid checks. The boss had gone ballistic.

She did remember, didn't she?

"Have a seat anywhere. I'll be with you in a minute," a woman in a black apron called out with disinterest. Jamie stared after her as she disappeared through the swinging door to the kitchen. The black uniforms were new. Hers had always been green. They'd had to wear black pants, a white button-down shirt, and the green apron. She hated white shirts. She had sworn that once she left, she would never wear a white shirt again.

"Where would you like to sit?" Eric asked her.

Jamie started. She had forgotten he was with her. But now that she heard his voice again, it too seemed a familiar part of the surroundings.

She glanced into a back corner of the room, the short arm of an L that wrapped around the bar. She walked to where she could see the booth in question: a circular corner unit that could seat eight or nine. It had been the law students' regular spot. They would drink Iron City draft and gorge themselves on buffalo wings and nachos. Neither appetizer was Italian, but they stayed on the menu anyway. Old Man Vermelli was a businessman, not a purist.

Jamie stopped short of the booth. There was no one else in the restaurant yet; the lunch hour always tended to be lean. She moved sideways and slid into one of the tall booths along the wall, positioning herself where she could watch the back corner. It held a fascination for her, yet she didn't want to be any closer.

Eric sat down opposite her, removed his coat, and laid it on the seat beside him. Jamie left her own coat on; she was anything but warm.

"Are you really all right?" he asked quietly, studying her. "I'm guessing that what Kirsten said back there came as a shock to you."

Jamie had no intention of discussing the matter. She was doing her best to beat back the fear in her gut, to wall it off, compartmentalize it. It would still exist, but no one else could see it.

"I remember working here," she announced. "It's all just like it was. Except for the uniforms."

The waitress approached, delivered two laminated cardboard menus, and left with their drink order. Jamie knew that she should be hungry, but her stomach balked at the selection. She tossed the menu back onto the table, a queer irritability growing inside her. "You'd think they could serve one thing I haven't personally seen defiled in the kitchen," she said sourly.

Eric peered at her over his own menu, his voice detached. "The oriental salads are new."

Jamie didn't answer. Her eyes were staring at the plastic salt and pepper shakers, but her mind was seeing something else. She remembered the place vividly now. Her first day, her first paycheck. It was the first chance she had ever had to earn tips, and she had milked it for all it was worth. For once, she had gotten paid to be a flirt. Her natural inclinations were no longer a distraction; they were a bona fide business plan.

She knew she had considered herself lucky to work here, and that for a while she had been relatively happy. Yet at the same time, the sight and feel of the place filled her with a smothering unease.

Was this all she had ever done? Served food and drinks, flirted for tips? She knew that she had gone to college, but she could not remember whether she had graduated. Maybe she had dropped out. Maybe teasing men for money was the only thing she had ever succeeded at. Her plan had always been to keep reaching higher, to keep moving up. So what had happened? What the hell kind of life had she been living to be dumped like garbage in a park?

"Jamie," Eric said heavily, his voice treading the line between concern and exasperation. "You're worrying me. What are you thinking?"

She raised her chin and looked him in the eyes. Obviously, he could tell that it wasn't the Vermelli's menu that had turned her stomach. She also supposed he was not going to leave the subject alone. That being the case, she might as well get some information from him.

"Tell me the truth," she demanded, her husky voice carefully controlled. "Was I really found in a blanket?"

Eric's sympathetic eyes didn't blink. "All I know is what Teagan told me. But that's what she said, yes."

Jamie stared back. Fear and anger battled within her, but it was anger she preferred, and anger that would have driven her to bang both fists on the tabletop if her arm didn't already ache. "Then why didn't she tell me?" she raged. "Nobody tells me anything!"

Eric slipped cleanly into lawyer mode. "Whatever decisions Teagan made, she made in your best interest. The police always hold back some details—in this case, they probably didn't want to bias your memory. Plus, I'd imagine that your doctors didn't want you stressed unnecessarily. Surely you can understand that."

The waitress delivered their drinks, took their stiffly delivered lunch orders, and left with haste. Jamie stared at her ice water in silence. It looked cold. Everything was cold.

She had been freezing that night too, hadn't she? Being bashed on the head and smothered wasn't enough...

"I had a nightmare," she blurted, unable to stop the traitorous words from escaping her mouth. She wanted to stop there, and she would have stopped there, if it weren't for the softly spoken words that echoed in her head—advice from a loving mother to a frightened child. *If you tell your nightmare out loud, Jamie, it won't seem so scary anymore.*

"This morning," she continued before she could think

better of it, "I dreamed I was wrapped up in something—that I couldn't breathe. And there was this noise, and a vibration. Like an engine." She stopped and took a breath. "I woke up in a sweat. I thought my mind was just making things up. But now I'm not so sure."

Eric said nothing for a long time. She didn't know what he was thinking. Her eyes were fixed on her hands.

"I don't know what to say to you, Jamie," he said finally, gently. "All this is way out of my league. I do think you should tell Teagan about the nightmare, because it might mean something. But even if it does, you know you're safe now, right?"

Jamie raised her eyes to his. She took in the sincerity of his expression, the compassion in his earnest eyes. She knew those eyes well. There had been a time when she adored them.

"You think so?"

"I know so," he said confidently. "You're going to remember who it was that hurt you, and the second you do, the bastard is toast." He offered an unexpected smile. "We'll plant evidence if we have to. I know one of the assistant DAs, and he's totally amoral, so he'll go along."

Jamie smiled back.

"No man gets the better of Jamie Meadows, that's all I know," he finished, taking a swig of cola from his thick glass mug.

Meadows. Of course!

Some measure of warmth returned to her. It started with a flush in her cheeks, then spread pleasantly to her fingers and toes.

"Is that so?" she baited.

He chuckled. "You, Jamie, are one of the most hardworking, motivated, independent, take-no-prisoners women I've ever met. You're also a master manipulator who can twist three quarters of the male population around her pinky on demand. That last part is a talent you were always quite proud of, by the way."

Jamie grinned broadly. Clear as day she could picture Eric with his law student buddies, sitting in the back booth, drinking beer and downing huge plates of greasy nachos with jalapenos. Eric loved the jalapenos. She always made sure the cook gave him extra.

"And were you in that three quarters of the population?" she dared. Whether he was specifically trying to make her feel better about herself or whether he was merely trying to distract her from her fears didn't really matter. Either way, he was succeeding.

His eyes narrowed playfully. "For a while."

Jamie cast another glance at the corner booth and was struck with the memory of the day they met—the first time Eric had joined the already regular crowd of law students she'd been flirting with since fall. She had liked all those guys. They talked about interesting subjects and they had the smell of future money about them. But she wasn't looking for any MRS degree; she wanted money of her own. She had wanted to drop her serving tray, slide into the booth, and *be* one of them.

Eric's appearance in the group had been an unexpected treat. She was drawn to him immediately, though she had been at a loss, then, to explain why. At twenty two he had been skinny and fresh faced, hardly the dark and dashing hero type she claimed to prefer. Looking at him now, she wondered if—in the back of her mind—she hadn't taken his sunny smile and red hair and converted him into a Walton. John Boy, Ben, or Jason—any of them would do. When her foster homes had cable, she had always found the retro show somewhere. The Waltons were the big, loving family she had never known, and she had watched their travails with rapt fascination, never admitting, even to herself, how she longed to step bodily into that fiction.

Goodnight, Jamie.

Goodnight, family.

Whatever the attraction, Eric had always stood out from the pack. At work she would flirt with anything bearing a wallet, but when it came to actual dating, she was very selective.

He had made the cut.

"I remember meeting you now," she admitted, feeling unexpectedly awkward. "Your friends were so much fun—very sweet. It almost made up for them being such lousy tippers."

Eric laughed. "None of us had any money, you know. Steve and Brian used to skip other meals just so they could afford your beer and buffalo wings. They were all half in love with you."

The smile disappeared from his face. Jamie felt a pang in her stomach, and squelched the question that sprang immediately to mind.

And were you?

Instead she reached for a packet of sugar, tore it open, and dumped it into her still untouched ice water.

She hadn't been in love with him, had she? She couldn't swear it, being that she still wasn't sure what romantic love was. She had been fond of him—very fond. He had been good to her. He had been fun. But in searching her databank of warm fuzzies, the memory of him failed to touch her the way memories of her mother did. That indefinable pull, that depth of connection that made her feel secure and vulnerable at the same time simply wasn't there. Whatever she felt for him, it hadn't been strong. Not half as strong, even, as what she felt for Teagan.

But still, there was something. She watched him as he sipped his cola, eyes averted, on edge, yet tolerant. She had hurt him, no doubt—as she seemed to hurt everybody. But he didn't appear to be holding it against her. Last night she had perceived some antagonism from him, but she felt no hint of it now. Rather, he seemed to be doing his best to help her. What he stood to gain from it, she couldn't imagine, except perhaps the appreciation of his wife. But he was just as likely to get grief from that corner, whether Teagan intended it or not. So why should he give Jamie the time of day?

She continued to study him as he sat, eyes focused on some distant point, his thoughts inscrutable.

I love you, Jamie.

The memory was sharp and crisp. He had said the words as they lay cuddled on a twin bed, their bare skin concealed in the darkness, sated, content. And what had she said in return?

She couldn't remember.

Her eyes followed the line of his jaw, tracing his neck down to the curve of his shoulder.

She hadn't been in love with him.

But maybe she should have been.

Chapter Fifteen

The detective appeared in Teagan's office within an hour of her call. He leaned his thin, forty-something body across the front of her desk, tapped at the edge of the card with a pen until it faced him right side up, and squinted. He was an unimpressive man physically, small in stature and pale skinned—a stark contrast to the impression formed by the deep, rumbling voice Teagan had heard over the phone.

"Clever," he mumbled, rubbing bony fingers over the smattering of gray stubble on his pointed chin. "I wouldn't have guessed that."

Teagan leaned closer, her heart beating loudly against her ribs. "What do you mean?"

The detective pursed his lips a moment before answering. "First impression on a case like this would be that we were dealing with a hot-tempered boyfriend, maybe an outside chance of a drug deal gone bad. Either way, we're looking for a bully—a thug. But this card doesn't fit. Somebody went to a lot of effort to get that message across confidentially. It was deliberate. It required a brain."

Teagan felt a shiver. Being beat up by a witless bully for no particular reason was bad enough. Being attacked by someone calculating, for a specific reason, was worse.

"There's also the fact that he seems to know about her memory loss," the detective continued grimly. "That wasn't reported by the media, which means he must have tapped into the grapevine here at the hospital."

"But we have—"

He held up a hand. "Don't lecture me about HIPPA. Staff talk; we both know it. What's significant is that he was savvy enough to get the information without tipping anyone off." The detective frowned. "This guy's obviously got a lot to lose if the victim comes forward and identifies him. Maybe his problem with her was personal, like he's married and needs to stay that way, or maybe the victim knew something about him and his business that she shouldn't have. Maybe he meant to kill her; maybe he only meant to threaten her originally, but things got out of hand. Either way, her pulling through just made his situation a whole hell of a lot worse."

Teagan nodded mutely. Her head swam with unpleasant scenarios as the detective carefully dropped the card into an evidence bag and then collected her fingerprints. There could be others on the card, he explained, that would match an existing criminal record.

He moved towards the door.

"Did you get a current address yet?" she asked anxiously. Jamie's going home now was out of the question, of course. Wherever she had been living would not be safe until her attacker was behind bars. But getting a good look at the place, even from a distance, could jump start her memory.

The detective shook his head.

Teagan's ire sparked. What was taking so long? It had been hours. "But you have her name!" she protested, sharper than intended. "You must be able to track some of her history."

The detective paused, one hand on the door knob. "We could find out everything we need to know in about five minutes if we had the *right* name. But it isn't Meadows any more than it was Knight. Which is why I need to talk to this woman again myself. She's lying to you, Ms. Hansen. And I'd like to know why."

Teagan felt as if she'd been slapped.

No, she assured herself. Jamie wasn't lying. Why would she?

"That's impossible," she said firmly. "The names didn't even come from her. I remembered what name she used when she was younger, and another acquaintance remembered the name she went by after high school."

Teagan squirmed at her own instinctive desire to hide that other "acquaintance's" identity. "Jamie must have changed her name recently. Maybe she got married."

The detective looked back at her with a gaze that bespoke sympathy—a sympathy Teagan didn't want. "Listen, Ms. Hansen," he began slowly. "It's not a matter of not having the victim's 'current' name. What I'm telling you is that there never *was* any Jamie Knight, or any Jamie Meadows. There are no records with either name that match any part of her history. The woman is using aliases. And if she used those names years ago, then she was using aliases years ago. Understand?"

Teagan stiffened. What the detective was saying made no sense. Why would Jamie lie about her name, on two occasions, years apart?

What else had she lied about?

"I have another appointment in half an hour," the detective explained, opening the door and letting himself out. "But I'd like to interview the victim again later this afternoon. She'll still be at the address you gave me?"

Teagan nodded. "I'll make sure she's home." Her mind flashed a picture of Jamie and Eric, laughing and reminiscing over plates of steaming pasta. Maybe Jamie had remembered more by now. Maybe she remembered living with him.

Teagan squelched the picture with a blink.

"Her whereabouts aren't known to anyone else, right?" the detective asked.

Teagan shook her head. "Just my immediate family. And the social services department here, of course."

He nodded, his voice solemn. "Good. Let's keep it that way."

"The salad you didn't finish was $8.95, so with your half of the tip, plus the coffee you had earlier, I'd say you owe me $15.75. We'll add 7% interest after a month," Eric teased, regarding Jamie with a mischievous look from behind his third glass of cola.

Jamie grinned. She hadn't said much during their lunch — neither one of them had. But the more time she spent in Eric's company, the more she realized how well he seemed to know her. He hadn't bugged her to talk when she got quiet. He had offered her the croutons off his side salad, which she promptly devoured. And now he was making clear that the lunch he had just paid for was nothing but a loan. Most women would be offended. Jamie was touched.

She had spent the meal watching him, thinking, trying to remember. The years after high school, still blurry this morning, came back to her easily now. But she had little desire to dwell on them. She had worked like a dog, and she had lived like one. While the people about her talked of partying and fun, she had gone home to her dreary basement and collapsed in exhaustion. There were boyfriends here and there, but none of the relationships had lasted. She had had neither the time nor the energy to concern herself with what anyone else needed — it was always, only, about her. Her working hard toward her goals and battling to keep her spirits up in the process.

Eric had helped with that. He had brought an infusion of lightheartedness, of cheerfulness, into her ordinarily dreary life. At least for a little while.

"Where was your apartment?" she asked, blurting out the question just as he was reaching for his coat. "The one where I stayed, too?"

He stopped what he was doing and looked at her, his eyes wary. His posture stiffened. "Not far from here. Why?"

His evasiveness made Jamie all the more resolute. "Because I want to remember it," she insisted. "Why else?"

Eric shook his head and stood up to leave. Jamie joined him. "Is there some reason I shouldn't remember your apartment?" she pressed.

He pulled on his coat and moved toward the door, his gaze avoiding hers. "You can remember anything you want, but my apartment isn't going to help you figure out what you need to know now. We should be focusing on when you went to school. I'll drive you by some of the academic buildings and you can see — "

He continued to talk, but Jamie ceased listening the instant when, in passing by the kitchen, she caught a glimpse of the staff exit. The sight of the deeply scratched, black metal door connected with her gut like a lasso.

Time to go home.

On its other side, she knew, was a narrow concrete alley and a rusted metal stairway leading up to the street. She had climbed those stairs hundreds of times, her feet and back already aching, dreading the ten block hike that separated her from the thin mattress on the floor of her apartment. In winter, she dreaded the trek so much she had once begged, unsuccessfully, to be allowed to sleep in one of the booths. At least then she would have been decently warm.

"Jamie? Are you coming?"

Eric stood at the bottom of the staircase, his voice impatient. The distant, guarded man he seemed now was not the one she had known. Young Eric had always been sweet to her, considerate and obliging; and when they were together, she had looked at that black door differently. She had moved through it, in fact, with a surge of anticipation…

A grin spread across her face. She caught up with Eric and passed him on the stairs. "Let's go for a walk," she suggested, her voice chipper. Not waiting for an answer, she exited the front door of the restaurant, rounded the corner, and began a determined march up the street.

She could hear Eric's footsteps behind her. "Jamie!" he called. His tone expressed displeasure, but made no particular demand. She ignored it. When she neared the end of the block she broke into a jog, heedless of the stinging sensation the bitter cold air brought to her lungs. She knew exactly where it was. Just two duplexes over.

Her steps didn't slow until she reached the building. She stretched out her good arm and leaned onto its concrete-topped brick newel post, suddenly conscious of a profound weakness in her limbs.

Eric appeared behind her at once. "Dammit, Jamie!" he swore, his voice distressed. "What are you thinking? Do you want to pass out right here on the street? You just got out of the hospital!"

Jamie looked away from him without comment. The truth was, she *had* forgotten what shape she was in. She concentrated on breathing slow. Creeping blackness flirted with the periphery of her vision, and for a moment she feared she would pass out.

Eric's hands came around either side of her waist, poised to steady her. "Are you all right?" he asked.

After a moment, Jamie nodded. She didn't move, but raised her chin just enough to take in the building's façade. Eric's apartment had been on the left, second floor. Shared with another law student who was never home. It had been sparse, but clean—far cleaner than Jamie's own communal living quarters. More importantly, it had had two bedrooms with doors that locked. And behind one of those doors, in a soft, comfortable bed, was Eric. Sweet, dependable Eric.

Jamie removed her hand from the post and straightened. She could feel Eric's chest behind her shoulders. His heavy breath tickled her ear. "I didn't mean to scare you," she apologized. "I'll be fine. I just wasn't thinking."

Eric stepped back. His withdrawal filled Jamie with a piercing sense of disappointment, and she turned to face him. "I remember this place," she announced. "I remember coming here after work all those nights."

Eric took another step back. His eyes flashed with the same mild hostility Jamie had seen last night at dinner, but this time, it spurred a more visceral reaction. Hurt.

"I'm glad you're remembering your life," he said coolly. "But this is one road we don't need to go down. Can you walk to the car, or do you want to wait here and let me pick you up?"

He doesn't want me to remember, Jamie thought to herself,

suddenly cognizant of the cold that stung her face and fingers. She shoved her hands in the pockets of her coat.

Correction: *Teagan's* coat.

"I want to stay a minute," Jamie said stubbornly. She turned back toward the building and focused on the second story window. Her inner vision penetrated the red brick, looking through it to see a tiny bedroom with scratched, unadorned, off-white walls. It contained nothing but a bed, a dresser, and a television.

You want breakfast? Morning light had streamed around the pull down shades, casting light on Eric's lean body as he pulled on a pair of jeans. He had looked good in jeans. He looked good without them.

No thanks, she had answered, stretching her arms, lifting her bare torso out from beneath the sheets. *I have to get to work.*

He had stopped and turned to watch her, his expression devilish. She had grinned back.

"Then why don't you just sit down on the steps and relax," Eric suggested, interrupting her reverie. "I'll go get the car."

It took Jamie a moment to regroup. She looked back into his clearly annoyed, present-day face, and a wave of unexpected sadness washed over her.

He had loved her once. Now he wanted to forget. She hadn't returned his love, but she was desperate, now, to remember what it had felt like. She knew that being with him had made her happy. She could remember enjoying everything about his company — his wit, his tenderness, his peculiar mixture of earnestness and sunny naiveté. She had felt comfortable, safe, and alive. So why hadn't any more come of it? Why had it ended so soon?

He was already moving away from her when she reached out and grabbed the sleeve of his coat. "Tell me why we broke up," she ordered. "I can't remember that part, and I want to know."

Eric's eyes narrowed with aggravation, and his jaw

clenched tight. But he did stop walking. "We wanted different things," he answered finally, his voice clipped. "You wanted independence and freedom. I wanted someone I could count on. End of story."

His words filtered through Jamie's brain, but they made no connection with her own recollections. "I don't get it," she said bluntly. "Did I cheat on you?"

Eric huffed out a breath. "Well, I wouldn't know, Jamie. But if you do remember anything like that, please keep it to yourself." He shook off her grasp and started walking again.

She followed. "Don't get angry," she cajoled. "I'm just trying to understand. Don't you think it's only fair we're on the same footing, memory wise?"

He stopped once more and faced her. "Are you going to stay here or not?"

"No. I'm walking back with you."

He exhaled and resumed moving, but this time his steps were slower. They walked in silence for several seconds before he spoke again. "I don't know why you wouldn't remember it," he said gruffly. "It happened right in the middle of Vermelli's. Half the people we knew witnessed the whole ridiculous scene."

Angry eyes appeared in Jamie's mind. Eric's eyes. His whole face was red. She had never seen him like that.

I wasn't doing anything! She had protested.

Not doing anything? He had argued back, bewildered. *You were practically giving that guy a lap dance!*

People had started to stare. Red heat had risen in Jamie's veins. Her pulse pounded. *I was earning a tip!* She had shouted back, incensed.

Eric had glared back at her, his eyes livid. She could see the hurt in them, too, but she ignored it. All she cared about was his anger. His anger and his possessiveness.

You don't have to act like that to earn tips, he had informed her, more coldly now, almost patronizing. *You're a waitress, not an exotic dancer.* He had moved closer to her then, taken her arm. His voice dropped. *And you belong to me.*

A pressure within her chest had built near to bursting. She shook him off with a fury, her whole body hot, his clingy touch searing her skin. *I don't BELONG to anybody!* she had raged, losing all sense of place, oblivious to their audience. *I flirt with who I want, when I want, and I'll do whatever I want — whether you like it or not!*

The restaurant had fallen silent. He had stared at her a moment, disbelieving. Then he had answered her with four words. Four words that had resonated in her head for a very long time.

Fine. You do that.

Jamie lowered her gaze to the cracked concrete. Her stomach felt sour. She could recall quite clearly what she had been thinking back then. How important it was to her to be her own woman, just like her mother had been. Her mother hadn't needed a man, and neither did she. The mere suggestion that any man thought he could own her, possess her — it had rattled every pole and vine in her clumsily constructed cage. She had rebelled with everything in her, against all reason. Against, even, her own desires.

I will!

She couldn't remember if she and Eric had ever spoken again. She only remembered watching his back as he stormed out the door of Vermelli's. A part of her had wanted to cry. But she hadn't.

Their slow steps were halted by the melodic ring of Eric's cell phone. He reached into his pocket and brought it to his ear. "Hello?" There was a brief pause. Jamie watched as his features softened with relief. His eyes twinkled, and his mouth drew into a smile. "Hey there, 'me.'"

Jamie felt a queer heaviness in her middle. She bounced on the balls of her feet to keep warm. She kept her eyes averted.

"We just finished lunch," Eric explained, his voice exuding a warm, familiar tone that made Jamie feel even colder. "Why? Did you need us to do something?"

The next pause was a long one. In the middle of it, Eric

laid a hand on Jamie's elbow and encouraged her to start walking again. He removed it promptly, and the two continued down the sidewalk. "We can be home in an hour, no problem," he offered. "I thought we'd just drive by some of the classroom buildings first." His voice dropped in volume, but Jamie could still understand him. "Did they find out something?"

She turned toward him, and as she watched his face grow pale, the blood seemed to drain from her own.

"Oh," he said in a whisper. He cast a glance toward Jamie, then looked away again. "Don't worry," he said more cheerfully, his voice back to full volume. "I'll have her home in time. And when will you be there?"

He grinned during the silence. "Can't wait. See you then."

He snapped the phone closed and replaced it in his pocket, then turned to Jamie. An artificial, tolerant smile had taken the place of his genuine one. "We'll need to head back pretty soon. The detective wants to talk to you again. Teagan thinks he may have some new information."

Jamie's gaze returned to the pavement. Her foot struck a clump of undissolved salt pellets, scattering them across the sidewalk and into the gutter. Teagan had told him something important, but he wasn't passing it on. Jamie wanted to be mad about that, but she was having a hard time focusing her thoughts. All she could hear was the love in his voice when he talked to his wife.

All she could see was that she had been an idiot.

Chapter Sixteen

Jamie felt tired. Bone tired. She leaned her head back against the car's headrest, her eyes drifting idly over the architectural mishmash of college buildings that filed by outside her window. She would have been content to go straight back to the garage apartment and take a nap, but since Teagan's phone call, Eric seemed to have been seized with new determination. He wanted Jamie to remember more, that was clear. He just didn't want her to remember anything else about him.

"Think about walking around with a backpack on your shoulder," he suggested. "Or picture yourself late for class, running, trying not to slip on the ice. Something around here's bound to ring a bell. It would be better if we could walk some of these streets, but you're obviously not up to that."

Jamie said nothing. She shifted in her seat, trying to stop the aching in her leg bones. The heavy feeling wasn't coming from any one place; she ached all over. She was weaker than she had realized, and it bothered her.

"Jamie?" Eric prompted after another long spell of silence. "Is something wrong?"

"I'm just tired," she lied.

"Do you want to go home now?" he asked, sounding disappointed.

She turned her head to the side and looked at him, wondering at his motivation. Most likely, he was anxious to be rid of her, and he knew that the return of her memory would be the best and quickest route to her departure from both his garage and his life. But maybe there was more. Maybe whatever Teagan said on the phone had worried him… and he did still care.

She chose to look on the bright side. "No," she answered, sitting up a little. She cleared her throat and looked out the window more purposefully. "I'll give it another shot. I remember being at Vermelli's after you left. I even halfway remember working with Kirsten. I'm thinking I started school not too long after I got fired."

The face of a nameless manager popped vividly into her mind, his face glowering with rage. Like most of the Vermelli's managers, he was a college graduate paid at least twice her salary. He was also a complete incompetent with no administrative ability, little common sense, and the social skills of a fourth grader, and she had responded to his expletive-filled reprimand by flipping him off.

I don't need this lousy job anyway!

Jamie smirked. Yes, she was definitely already set for school the day she had burned her bridges at Vermelli's. She wasn't *that* stupid.

"I remember wanting to be a manager," she confessed. "Walking back into Vermelli's and telling all those morons everything they were doing wrong. The managers never listened to the wait staff, you know. They thought they didn't need to. But they missed so many opportunities…"

Her voice drifted off as she became lost in thought. When she realized Eric was smiling at her, her mind trained back to the present. "What?"

"You were always brainstorming something or other," he explained. "If not how to do things better at the restaurant, then how you were going to make your million. For a while there you were talking about law school, most likely because Steve and Brian kept pushing you about it. They thought you'd make a great litigator."

A warmth pulsed through Jamie's limbs. She knew she liked those guys. They hadn't eaten all those buffalo wings just to ogle her cleavage. They had respected her. And so, she was certain, had Eric.

"Did you think I should go to law school?" she asked.

His mouth drew into an odd half smile. "Actually, no. I

thought you'd find it boring. You were more of a hands-on person. You liked what was concrete and practical, as opposed to legal lingo and theories."

Jamie considered. He was right. "So you advised me against it?" she asked, curious.

To her surprise, he laughed out loud. "*Advising* you was pretty pointless, Jamie. But I did point out that a business degree would take four years instead of seven. Besides, it was clear you had the savvy for it. Your ideas about how Vermelli's could be made more profitable made a lot of sense."

Desks. Chalkboards. Papers. Books. Computer lab. Library fines. Grade reports in the mail. Straight As. One completely undeserved B in astronomy. But she would show that asshole, wouldn't she? The nerve!

Jamie's eyes widened as the images came on at light speed, tumbling over one another in a massive, chaotic rush. "Oh, my God," she whispered.

Eric turned his head toward her. "What is it?"

She swallowed hard. "I just remembered all these things about school... all at once. Here I've been trying all day and couldn't remember squat about going to Pitt, and then I'm just sitting here and all of sudden—" she broke off, unable to find the right words. "It's just so strange how it happens. I can't describe it."

She looked over at Eric. "I thought college would be hard, but it wasn't. I hardly studied at all."

"I'm not surprised. You were great at memorizing things. You never wrote down an order." He offered a good-natured smirk. "I was plenty jealous of that talent."

Jamie grinned back. "That's right. I would sit down the night before a test, memorize everything, and then spit it right back out. I didn't have any trouble working at the same time, either. Heck, school was like a break for me. And then, I got that job..."

Her thoughts moved forward swiftly again, too swiftly for her voice to follow. She was quiet for a moment, thinking. Eric didn't interrupt. "I got some kind of a desk job," she finished finally. "But I can't remember where. I just remember that doing it was so easy I couldn't believe I was getting paid."

"You mean after you graduated?" he asked hopefully.

"No. Before that. It was a work/study thing." She concentrated hard, attempting to remember graduation, a job hunt, anything that might bring her closer to the present. Her last, precious paycheck. Her bank account. Her apartment? But her most recent images still fell short. All her memories were of being a student.

"That's all," she said finally, releasing a pent-up breath. She was disappointed, but not very. She had remembered one thing that meant a lot to her. "I know I did well," she announced, aware that her cheeks were reddening. "I made the Dean's List every term." *So there.*

Eric chuckled. "Of course you did. You're smart, and you're a fighter. You always did get whatever you set your mind to."

Jamie relaxed in her seat. Maybe he was right about her. Once she set her goals, she was as relentless as a pit bull. She had been determined to finish college, get a business degree, and get a good job managing a restaurant—or some other sort of business. But restaurants were what she knew, and what she had a passion for.

Just not waiting tables. She would never wait tables again.

"I wanted a job managing a restaurant," she proclaimed. "But I don't know if I ever got one."

Eric turned his head toward her, and for a second his eyes held hers with a glimmer of affection. "Believe me," he responded. "If that's what you wanted, that's what you got."

His gaze returned to the traffic, but Jamie continued to watch his face. He was a good guy. A good man. No doubt she had treated him badly once, and her reappearance now hardly delighted him. But still, he was willing to help her. To boost her spirits, make her feel better about herself.

He *was* right about her. She did always get what she wanted—eventually. No matter how tough the effort. No matter how long it took. She was the queen of delayed gratification, an anomaly in her generation, apparently. She had always known what she wanted. She had always been willing to work for it.

For one heady moment her ego soared, but all too soon it deflated again. The other thing was still there, brooding. The closer her memories came to the present, the more she could feel it—a deep, festering worry lurking just around the corner of her brain, reminding her that everything had *not* turned out all right. That after so many years of single-minded scratching, clawing, and striving, somewhere along the line, she had made a mistake.

A mistake that had almost killed her.

Jamie followed Eric into his warm, quaint old house, feeling more awkward with every step. She shouldn't have accepted his offer to come in for something hot to drink. She should have gone straight back to her garage apartment and waited for the detective there.

But she didn't want to. The preferences of her mood usually won out over any desire to be polite or appropriate, and today was no exception. She wanted to stay with Eric a while longer. She didn't care to examine why.

He stepped into the dining room and picked up a note lying prominently on the center of the table. As he eyed it, his face hardened into a frown. He crumpled the paper in his hand and tossed it into the trash can as he moved into the kitchen.

"Was that from Teagan?" Jamie asked, aware that she didn't deserve an answer.

"No," Eric grumbled, his expression still sour, "it was from Sheryl."

Jamie turned to the side a little, hiding a smile. Sheryl had been pleasant enough at dinner, but Jamie knew Teagan's mother didn't trust her. Women like Sheryl never did. And with good reason, generally.

She needn't have worried about concealing her amusement. Eric wasn't watching her; he was busy filling the tea kettle.

She knew that he had offered her a drink only to be nice, and that he would probably prefer to relax and unwind alone. But she couldn't face her sterile apartment just yet. She liked this strange little house with its tight corners, circuitous floor plan, and decades of heirloom accumulation—though she was at a loss to explain why she should. It certainly didn't reflect her own tastes.

Whose tastes it did reflect, she wasn't sure. Certainly not Teagan's or Eric's. The wallpaper in the dining room was covered with faded cornucopias, and the woven drapes were adorned with an equally faded checkerboard pattern. An antique china cabinet was full to bursting with dated curios: an assortment of painted ceramic bells and figurines of large-eyed children and women in frilly dresses. As Jamie studied them, it occurred to her that Teagan had mentioned the house was a gift from Eric's grandparents. Evidently, the older couple had donated it lock, stock, and barrel.

The wall opposite the window was covered with family pictures. Not having noticed them before, Jamie skirted the table and stepped in for a closer look. Eric and Teagan's wedding picture had been placed front and center, but Jamie gave it only a cursory glance. Her eyes moved instead to a series of pictures of Eric and a red-headed girl, presumably an older sister. Most were inexpensive studio pictures with a Christmas backdrop; but the most recent appeared to have been taken at Eric's law school graduation. One large, more professional portrait featured the red-headed girl—now grown up—with a husband and baby son. Older pictures showed Eric's mother as a child and as a young woman, including her wedding portrait. Both Eric's parents appeared to be blond, and Jamie wondered idly how the red-headed offspring had come about, and whether they were a surprise.

She was standing there, still wondering, when she felt Eric's gaze upon her. He had finished whatever he was doing in the kitchen and was leaning against the doorway.

"Did I know you had a sister?" she asked absently. She sensed, rather than saw, him shrug his shoulders.

"I can't remember you ever asking about my family," he responded, his tone deadpan. "I asked plenty about yours, but you wouldn't answer me."

Heaviness pressed Jamie's gut. She didn't doubt he was telling the truth. She had never wanted to talk to anyone about her family — or lack thereof — and hearing other people talk of their good fortune had always felt like rubbing salt in a wound. Her curiosity now was out of character.

"What's your sister's name?"

"Meghan," he obliged, his tone still flat.

"And her baby?"

"Brendan. They live in Ohio." He stepped forward and walked around the table, passing her and moving out into the hall. "I'll be back in a minute."

He was gone. The staircase squeaked as he made his way upstairs. Jamie turned from the wall, planning to go into the kitchen herself and mind the tea kettle, but she stopped short at the trash can. What exactly had Sheryl written?

The crumpled paper lay conveniently on top of this morning's breakfast bar wrappers and saturated tea bags. Without a second thought, Jamie stooped and retrieved it.

Eric,

Just stopped by to see if Jamie needed anything while Teagan was at work. I'd be happy to help out if you have other things to do — I'm sure she's getting pretty lonely and a little female company is exactly what she needs. Call me! You know I'd do anything for the man of my little girl's dreams.

Love,

Your doting mom-in-law

Jamie chuckled ruefully as she recrumpled the note and tossed it back into the can. Sheryl was *so* subtle. She might be doting as well, but Eric had clearly been irked by her lack of faith, as well he should have been. So far he had been the soul of propriety.

Then again, so had Jamie.

Her eyes rested on yet another portrait, this one sitting separately on the antique buffet. She crossed over to it, and her smile faded. The portrait was packed with Eric's family members—four generations, to be exact. And this one included Teagan.

Jamie stepped forward, stretched out her left hand, and picked up the frame. Eric's wife was sitting on a white couch—not their own, but one in a studio somewhere—right next to his grandmother. The elderly woman held Teagan's hand in both of hers. Eric stood behind, beaming.

Jamie set the picture back down.

So Teagan has two families now, she thought, prickly heat suddenly itching beneath her heavy fleece top. *The one wasn't enough for her.*

She stood a moment, not moving, looking at nothing. Her jaws clenched.

She knew she was jealous, and she recognized the emotion for exactly what it was: both petty and destructive. In the past, no matter how little she had possessed herself, she had always managed to avoid envy—usually by denigrating whatever it was other people had. Sure, it was a nice car, but the insurance payments must be a fortune, and it would get stolen in a heartbeat if you parked it in on the wrong curb. Sure, that woman's boyfriend was rich, but his fingers were stubby and he had no butt. There were always ways Jamie could make herself glad of her own situation. Always.

So why couldn't she do it now?

Her eyes moved back to the portrait, almost against her

will. She and Teagan had so much in common that summer on Indian Lake. Single mothers. Absent fathers. Constant moves from school to school. But there were differences, too. Big differences. Teagan's mother might be flighty, but at least she was alive; and Teagan's grandparents had both loved and wanted their only granddaughter. Now Teagan had a second family as well, complete with extra grandparents, a sister-in-law, and a nephew.

They're probably a pain in the butt. Interfering all the time. Quarreling.

They probably get together at Christmas.

Jamie tore her gaze from the photograph and stepped away. Dear God, how she hated Christmas. Every year the sound of those damnable carols spurred acid in her gut, and the corrosion didn't stop till New Years.

It's your own fault, you know. All you ever do is push people away.

Jamie's eyes closed. The argument inside her head was an old one. Most of the time she could beat it, but it had the hateful knack of resurfacing whenever she felt her weakest.

The only person she could count on was herself. She had learned that lesson the hard way when her mother smoked her way to lung cancer at the age of thirty. No matter what anyone promised, no one could always be there. Teagan had promised a lifetime of friendship, and Teagan had disappeared. Every foster parent or sibling she ever even started to get close to she had lost; and it hadn't been long before she quit trying. She had come to understand that the only insulation against heartache was not caring at all. She hadn't put her strategy into words back then; she hadn't even realized what she was doing. Only as she grew up did she begin to understand the defensiveness that drove her. But that didn't mean she could change. Her fears, her phobias, would always be with her; her relationships would always be booby trapped. Whenever anyone got too close, she felt it—that horrible, creeping, worry. She never gave anyone the chance to hurt her. Before they could, she was gone.

She wanted to be strong, like her mother. She wanted to live her life without needing anyone. But despite all her steely determination, despite all the excuses she came up with for her fascination with cheesy retro shows like *Little House on the Prairie*, she understood all too well the conflict that raged inside her.

She wanted a family. She just didn't want to *need* one.

The staircase creaked under Eric's weight, and Jamie's eyes sprang open. Moisture clung to her lids, and she raised her hand to swipe it away. But in her haste she clopped her cast hard against her cheek bone.

She swore.

Eric stopped short in the entrance to the dining room. Before he could ask if she was okay again, she spoke.

"I keep forgetting about this stupid cast," she explained quietly. "It's a wonder I don't knock myself out."

The tea kettle whistled. Eric headed toward the kitchen first, but Jamie, desperate for a diversion, also whirled to fetch it herself. They collided just outside the kitchen doorway, standing toe to toe.

"I'll take care of it," Eric offered.

A tremor of weakness swept through Jamie's legs. She must have whirled a little too quickly—the corners of her vision were darkening again. She felt herself sway.

"Oh, no you don't," Eric warned as his strong arms moved to support her. "Don't you dare pass out on me. Sit down."

He began to guide her towards one of the dining room chairs, but Jamie planted her heels. She didn't want to move. She wanted to stay where she was—where she had been six years ago. If she hadn't been so damned stubborn back then, things might have been different. This one relationship, at least, might have kept going. If it had, there might be smiling pictures of *her* on the walls right now. She might be part of a family—a family that would actually notice if one of its members went missing for three whole, freaking days.

So tired.

The gnawing weakness that had threatened her all morning seemed at last to take hold, draining whatever strength was left in her, both physically and emotionally. A queer sorrow overwhelmed her, but she had no reserves with which to fight it. She wanted to curl into a ball, hide under a rock—yet she didn't want to be alone. She craved the warm comfort human arms could give her, the ardent male attention she knew was not affection, but which could sometimes pass for it if she closed her eyes and dreamed.

She wasn't thinking any further than that when she slid her arm around Eric's neck and pulled him closer. She leaned into his chest as naturally as if she had done it a thousand times. Then she stood on her tiptoes and pressed her lips to his.

Chapter Seventeen

Teagan approached her front door with quicker steps than usual. She was always eager to get home and relax after work, but the strain on her nerves this particular day wasn't going to ease at the threshold. She and Jamie had business.

The absence of an unknown car in her driveway told her that the detective had not yet arrived, which was good.

She pushed open the unlocked front door to a familiar sound: the whistling of a tea kettle. The noise continued unabated as she took off her coat and hung it in the hall closet. Puzzled, she closed the closet door and moved into the dining room toward the kitchen.

The sight that met her as she rounded the corner was objectively nothing. Jamie was dropping into a dining room chair; Eric was moving away from her. He stopped at the doorway to the kitchen and looked back at Teagan with wide eyes. His face was flushed.

"Teag," he said breathlessly. "You're home."

Foreboding socked her gut like a blow. She didn't need eyes to sense the charge that arced between him and Jamie, linking them even as they parted, its invisible sparks still crackling in the air.

Teagan's shoulders instinctively drew back. With a mighty effort she refused to assume the worst, instead focusing intently on her husband's face, searching desperately for some simple, nonthreatening explanation.

What's going on? Her eyes asked.

It's all right, his answered swiftly. *Don't worry.*

Teagan attempted to steady herself. She would not overreact. She trusted him, didn't she? "Yes, I'm home. So, were you waiting for me to get the tea kettle, or have you both gone deaf?"

It would have been a good line if she could have delivered it without her voice quavering.

Eric moved into the kitchen. "Sorry," he called out as the whistle muffled, then died. "Jamie looked for a second like she was going to pass out, but I think she's all right now."

Teagan's gazed turned toward the blonde sitting at her table. Jamie's skin was pale, but each cheekbone sported an incongruous patch of red that only served to magnify her perfect bone structure. "I'm fine," Jamie mumbled. "Just a little worn out. Your husband's a real slave driver when it comes to this memory thing."

Eric appeared in the doorway. He threw Jamie an odd look that seemed half indignation, half admiration; then he hastened to Teagan's side. "Don't listen to her," he said lightly. "It was her own fault she took off running — not my idea." He pulled Teagan to him and held her tightly.

Teagan hugged him back. He and Jamie were clearly covering something up, but the fervor of his embrace bolstered her. Whatever was going on, he would tell her the truth about it later — she was certain of that. She was also certain that right now, all he wanted was to get the hell out of Dodge.

"I'm going to the workshop for a while," he proclaimed, releasing her with an uncharacteristic kiss on the cheek. "Call me if you need me." He stepped back briskly, threw Jamie a perfunctory parting wave, and disappeared into the hall.

Teagan watched after him for a long moment, her mind racing. His embrace had been reassuring; his kiss, not so much. In fact, something about it had been distinctly disturbing. But she could not — and would not — think about that now.

She took a deep breath and turned, slowly, back to Jamie. She hadn't faced her erstwhile friend since learning the truth about their shared history, and that prospect had been harrowing enough without this debacle added on.

Just don't think about it. Any of it.

She pulled out another chair and sat down. Jamie regarded her hostess studiously, as if trying to remind herself who she was.

"You almost passed out?" Teagan inquired. Her voice sounded harsh. Cold. She should probably get a grip on that.

Or not.

Jamie's golden eyes were swimming with emotion, and at first she seemed unable to speak. "I guess I was pretty close to it, yes," she answered finally. Her tone was breathy and fatigued, without a trace of defensiveness.

Its candor was unexpected. Teagan found herself taken aback.

"I tried to jog, earlier," Jamie continued wearily. "It was stupid, I know. It really wiped me out. Is the detective coming soon?"

"He should be," Teagan answered. Her eyes were locked on Jamie's. She studied every glimmer, every nuance of expression. She was looking for guilt. All she saw was discouragement.

She cleared her throat and regrouped.

Innocent until proven guilty.

"I'm glad he's not here yet," Teagan continued, her voice, if not all her feelings, back under control. "It's just as well if you and I talk alone first."

Jamie's face remained passive, almost disinterested. "About what?"

Teagan continued the eye contact. "About your name. You told me it was Knight. You told Eric it was Meadows. Neither one was right. You have any explanation for that?"

Jamie's eyebrows rose. She blinked once, then twice. Then, to Teagan's amazement, she burst out laughing. "Oh, my God," she chortled, her eyes watering heavily. "No wonder nobody knows who the hell I am."

She chuckled until Teagan interrupted her. "So, you remember your real name now?"

"Oh, yeah," Jamie answered with a snort. She attempted to wipe her eyes, but banged her cast against her face instead. She swore, then switched hands. When she finally looked back at Teagan, her tone was apologetic. "Sorry about that—I didn't mean to make you mad. It wasn't anything personal. I've been lying about my name since kindergarten."

Teagan's brow furrowed. "Why?"

"Because it sucks. It's the most horrible name in the world—one kids can't resist pronouncing the wrong way to make it crude. It made my school days a living hell. I could never understand why my mom didn't ditch it. I sure did. I wrote it down on official papers, but anybody who didn't have to know, I told different. I always wanted to change it legally, but I wasn't sure how, and I was afraid it would cost too much. So whenever I could get away with it, I just lied."

"What was it?" Teagan asked.

Jamie grimaced. "Fukas."

Teagan thought a second. "Gotcha."

"Meadows was what I used the most," Jamie explained. "I liked the sound of it. That's what everybody at Vermelli's called me. Only the management knew otherwise, and as long as I used the right name on my bank and tax stuff, they didn't care. I didn't have a driver's license or a credit card, so it wasn't like anyone else could find out that easily." She paused. "What name did I tell you again?"

"Knight."

Jamie smiled. "You must have caught me in the middle of my *Brady Bunch* phase. I had a crush on Peter—Christopher Knight."

The feeling overtook Teagan despite her resistance. The same warm, companionable sentiment that always swamped her when she thought of Jamie the girl. Never mind the justifiably mixed feelings she had for the adult. Sitting here now, listening to a Jamie who looked twenty-six but sounded twelve confess to having been smitten with the curly haired Peter Brady, the two women could just as easily be back in the canoe, wearing mud-spattered swimsuits and swerving to avoid imaginary manatees.

"I had a thing for Peter, too," Teagan admitted, allowing herself a grin. "Of course, that show was so old the actor was probably forty by the time we saw it. Hopeless cable junkies, that's what we were—at least during the school year. We probably should have been reading."

"Speak for yourself. I read *Tiger Beat*."

They shared a laugh, and a pang struck Teagan's middle. Why did her relationship with Jamie have to be so blasted complicated?

Just don't think about it.

Teagan straightened in her chair. She could do this. Really, she could.

"So, tell me," she began, trying hard to keep her voice businesslike. It was the only way she knew to discuss anything even remotely related to Eric without degenerating into a screeching harpy. "How much did you remember today? What's the closest thing to the present you can recall?"

Jamie's eyes flashed disappointment. "Well, having my name come back is something, I suppose. The details are filling in. But I still can't remember anything recent. I remember starting classes at Pitt not long after I left Vermelli's, but that would be four or five years ago."

Teagan considered. "You might still be in school now, then."

Jamie's brow creased. "Maybe. But I don't think so."

"Why not?"

Jamie didn't answer. She stared into space across the table, her eyes distant. "I can't explain it," she said finally. "I just have this feeling that even before I wound up in the hospital, something had changed. That I was... someplace different."

She said no more, but the hollowness in her voice spoke volumes.

Teagan's natural empathy was immediate, and involuntary. "A good place, or a bad place?" she prompted.

Moisture returned to Jamie's eyes. She shook her head

slowly. "It's like… I'm afraid to think about it."

Silence descended. Teagan mulled the vague answer as Jamie made an obvious struggle to control her welling tears. She did look tired. Perhaps the day had been too much for her.

Unfortunately, it was about to get worse.

Now was obviously *not* the ideal time to remind Jamie of the assault, much less inform her of how anxious her attacker was to renew their acquaintance. But Teagan didn't feel she had any choice. Either the news would come from her, now, or from a man Jamie barely knew in about ten minutes. "Jamie," she began softly. "There's something you need to know. About the person who assaulted you."

Jamie huffed out a breath. "Sure. Why not? Lay it on me."

Teagan chose her words with care. "Someone who watched your story on the news sent a get-well card to the hospital, addressed to 'The Woman from the Park.' It was routed to me, and I opened it."

Jamie's eyes showed no emotion. "Yeah? So? I don't mind."

"It wasn't really a get-well card. Someone wanted to deliver a message to you, but they didn't want anyone else to see it. So they hid the words in the middle of a hand-written note that looked like it was coming from an elderly lady."

Jamie's eyes widened. A flush of color returned to her face, and she sat up straight in the wooden chair. "What did it say?"

Teagan hesitated. "I didn't memorize it, and the detective came and picked it up for testing. But the gist of it made us both believe that it was written by the person who assaulted you."

Jamie's expression didn't change, but a tremor in her shoulders made the fiberglass cast bobble on the tabletop. "What did it say?" she repeated.

"It claimed that what happened was a misunderstanding," Teagan explained. "An accident. The individual seemed to know that you had amnesia, but suspected that you would remember him soon, and he wanted you to call him before you talked to anyone else. He said he would make it worth your while."

For a moment, Jamie's body seemed frozen. Then slowly, her golden eyes began to gleam. Behind them, Teagan could see hot anger sparking up like a flame, and she found herself fighting an urge to recoil. But she managed to stay calm and silent, even as the fire grew to an inferno.

Jamie bolted up from her seat and stood in place, one hand still in contact with the table for support, her chest heaving with uneven breaths. "So, on top of everything else, he thinks I'm *stupid?!*" she roared.

Teagan remained sitting, trying hard to stay composed as she struggled with a near-nonsensical urge to laugh. Only Jamie, in the face of an attempt at murder in cold blood, could be more offended at the insult to her intelligence than to her person.

"He's the stupid one, Jamie," Teagan responded evenly. "And we're going to get the bastard. You know we will."

Jamie made no response. Her eyes glowed like embers as she stared straight through Teagan, the wheels in her brain seeming to spin at warp speed. "I *should* call him," she said finally. "Damn, I can't wait. I'll tell him I'll keep my mouth shut for oh, say… a hundred thousand in cash? We'll set up a meeting somewhere, and the second he shows the cops will bust his ass." A grim smile spread across her face, and her voice turned suddenly hopeful, almost childlike. "You think they'd let me keep the money?"

Teagan could contain herself no longer. She burst out laughing.

"What?" Jamie demanded, sounding near her usual self again. "You don't think I'd do it? Or you don't think I deserve the money?"

Teagan wiped her watering eyes. Today of all days, the relief of a laugh felt amazingly good. If nothing else, it could keep her from crying.

All at once, she knew that Jamie felt the same.

"I *know* you'd set him up," Teagan assured, playing along. "I just don't know if you could wait for the cops to get there before you smacked him upside the head."

Jamie studied her with a smirk. "Beating men up is more your style, Teag. I prefer to torture them, slowly, with my superior intellect."

Teagan grinned. "In that case, the man is toast."

Jamie's tone was steely. "A chunk of smoldering ash, baby."

Is the king purple, too?

No, his body is purple, but his head is green, with fish scales.

Teagan gave her head a shake. Connecting with Jamie could bring back the most ridiculous mental images — things that meant nothing, things she would have thought were long since forgotten. Her conscience seemed to be goading her toward the unacceptable conclusion that Jamie the girl and Jamie the sexpot were the same person. She could not divide them; she could not be nice to one and stick pins in the other. It was *this Jamie*, and no other, with whom she had fantasized about enchanted fish and the curse of the flipper people.

"Teag?" Jamie asked tentatively.

Teagan started, her mind still clouded in thought. "Yeah?"

"Are you going to answer the door bell? Or do you want me to get it?"

Teagan sat up. She had heard the doorbell, hadn't she? "Someone must be at the door."

"A brilliant deduction," Jamie quipped.

"Shut up!"

We'll be just like real sisters.

Teagan shook her head again. She rose.

Chapter Eighteen

Teagan picked at her dinner. She had no appetite. From the look of Eric's equally untouched plate of microwaved frozen lasagna, she figured he didn't either. She had expected they would talk over the meal, but so far, they hadn't gotten around to it. They were both walking on eggshells.

The detective's visit had been brief. He had arrived looking flustered and exhausted, then took down Jamie's real name and discussed the greeting card in an almost robotic manner. Once he had ascertained that Jamie's returning memory still fell short of identifying her attacker, he asked no further questions.

He did assure her that the station would run a thorough check on her ID. But he did not, Teagan noticed, promise Jamie they would share that information immediately. Rather, he admonished her not to move back to wherever she had been living before the attack—no matter what she thought she remembered—until the police had a chance to investigate the premises. He would be off-duty tomorrow, but he had left her with the name of another detective in the department to call in case of any significant developments. Otherwise she was to sit tight until he contacted her on Monday.

Overall, it was a less than encouraging interview.

"I hope the microwave in the apartment still works," Teagan said idly, disengaging an unappetizing strand of orange-stained mozzarella from the tines of her fork. "Cold soup isn't much of a meal."

She hadn't been looking forward to an awkward dinner for three, and evidently Jamie hadn't either. No sooner was the detective out the door than Jamie had begged off, pleading fatigue. She had headed to her apartment with a can of soup, a package of crackers, and a two-liter of cola, and Teagan hadn't argued. She had been too relieved.

"The microwave works fine," Eric answered, his voice deadpan. "I heat coffee in it all the time."

Teagan set down her fork. Her husband had barely made eye contact since returning from his workshop, and she could tolerate the gnawing in her middle no longer.

"So, tell me," she began, taking care to keep her voice even and free of accusation, even as her pulse skyrocketed. "Did Jamie remember the time you spent together?"

Eric's gaze met hers only briefly. He set his fork on his plate with a clank, picked up both, and took them into the kitchen. After a brief moment that felt like twelve eternities, he returned, pulled out the chair beside Teagan and sat down.

He laid an arm across her shoulders and entwined his fingers affectionately in her hair. "Yes, she remembers," he admitted. "But it doesn't matter. She doesn't need me to get her life back. She needs you."

Teagan felt another twinge of pressure building behind her eyes. He was trying his best to make the situation easier for her. But she had hardly been doing the same, had she?

She caught his hand in hers and planted a kiss on his workshop-roughened knuckles. "I'm sorry," she said sincerely. "When I sent you out with her this morning, I didn't think about how awkward it could be for you."

"It was fine," he said dismissively.

He was unconvincing.

Teagan caught his eyes. "No, it wasn't. I'm not blind. I know I walked in on something when I came home. Do you want to tell me about it?"

He leveled a gaze back at her. "No," he said firmly. "I don't."

Teagan blinked in surprise. She sat still as he rose and took her dishes away to the kitchen. When she heard sounds of the dishwasher being loaded, she got up and followed him. She stood by mutely as he collected the day's worth of assorted tumblers, tea cups, and stray forks from the far ends of the counter and dropped them into the racks. Only when he stopped and straightened did his eyes meet hers again, and when they did, he pulled her into his arms.

His embrace was strong and affectionate, and it should have been comforting. But for the first time she could remember, the gesture only increased her unease.

"I don't mean to be mysterious," he explained, seeming to sense the tension in her. "I just don't want to talk about it. I honestly think it would be better for everyone if we didn't. Are you okay with that?"

Teagan breathed in deeply. The answer was no. Ancient history was one thing, but she was *not* okay with him and present-day Jamie keeping present-day secrets. Not when every single thing Eric had done and said since Teagan got home only confirmed that she actually *had* walked in on something.

Still wrapped in his arms, she started to answer, then stopped herself. She did the same thing two more times.

What could she say? Either she trusted him, or she didn't. And she did trust him. She had no doubt whatsoever that if anything physical had happened, Jamie had started it, and he had ended it. There was also not a doubt in her mind that something physical had happened.

So what was there to ask?

How good is she?

Her stomach threatened to heave.

Eric relaxed his hold, brought a hand to her chin, and lifted it. "Look at me," he said gently.

She complied.

"You *know* you have nothing to worry about with me. You know I'm madly in love with you. Is it too much to ask for you to give me some credit and just let this thing drop?"

Hell, yes.

"Of course not," she heard herself lie, "Not when it was my own stupid fault for throwing the two of you together in the first place."

In one swift movement, he pulled her close again and kissed her soundly.

He seemed determined to prove how much he wanted her, and his effort was impressive indeed. It would have been the perfect tonic had she not been reminded of the considerably less impressive peck on the cheek he had delivered a few hours earlier.

It had bothered her then, but she hadn't been sure why. Now she knew. Pecks on the cheek were not her husband's style, regardless of circumstances or audience. He had avoided kissing her on the lips because his own had just been elsewhere.

"Teagan! What's wrong?"

She had pulled away from him without thinking.

He exhaled with frustration.

The annoyance in his eyes jerked her back to reality. Yes, of course Jamie had wanted to kiss him; he was gorgeous, what woman wouldn't? And of course he wouldn't want to make things any more complicated between the two women than they already were.

It didn't matter, did it? He hadn't kissed Jamie back.

Not even for a second?

Teagan forced back the unwelcome thought. Eric was her best friend, their marriage was rock solid, and if she was stupid enough to risk alienating him over a crime he didn't commit, she didn't deserve a faithful husband in the first place.

She did not answer the question, hastening instead to pick up where they had left off. But although Eric was cooperative, his ardor seemed to have cooled, and when they broke apart he turned away from her and wordlessly fetched the box of dish detergent from under the sink, poured it in the holder, and shut the dishwasher door.

Teagan stood silently herself, her heart thudding. She wasn't used to things being awkward between them. She certainly wasn't used to his being angry.

But he was. He did not look at her as he pushed the start

button on the machine and then turned around to lean against the counter. He folded his arms over his chest, his eyes focused on some distant point in space.

"Just ask me," he said finally, his voice brusque.

Teagan lifted her head to look at him, but his gaze remained elsewhere. "Ask you what?"

"Whatever it is you want to ask," he retorted. "You obviously can't let it go."

En garde!

Teagan's ego may have been cowering since the tea kettle whistled, but with that accusation of weakness, it rallied and sprang back for the challenge.

She turned toward him and placed her hands on his shoulders. "I *can* let it go," she declared. "I said I trusted you, and I mean that." Her voice caught a little, despite herself. "I know you can't control what Jamie does."

Eric's gaze softened. He smiled at her. "Thank you for that."

She should have shut up then. She really should have. But there were too many other unanswered questions torturing her mind, and the elephant was already in the room. She might as well get a good look at it before shooing it away.

"I do want to ask you something else, though," she said quickly, before she could think better of it. "You don't have to answer me if you don't want to."

Eric exhaled uncomfortably. "What's that?"

Fabulous. Now he's mad again.

Teagan forged on. "It's about the past; not the present. I just want to know why the two of you broke up."

Eric's eyes rolled. "Why is it that both —" he bit off the words sharply. Only after several second's worth of inner struggle did he begin again. "If I satisfy your curiosity on that one point, will you promise to drop the subject?"

Teagan nodded mutely.

He stared back at her with skepticism, but to her relief, he kept talking. "It was pretty straightforward. When she was working as a waitress she flirted with all the men, but with the biggest tippers, she could be shameless. If you know her at all, I'm sure that won't shock you. But one night I walked in and found her sitting on some middle-aged man's lap, and I called her on it. I thought I was being protective; honestly, the guy looked like bad news to me. But she thought I was being controlling, and she flipped out. We got into a shouting match right there in the restaurant, and that was the end of it."

Teagan digested the information silently, trying to picture her mild-mannered husband yelling at a waitress in a restaurant. She had a difficult time doing so. The fleeting thought that perhaps he had been more passionate back then made her guts twist, and she dismissed it.

"Did you talk afterwards?" she asked carefully, not knowing how long his willingness to share was going to last. "Try to patch things up?"

"No."

He said nothing else immediately. His brow was creased in concentration, as if he were trying to figure something out for himself.

Teagan was leaning against the counter beside him, and although her body was within inches of his, every millimeter seemed a mile. She wanted to press herself against his chest and feel his arms around her, but she feared that any move on her part might make him stop talking.

"I thought about it," he said finally. "But I guess I figured that if she cared about me at all, she would have understood why I reacted the way I did. I could have made the first move myself, apologized for making a scene. But at first I was too angry; I really did think she was out of line."

"She was," Teagan agreed. Possessive behavior was a red flag every woman should watch out for, true. But how Jamie could mistake a simple case of jealousy and wounded male pride for anything more sinister was beyond her—not when Eric clearly hadn't a controlling bone in his body. If Jamie hadn't realized that, she didn't know him at all.

Eric turned to his wife with a smile, and her heart warmed. He reached out a hand and brushed a lock of hair behind her shoulder. "You've never been one to play mind games, Teagan. That's one of the things I love about you."

She grinned back. "Name something else."

"That you don't ask me a lot of dicey questions about my past?"

She pursed her lips. "Hmm. Better try again."

He frowned. "I was hoping we were done."

"Almost," she said quickly. "But you were about to say something else. After you got over being angry, what then? You—" Teagan swallowed. Damn, this was hard. But she had to know. It was the wondering that was killing her. "You don't usually give up easily, and you obviously felt something for her."

Eric rubbed his hands over his face in a gesture of weariness, then turned again to face her. "Look, Teagan. If you want to know the truth, what attracted me the most about Jamie was the same quality that attracted me to you. You both have this… fighting spirit, I guess, that's incredibly strong. You're independent, you're self-confident—you make a person believe that if you set your mind to it, you can move mountains. I like that. If you think about it, it's probably a big part of why you like each other."

With a swift movement, he put one arm around her waist and brought her closer. "But hear this. There are also huge differences between the two of you, and one of the biggest is that whereas *you* feel this crazy need to save the world, all Jamie's drive and ambition is dedicated to Jamie. I knew the woman was self-absorbed five minutes after I met her, but it took that ridiculous argument to bring home just how little I really mattered to her. She had no interest in committing herself to a long-term relationship—not to me, maybe not to anybody. Not that I was looking for marriage at that point, but I knew what I wanted down the road. I *am* the marrying kind, as you know."

Teagan smiled and melted against him.

He kissed her lightly on the lips. "Now are we done? Are you satisfied?"

I wish.

She could not think what to say. She was relieved to know that the breakup had been mutual, that Eric wasn't still holding a torch for a woman who had dumped him. She was deeply touched by his perception in comparing her character to Jamie's, and she even appreciated his unwillingness to sow further discord between the women by dwelling on Jamie's misbehavior.

But she still felt sick inside.

Eric did not wait for an answer, but pulled her to him and kissed her again. He seemed more relaxed now, no doubt relieved to be done with the burden of talking. Teagan should have been relieved too. Yet as much as she craved the comfort of being close to him, she remained inexplicably uneasy. The more passionate he became, the more she felt herself stiffen, her mind plagued with thoughts she had no business thinking.

Jamie didn't want him then. But what if she does now?

He knew what she was like — he slept with her anyway.

She had ways of keeping him happy.

Eric let go of Teagan abruptly and walked out of the kitchen.

Teagan stood frozen a moment, staring after him, her pulse pounding in her ears. He hadn't rejected her; she had just rejected him. She'd been fighting him the whole time, could she really expect him not to notice?

"Eric, wait!" She followed him into the living room. He dropped onto the couch without speaking, and she hurried to his side.

"I'm having a hard time with this," she confessed, all ego temporarily banished. "I'm not blaming you for anything, I swear. But I can't stop thinking about it. I can't get these images out of my head."

He turned to face her. His blue-gray eyes were angry, but she knew his anger wasn't directed at her. She understood it because she shared it. Having the specter of Jamie drive a wedge between them in such a primal way, despite both their best efforts, was beyond infuriating.

"She has a better body than I do," Teagan blurted.

The words reached her own ears before she knew she was saying them. The voice doing the talking was so pathetic, so insecure, she felt a strong urge to hit the floor running and not stop till she was out the front door. Eric did not respond immediately, and in the single second before he turned to her with an expression of shock, she fantasized that maybe he hadn't heard her.

But he had, of course. And just as she was deciding that the best course of action was indeed to run for the door, he caught both her arms and swiveled himself to face her.

He shook his head in disbelief. "What did you just say?"

Teagan sighed and gave up. "You heard me."

He had every right to look shocked, and not because what she had said was untrue. That she was flat-chested and had hips as straight as a boy's was a fact. What she shouldn't be, what Teagan Raye Hansen had *never* been, was insecure about herself. Other women might throw out such statements of humility just to fish for a compliment, but Teagan loathed such neediness. She was perfectly happy with, and proud of, her own body—whatever its imperfections.

Just so long as she was *not* imagining her husband running his hands over a better one.

Eric's mouth opened, but she seemed to have left him speechless.

She stood up. "Can we both just forget I said that?"

He found his voice and stood up next to her. "Is that *really* what's bothering you?" His tone was suddenly lighter, almost humorous.

She didn't know whether to be offended or relieved.

"Yes. No. Maybe. I don't know."

"Teagan," he said incredulously, "I'm sitting here thinking that deep down you're hating me, that you're never going to forgive me for all this mess… and you're worried about—"

"Don't say it," she barked. "Once was enough." She forced herself to hold his gaze, even though a part of her still wanted to bolt for the door. How had this conversation gotten so out of control? "I do *not* hate you. How could you even think that? I told you I don't blame you for any of this."

"And I told you that you have nothing to worry about," he retorted. "But you keep pulling away from me. What am I supposed to think?"

"That I've lost my freaking mind? I don't know!" her strangled voice was catching again. Embarrassed, she launched herself into his arms and pressed her forehead to his shoulder, hiding her face. "Why, Eric?" she muttered into the fabric of his shirt. "*Why* do you have to have an ex with the body of a *Sports Illustrated* swimsuit model? How am I supposed to compete with that?"

She could feel laughter rumbling in his chest; his arms squeezed her tight. "You don't have to," he said gently. "You've already won."

Good answer.

"But," he continued more sternly, pushing her away from him just enough to look at her. "I should be insulted you think I'm so shallow. You can't seriously think body type is all I care about?"

If it is, do I still win?

He pressed her close to him again, and the last of Teagan's defenses, if not her mental qualms, were overpowered by his sheer physical allure. "If you're going to accuse me of not being attracted to you, Mrs. Hansen," he murmured in her ear, "you've got a very poor case. Have I not been presenting clear evidence to the contrary, at least once every twenty-four hours for the past six months?"

Teagan let out a chuckle. He had her there. God knew she wanted him just as badly—to hell with the rest of it.

She looked up at him with a wet-eyed smile. "Case dismissed."

Chapter Nineteen

Jamie got up and turned off the ancient television. She had hoped that the lame antenna with its digital converter box might pick up something that would capture her attention, but it had not. Her attention remained where it had been all day—inside herself. The process of rediscovery was brutal, heady, and exhausting at the same time. She had enough of her memory back that she knew where she had come from, and she knew who she was. But the closer her memory inched toward the last year of her life, the more the same vague, haunting fear gnawed at her insides like a piranha.

She knew who she had been, yes. But she was not at all sure, on the night she nearly died, who it was that she had become.

She sat back on the bed and chewed a fingernail. It was Saturday night. She had been taken to the ER in the wee hours of the morning on Thursday. If she had a job, she had missed at least two days of it. If she had friends, they had been out of communication for three. Her neighbors wouldn't have seen her, either. Surely a roommate would be wondering.

Did she have a roommate?

Her brow furrowed. She had always had roommates; ever since giving up that first apartment she couldn't afford. But she had never wanted them. Having a place of her own was another fantasy of the future, along with managing a restaurant and telling other people where to shove it. Had she gotten her wishes?

Or was her "roommate" the one who had split her head open?

Her good hand flew to her scalp. The stapled wound was less sore now, but it was beginning to itch. Ten staples had been required to close the skin; she must have bled like a gusher. Her arm ached almost constantly, but she was getting used to that. She had a high pain tolerance, born of years of aching back and feet and a deep-seated fear that medication would dull her much needed wits.

She fell back on her pillow with a bounce. She was exhausted, but she couldn't sleep. The hot soup hadn't helped, and neither had the shower. An urge persisted within her, an urge with which she was unfamiliar. She wanted to talk to someone.

She was lonely.

She stared up at the ceiling in the darkness. She and Teagan had often talked late into the night while gazing up into the rafters of the loft in Teagan's grandparents' cabin. Jamie had slept over nearly as often as not, and it was at night that they became real confidants. Teagan didn't ramble and boast so much when she was tired, and Jamie was braver about voicing her fears. Never mind her grief.

It meant a lot to her, in those first horrible months after her mother's death, to have Teagan to cling to. Even though Jamie didn't always talk about exactly what was bothering her, Teagan had been willing to listen and had always seemed to know—whether with a touch of the hand, a smile, or a laugh-out-loud joke—just how to make her feel better.

That Teagan should amazingly appear again now, in the midst of the second most traumatic event in Jamie's life, was enough to make her reevaluate her doubt of the supernatural. Without Teagan, she would be living in some women's shelter now, listening to other people's babies cry and begging for cab fare. With Teagan, she had more than safe shelter. She had a sister again.

The image of mud raining down on two giggling twelve-year-olds made Jamie chuckle to herself, shaking the mattress. Did Teagan remember that, too?

The ceremony might have been done in fun, but Jamie had meant every word of it. She had wanted Teagan as a blood sister, even more than she wanted an adoptive parent.

No one could ever replace her mother, but the link to Teagan and her grandparents would have been enough, had it lasted. It doubtless would have served her far better than the parade of uncommitted foster families with which she had actually grown up.

Jamie's heart warmed at the memory of sit-down meals with Teagan's grandparents. She had had her own spot at the table, where she sat every time, and Teagan's grandmother had always made sure the pepper shaker was within reach. She had not only felt welcome, she had felt wanted. She wondered if the whole family got together for holidays. It would be so wonderful if—

Oh, hell.

Jamie groaned and rolled over onto her side.

How could she forget?

It was like one big, cruel joke.

Why, oh why, did Eric have to turn out to be Teagan's husband? He could have been her brother, her neighbor, her boss, her plumber... but no. He had to be the one thing standing in the way of Jamie's second—and perhaps last—chance at family.

Her thoughts flew unwittingly to the feel of his lips in that accidental, ill-advised, and yet very satisfying instant before he had pushed her away. It had taken him at least a second to do so. Perhaps because he was shocked. Perhaps because he was enjoying himself.

He had loved her once; she was sure of that. If not for Teagan, Eric might be back in Jamie's bed right now. And this time around, things could be different with him. She wouldn't freak out over a little possessiveness; maybe she would even encourage it. What if, instead of guarding her independence so fiercely, she allowed herself to return his feelings? Surely, if she made a point of trying—

Jamie sat up. She took her good hand and slapped herself on the cheek.

What was she *thinking?* That she could come and live at the house and sleep with Eric and Teagan would move over the garage? Of course! Then they could all be one big, happy family!

She slapped her other cheek, too.

Then she stood up, crossed to the window, and lifted the shade at its edge. She had to put Eric out of her mind.

Her eyes passed over the wooden frame of Teagan's house, silhouetted against the winter sky. A bright moon reflected off the snow on the roof; a thin curl of smoke rose from the chimney. All the lights in the house were out except the back porch light.

Jamie's lips curved into a smile. She wasn't completely removed from this paragon of warm domesticity. The porch light had been left on for her. In case she needed anything. All she had to do was knock, and Teagan would be there.

Someone did care.

A second light began to dance in Jamie's vision, and her gaze moved upward. This light was much dimmer, not as steady. It was shining through the window at the far right corner of the house, outlining a valance through closed blinds. The light was orange-red rather than white, fainter than the moon, and flickering.

Candlelight.

A lump swelled in Jamie's throat. Her jaws tightened.

The light was coming from Teagan's bedroom. The room she shared with Eric.

He's making love to her.

Jamie dropped the shade and turned around.

To her.

She walked back to the foot of her empty double bed and fell forward onto its mattress. She closed her eyes and dropped her face into her pillow.

You'll always be alone.

No tears came.

She didn't have the energy.

Late, late, late!!!

When the sun shone again, it did so with a vengeance.

Jamie awoke to find herself already at the window, rolling up the shade with a snap. The winter sun was shining full force on a smooth new blanket of snow, creating a glare so bright she winced. She couldn't remember waking up and crossing the room—all she knew was that light meant morning and morning meant she was supposed to be somewhere. This much light was unusual. She had to be horribly, desperately late.

Her pulse pounded in her temples. Why hadn't her alarm gone off? She would get fired. She whirled from the window and began to pull off the loose flannel top and sleep pants she was wearing. She couldn't imagine what had possessed her to buy such a frumpy outfit—she loathed pajamas.

She was late, late, late…

A wave of unexpected relief washed over her.

No, she wasn't late. She worked evenings now. She was the boss. She fired other people when *they* came in late. Remember?

She slipped the pajamas the rest of the way off and let out a breath. Of course. She must have been dreaming. Things were different now. Things were—

Her pulse raced anew. None of the sweatshirts laid out on the dresser were hers. Neither was the stretchy one-size-fits-all sports bra. She wasn't in her apartment. Where was she? What the hell was going on?

Her brain clicked into gear with the same gratified, yet embarrassed feeling one has when being the last one to get a punch line. Mere seconds had passed between her awakening from a sound sleep and her realization that she was at Teagan's place. But to Jamie, the confusion had been interminable. Not only had her mind been straddling three places, but she hadn't landed where she wanted to settle.

She wanted to be home.

The images flew before her eyes, fast and furious. She had an apartment. It had her stuff in it. It wasn't much, but it was hers. She had a job too, a real job. People liked her. People respected her. People counted on her.

So why wasn't she there?

It was a restaurant with white tablecloths. China plates. Candles. A hardwood floor. The kitchen was huge—her office was tiny. *Her* office. Hers and… somebody's.

She bit her lip, hard. She tried to remember more of the business, to see its storefront, to read its menu. But the more she attempted to focus on the place, the time, the more hazy her awareness of it became. Had she been remembering something real—or was it all just another dream?

She blew out a frustrated breath, then dropped the pajamas in a heap and headed for the shower.

Within minutes jets of hot water were massaging her back, enveloping her in a comforting curtain of steam; and as her wits sharpened, she began to feel suddenly, newly alive. Her arm still ached, and the portion of her scalp that had been stapled was still tender. But there was a lightness to her mood that was unfamiliar. She had gained something overnight. Something important.

She *did* have a home, and a job. She hadn't been making them up. She couldn't have, not when the memories seemed so much a part of her. Although critical elements of her past still retreated from her conscious mind, she believed now that all the information she needed *was* still within her, whole and complete. Extracting it was only a matter of time.

She finished her shower in a rush, pulled on the better-than-nothing bra and the last of the non-white sweat suits, and dried her hair. She didn't bother with makeup. The sight of her yellow eyes in the mirror bothered her, and she made a mental note to acquire more blue contacts ASAP. But right now her appearance didn't matter. All that mattered was getting home.

She wrapped herself up in Teagan's coat and headed out the door to the stair landing. The steps were covered with snow, but she crunched down them anyway, holding tight to the rail with her good hand. As anxious as she was, she had no desire for any more broken bones. She cut a new path to the back door, entered the screen porch, and brushed the snow off her shoes and pant legs and onto the worn outdoor carpet. She knocked on the house door, but left little time for anyone to appear before retrieving Teagan's key from under the ceramic squirrel and opening the door herself.

She could barely see. The house seemed dark after the glare of the snow, and she found her way to the kitchen as much by feel as by sight. Everything was quiet. The rooms were empty. She laid Teagan's coat over the back of a dining room chair, moved into the kitchen, and sank down onto a stool.

I want to go home now.

She drummed her hands impatiently on the counter, wondering if Teagan had heard her come in. It was 9:30 AM. She could not wait forever. She would simply have to wake Teagan up. Perhaps with a little innocent, unavoidable noise?

She put the teakettle on to boil and returned to her stool.

Each quiet moment that passed found her attempting, anew, to reason out where home might be. But she could see only parts of it. Flashes of furniture, flashes of things that were hers. Images of the restaurant where she worked were just as elusive—a table here, a spreadsheet there. She suspected she could piece it all together fairly quickly if, as at the university, she had a concrete visual or two to spark her gray matter. She should be out on the streets right now—looking, searching. Doing nothing was torture.

"Morning."

Jamie jumped as the gruff voice reached her ears. Teagan appeared at the doorway wearing a navy fleece robe and hot-pink slippers, trudged around Jamie at the counter, and shuffled into the kitchen. Her puffy eyes didn't meet those of her guest. Her hair hadn't seen a brush since nightfall.

"Good morning," Jamie answered pleasantly, trying not to sound as eager as she felt. She hated being dependent, asking favors of other people. If only she could borrow a car...

"You're up early," Teagan commented.

Jamie felt a sharp twinge of concern. Her friend's voice was devoid of its usual cheer. It was devoid of any sort of cheer. Perhaps Teagan had insomnia.

Or perhaps Eric had stabbed Jamie in the back again.

The tea kettle began to whistle. Teagan dove toward the offending noise immediately, slapping the kettle onto a cool burner before the sound could escalate.

Jamie drew in a breath. Either Teagan was trying to avoid disturbing her husband, or the sound had taken her, as it had just taken Jamie, back to yesterday afternoon.

Teagan's back was turned. She opened various cabinets and drawers, then slammed them shut again.

Dammit, Jamie thought. *She does know.*

Why did Eric have to be such a ridiculously straight arrow? The kiss had meant nothing, surely anyone who knew Jamie should realize that! She had been upset; she had sought comfort from the nearest man around. Eric had been a poor choice under the circumstances, but he shouldn't have taken it personally, and neither should Teagan.

Jamie released a sigh. She was not unaware of her insincerity. A neon sign flashing the word "liar" played prominently in her mind's eye even as she rationalized. How much of an "accident" the kiss had been was debatable—even in her own mind. She had no defense. All she knew was that she could not lose Teagan again. Not over a man; not over anything.

"I don't want to impose," Jamie began meekly. "But I was wondering if I could ask a favor. I'd like to do some driving around again today. I remember some things about my apartment and the place I used to work, and I think I would know them if I saw them."

Teagan stopped rooting about in the cabinets and turned sharply. "So you want me to drive by every apartment and business in the Pittsburgh area?"

Jamie swallowed. She wasn't afraid of many people, and she had never been afraid of any woman lacking a weapon.

But despite the strained equanimity of Teagan's tone, the look in her eyes struck a chord that ran deep. It was the same look the twelve-year-old Teagan had sported when she had caught Jamie's foster brother, Ty, trying to peel the shell off an injured box turtle. Ty was two years older than either of them and built like a train, but Teagan had nearly scratched his eyes out before the Renicks could intervene. Ty had avoided Teagan the rest of the summer, even as he was repeatedly disciplined for bullying every other kid on the lake. Jamie had considered herself lucky to be on Teagan's side.

If only she could be there now.

"I know it sounds silly," Jamie said carefully. "That's why I don't want to waste your time with it. I thought that maybe, if you could lend me your car, I could manage by myself."

"You don't have a driver's license."

"I've driven without one before."

"Not my car, you haven't!" Teagan snapped.

Jamie lowered her chin. She could think of no good rebuttal. But she couldn't just sit around all day. She had to *do* something.

She looked back up at Teagan, who was now pouring herself a bowl of cereal.

Cocoa Puffs.

An unexpected warmth flooded Jamie's veins. Young Teagan had adored Cocoa Puffs. She had eaten them for breakfast every morning. Whenever Jamie had slept over, the two of them had welcomed the next morning with "Cocoa Puffs Supreme"—the addition of excessive amounts of chocolate syrup to the already brown milk in their bowls. Two sleep-deprived girls on a chocolate high, giggling themselves into gear. Teagan's grandparents were pushovers; they let Teagan eat anything she wanted. Jamie had wished that she could stay with them every night. She had hoped they would adopt her.

She stiffened suddenly, pulling herself up straight on the

stool. There was moistness behind her eyes again, but she refused to give into it. Since when had she ever been sentimental? Of course Teagan's family wouldn't want to adopt her. They already had one fatherless girl to worry about, didn't they? Reliving that particular disappointment now made no more sense than lamenting a long-lost Barbie doll. Jamie was an adult, and she didn't need anyone to adopt her.

But she did want a friend. "What?" she asked lightly, teasing. "No chocolate syrup?"

Teagan's hand stopped moving in midair. She stood frozen a second, her back still to Jamie, before she whirled around.

The gaze that locked on Jamie's was piercing. Teagan's muscles were tight as a drum, her expression hard. But within the depths of her eyes, Jamie could see two things quite clearly. A heart that was hurting, and a temper that was about to erupt.

Jamie sat silently, waiting, for several uncomfortable seconds. Then she decided to uncork the bottle.

"Go ahead, Teag," she suggested. "Say it."

Teagan released a breath like fire. "You've got a hell of a lot of nerve!" she hissed. "Eric told me the two of you were involved before. He told me everything. And I didn't like it, but I dealt with it. Why? Because I'm a nice person, that's why. Because I wanted to help you, and I didn't figure it was anyone's fault. It was just a coincidence, after all. Right?"

Teagan's volume escalated. "But you couldn't leave well enough alone, could you? Never mind that I invited you into my house. Never mind that I overlooked the past and tried to help you anyway. You couldn't just appreciate that and be even a tiny bit sensitive to my feelings. Oh, no. Not Jamie! It's always, only, about what *you* want, about what *you* need! No matter how awkward you made things for Eric — no matter how much you knew it would irritate me!"

Teagan's voice had become a shout. Her eyes blazed. The knuckles that clenched her spoon were white.

Jamie remained silent.

"What the hell is wrong with you?!" Teagan railed, gesticulating with the now-threatening spoon. "Do you have some kind of death wish? If you remember the stupid Cocoa Puffs, you should remember who you're dealing with!"

Jamie took in the enraged woman before her, her fleece robe open to reveal pink and blue flannel pajamas decorated with coffee cups, her dark-blond hair mussed, a drop of brownish milk trickling from the spoon down her raised wrist. The image took Jamie back.

I am Zanzibar! Queen of the Jungle People. You have landed on sacred ground and defiled our coconuts. Back in the water with you — you will swim with the snakes!

A queer feeling erupted in Jamie's middle. Before she knew what was happening, a gush of air rushed up her throat and out her nose. She let out an indelicate snort, followed by a chuckle.

"What the *hell* is so funny?!" Teagan raged.

Jamie's eyes began to water. She dabbed at them with a finger, narrowly avoiding another clop on the jaw from her cast. Her mouth was smiling behind her hand, and her voice, though strangled sounding, was uncharacteristically warm.

"God, I've missed you."

Teagan's eyes widened. She stood, her spoon still in the air, staring at Jamie as if she'd gone mad. Then she lowered her arm and jabbed the utensil outward. Her voice remained grim, but Jamie could see a twitch of amusement playing on her taut lips. "You think I won't impale you with this?"

Jamie took another chance and grinned. "Oh, I'm pretty sure you would."

Teagan breathed out heavily. "You make one more move on my husband, and so help me—"

"I won't," Jamie said firmly. She caught Teagan's eyes with her own and held them, pleading. "I *won't*. I didn't mean to hurt you, Teag. And I don't want to cause trouble for Eric, either. I've been feeling a little lost lately; I admit that. I've been out of my mind in more ways than one. But that's going to change, now that I'm remembering who I am."

Teagan looked back at Jamie without comment, her expression still guarded. She set down the spoon. "I don't trust you," she proclaimed.

Jamie pursed her lips, then nodded. "I know."

"And I *hate* the fact that you turned out so damned sexy."

Jamie smiled. "Yeah, I know that, too."

Teagan looked away, and her voice turned hard again. "I'm not putting up with any more crap from you, Jamie. I don't care what the circumstances are. From now on, if you so much as look at Eric sideways—"

"A waste of my valuable time," Jamie agreed. "He's in love with you."

"Damned straight," Teagan huffed.

Both fell silent.

Jamie's heart continued to pound. It felt good to laugh, to smile—to defuse at least some of the tension. But she meant was she was saying, and she needed for Teagan to believe it. She needed Teagan, period. "Teag," she said soberly. "I am sorry. Really."

Teagan's eyes continued looking ahead. Her tone remained surly.

"You'd better be."

Chapter Twenty

"All right, here's the plan," Teagan began some time later, when she and Jamie at last buckled themselves into her car. Jamie looked so anxious she was practically bouncing; Teagan had deliberately been taking her time. "Eric and I went over what you've remembered about your restaurant, and it sounds like an upscale one. Odds are it's either downtown or in Shadyside, but it could be on the South Side, or even out in the suburbs, and we can't look everywhere. So you're going to have to narrow it down. Any memories of the *outside* of the building? Of how you got there, maybe? What the neighborhood was like?"

Teagan was aware that she was using her detached, professional tone. She was also aware that making specific reference to the conversation she'd had with Eric, which Jamie had not been a party to because Teagan had banished her from the main house immediately after breakfast, was an intentional jab of the "he's mine and don't you forget it" variety.

She didn't care.

"I told you all I can remember so far," Jamie insisted, her voice subdued. "I wish I could do better, but specifically thinking about a question never helps. I need to *see* something. Otherwise, it just comes back randomly. Sorry."

Teagan blew out a breath. She was low on gas, and she had no desire to waste more driving circles around the county. But she also wanted Jamie the hell out of her garage.

"So tell me about the inside again," she said shortly. "What do you remember?"

Jamie closed her eyes and smiled. "There were round tables, with white linen tablecloths and fine china plates. The chairs were dark wood, very elegant. The waiter's outfits looked like tuxes. They were all men, though... that irked me. Most of them were older than me. I had a problem with—"

Her voice broke off.

"Yeah," Teagan murmured uncharitably, "I bet you did."

Jamie's eyes opened. She sat up. "I did *not* screw around with my wait staff!" she said defensively. "I knew my damned job."

Teagan's conscience began to prick at her. A little.

"I just had trouble earning their respect at first, that's all," Jamie continued. "It was a rocky start, but I'm pretty sure things got better." Her tone turned pensive. "They must have, because I can see myself being happy there. I looked forward to work. But then—" She hesitated a moment. When she spoke again her voice was uncharacteristically insecure. "There's something else too, Teag. It's the same vague, bad feeling I've had ever since I woke up in the hospital. The closer I get to remembering the present, the more I feel it. It's not like one particular thing that happened. It's more like something was bothering me. Something... something awful."

Teagan stole a glance at the passenger seat. Jamie's brow was furrowed, her hands clenched. Her eyes gazed blankly ahead of her. She nibbled at her still-puffy lower lip.

"Tell me," Teagan urged.

Jamie groaned and rubbed her face in her hands. "I can't!" she said with frustration. "I think a part of me doesn't *want* to remember."

They rode in silence for a while. Teagan pulled into a gas station and filled her tank. Her hands were unsteady. She wasn't used to being angry, at least not at a friend. Ranting and raving over social injustices was different—*that* felt good for the soul. Her anger at Jamie for having intentionally caused grief to her marriage was justified, no doubt, but it was considerably less satisfying.

She needed to let it go.

Don't look at whether the choice is right or wrong, she quoted to herself from her training. *Just try to understand where it's coming from.*

She got back into her car and buckled up again. "You never told me," she asked without preamble, "what you remembered about foster care. What it was like growing up with other families, after having been with only your mother before."

Teagan felt Jamie's eyes studying her as she pulled back onto the road. "What's that got to do with anything?" Jamie asked. "Are you trying to psychoanalyze me?"

"Yes," Teagan responded. "Deal with it. Answer the question."

There was a long pause. Then Jamie merely shrugged. "Foster care wasn't horrible. In a lot of ways, I was lucky. All my placements were families; I never wound up at a shelter or in a group home. I was never abused in any way. It was just bad luck I had to move so much. One of my foster fathers got transferred out of state. One younger family had a premature baby of their own with huge problems, and they couldn't handle the fosters anymore. One couple hit retirement age and got out of the biz altogether. Another woman decided she only wanted younger children. They were all decent. They just weren't home."

And none of them loved me.

The words were unspoken, but as they lingered in the chill air, Teagan's conscience pricked at her again. Aside from Jamie's mother, who *had* ever loved her? If Jamie had extended family, they had obviously not offered to take her in. She had aged out of the system at eighteen and been on her own ever since. She seemed to have no adult female friends. Her romantic relationships, Teagan chose not to dwell on. But it should come as no surprise that Jamie didn't know, or understand, what a two-way street even looked like.

Teagan shifted in her seat uncomfortably. She herself could afford to love, because she had always felt secure. There had always been someone who loved her unconditionally. But Jamie had only Jamie. Was it any wonder she put herself first?

"That's it!" Jamie exclaimed suddenly, startling Teagan so much the car lurched. There was no restaurant in sight; they were merely cruising down the Parkway North toward the city.

"What's what?" Teagan asked.

"The city!" Jamie said gleefully, pointing at the skyscrapers whose profiles were just now coming into view. "You could see the city from our windows! Gorgeous, sweeping views of the rivers and the stadiums. Customers always wanted the tables by the windows!"

Teagan smiled. "You mean you were up on Mount Washington?"

Jamie smiled back. "I'm sure of it."

Teagan set her course for the mountain ridge that loomed high above Pittsburgh's "Point," where the Monongahela and Allegheny Rivers meet to form the Ohio. Her spirits rose. They could hit almost all the nice restaurants in that area with one cruise down Grandview Avenue. Surely Jamie would recognize the right place when she saw it.

Jamie's heart thudded in her chest. Despite her looming apprehension, the sight of the *La Veduta* had buoyed her spirit with an almost childlike excitement.

"The name's Italian, but we served all sorts of food," she prattled to Teagan as they approached the staff entrance. They were making their way carefully down a steep ramp to the side of the aged, yet grandiose building, which was perched precariously on the sharp slope of Mount Washington's city face. Teagan had lucked into a prime spot of on-street parking only two blocks away, but new snow had started to fall again, and Jamie couldn't move nearly as fast as she wanted to.

"I hope someone's here at this hour," she continued. "There isn't always, but the general manager sometimes comes in on Sundays to catch up on paperwork. Maybe we'll get lucky." She reached the nondescript entrance, gave the doorknob a perfunctory try, then rang the service bell. Anxious beyond words, she leaned forward and laid her ear against the cold metal door.

She heard footsteps. "Someone's here!" she said excitedly, jumping back so quickly she nearly collided with the silent figure of Teagan behind her. Whoever it was, Jamie knew, would be looking through the peephole first. Management took security very seriously.

As the locks began to click open, Jamie felt a new flash of anxiety. Did she really want to meet the general manager? She could picture a thin, sallow man with a pointed nose and absolutely no sense of humor informing her of her duties and berating her for her alleged mistakes. But she also remembered that he had been fair... and he'd had the good sense to hire her in the first place. What was his name? She braced herself.

The heavy door swung open with a groan. The sight of the man behind it filled Jamie, quite unexpectedly, with joy. The muscular torso, bald head, multiple earrings, and impish blue eyes were a slam dunk, even for her ailing brain. "Richard!" she exclaimed, as her memory of both the sous chef, *and* his name, came back in a rush that was dizzying. She must have swayed a little, because she could feel Teagan's hand suddenly clasp her upper arm, supporting her.

"Jamie?" he responded, his gaze sweeping down over both her frumpy clothing and her cast with a look of surprise. His voice rang with friendly greeting, but confusion creased his brow. "What happened to you? What the hell are you doing back here today?"

Jamie grinned and pushed past him to enter, motioning for Teagan to follow. "What the hell am I doing, period? That's a better question."

Richard shut and bolted the door behind them. Then he turned to Jamie with a smirk. "Darling, there's no one alive who can answer *that* question."

Jamie smirked back. *Richard.* God, she adored the man. He had been her first friend here. And she had paid him back by helping to set him up with the man of his dreams — the florist who supplied *La Veduta.* The two had moved in together over Thanksgiving.

Her body warmed, and not just from the marginal heat in the hallway. Her memory was coming back. It was coming back beautifully.

"Why *are* you here?" Richard repeated. "If I'd known you were coming I wouldn't have wasted half my day doing your job for you. And who is your overly protective friend?"

Jamie cast a glance at Teagan, and was surprised to see the social worker glowering at Richard with suspicion. "This is Teagan," Jamie introduced, feeling a rare surge of sentimental pride. "She and I have been friends forever."

"You don't say," Richard said slyly, nodding to Teagan. "Under the circumstances, that's quite an accomplishment."

"Oh, stuff it," Jamie retorted gaily. "Is my office unlocked?"

"Probably," Richard answered as he followed her down the hall and around the corner. "Preston was here, but he went out a minute ago. Where's your key?"

"No idea," Jamie quipped. She opened the unlocked door and stepped over the threshold into the tiny, cluttered office. Her pulse pounded with elation.

My office. MINE.

She had been the boss here. Almost. At least when the general manager wasn't around. She had managed the wait staff and the valets, smoothed over issues with guests, managed inventory, worked with the chefs to keep the kitchen on track...

"FYI," Richard said pointedly, "Preston's plenty pissed he had to cover for you on Thursday. Where the hell were you? Did he get the dates wrong, or did you?"

Jamie's happy reminiscence came to a sudden, shuddering halt.

After an awkward moment of silence, Teagan stepped forward. "Maybe I can explain. Jamie received a head injury last week, in addition to the broken arm. For a while, she couldn't remember who she was or where she worked. She's getting better, but we're still trying to piece a few things together. You said you were expecting her at work on Thursday?"

"A head injury?" Richard turned to Jamie, his face a mask of concern. "What happened, love?"

Jamie felt a flush of warmth in her cheeks, even as the horror of struggling for air within a stifling blanket hovered ominously just outside her thoughts. *Someone did care.*

"She's not allowed to talk about the details yet," Teagan interjected.

Jamie turned with a frown. If Teagan was thinking that Richard had anything to do with the assault, she was off base by a mile. He was tall, strong, and had tattoos, sure. But he was a total sweetheart. She opened her mouth to say so, but Teagan cut her off with a warning look.

"You said you were expecting her on Thursday?" Teagan repeated, her manner all business.

Richard looked from one woman to the other with a confused expression, then sank down on a corner of the general manager's desk. "Yes," he answered quietly. "She was marked off for a four-day weekend—we weren't expecting her back until Tuesday. But she was supposed to be here Thursday. When she didn't show, Preston figured there must have been some confusion about the dates. It wasn't like Jamie to be AWOL, and her phone was off—we figured that had to mean she was on the plane already."

"The *plane?*" Jamie repeated sharply. Something dark flirted with the edges of her consciousness, but when she tried to grasp it, it disappeared like smoke. Her brain was only teasing her.

"Yes, angel," Richard said with sympathy. "You were going on a vacation. You were outrageously excited about it. Never mind that you wouldn't tell your nearest and dearest coworker a single thing about it. I knew it was big. My money was on a whirlwind weekend in Europe. I did catch you looking at pictures of castles in a travel magazine."

It was Jamie's turn to sink down on a desk. She was pretty sure she landed on top of a stapler, but that didn't seem important. "Europe?" she repeated dumbly. "With... with a man?"

Richard's eyebrows arched. "Can't see you going any other way, my dear. Can you?"

"Did you know who she was going with?" Teagan asked sharply.

Richard turned and looked at her, then cast a questioning glance back at Jamie. "Do you really not remember? Do you want me to talk about it?"

Jamie smiled at his sensitivity. Teagan was playing quite the tigress; it was nice to have two people on her side, even if they didn't trust each other. "Yes, please," she answered weakly. "I have to know. And no, I don't remember."

Richard blew out a breath, then settled himself farther back on the desk. "You've been seeing this mystery man for the last—oh, I don't know—six weeks, maybe? I don't know who he is because you wouldn't tell me. You wouldn't tell anybody. I suspected he was a customer here, but if so, you never let on in front of the staff."

Teagan let out a sound suspiciously like a groan. Jamie could sense her frustration, but her own response was oddly the opposite. She was glad Richard didn't know. She hadn't wanted anyone to know.

To know... what?

"Why would Jamie want to keep the man she was dating a secret?" Teagan asked.

Richard kept his eyes on Jamie. His expression was sympathetic. "She wouldn't say," he explained. "But I had my suspicions."

Jamie wanted the conversation to stop now. The general manager could be back any minute, and she didn't want to run into him. He would be furious with her for skipping work on Thursday, and she had no interest in defending herself right now with some lengthy sob story. Her personal affairs were none of his business. She walked around to the other side of the desk, pulled open a drawer and dug through its miscellaneous contents to the back right corner, her fingers fishing for her extra set of keys. *Eureka.*

"And what did you suspect?" Teagan asked.

Jamie slipped the keys into her coat pocket.

"Isn't it obvious?" Richard responded, sliding his eyes over to Jamie with a wry expression. "Methinks my blond beauty was dallying with a married man."

No!

Jamie straightened with a start, slamming the drawer shut with a bang. Her body flushed with heat. Her mouth opened to protest, but no words came out.

The silence that followed was deafening.

It was Teagan, at last, who broke it. "And what made you think that?" she asked stiffly.

Richard's expression was all remorse. "Heavens, Jamie, don't get so upset! It isn't murder. Of course, it was less than you deserved, and I did suggest as much, but you refused to even talk—"

Jamie's voice returned. *"I do NOT date married men!"*

Richard recoiled as if a wind had blown him. "All right, love. Don't go popping any vessels on my account! You know perfectly well *I'm* not going to judge you. It just fit the usual pattern, that's all. The secrecy, the expensive gifts—"

"Expensive gifts?" Jamie sputtered, her insides burning. What Richard was saying wasn't possible. It couldn't be true. She *didn't* date married men. *Ever.* Why should she? She could have any single man she wanted. Her mother had fallen in love with a married man, and where had it gotten her? Deserted, broke, disowned, and pregnant—forced to waste the best years of her own too-short life raising a child without a father.

"I don't take 'gifts' from men! I don't take anything from anybody!" she protested hotly.

The dark mass of foreboding that had dogged Jamie for days hovered suddenly closer. It was thicker, more ominous.

Stifling.

Get away from me!

Richard had risen from the desk. His face was ashen. "I'm sorry, Jamie—I'm sorry! Never mind me, I'm just spouting the daily drama. What do I know?" He turned to Teagan with a pleading look. "Has she seen a doctor?"

"Several," Teagan answered, her voice sounding, for some reason, as unsteady as Jamie's own.

What was wrong with everybody?

"There's a chance that the man she was with is responsible for causing her injuries," Teagan explained. "The police are trying to locate him. Do you have any idea who else they might talk to? Did Jamie have a roommate or another friend who might know his name?"

Richard shook his head. "She had her own place. I don't know about any friends outside work. I didn't know about you."

"I'm a social worker at Northside General," Teagan began. "I know Jamie from a long time ago. Do you happen to know..."

The voices in the room seemed to fade in and out of Jamie's hearing as the gray mass closed in on her, transporting her to another time, another place...

Expensive gifts.

Olive-skinned hands slid over her head from behind. They were strong hands, virile hands. Between their fingers sparkled a bauble... gleaming silver, shining stones. She glanced down at her neck to find it bejeweled like a princess's. The hands slid back over her bare shoulders, caressing now. Her eyes caught sight of another gleam. A golden ring, on the left hand's fourth finger—

"*Dammit!*"

Both Teagan and Richard stared back at Jamie.

"Damn what, exactly?" Teagan asked.

"Damn—" Jamie faltered. Her energy was gone. She felt

suddenly empty, light headed. "Just dammit," she said miserably, sinking back into her desk chair.

"We can leave anytime you're ready, Jamie," Teagan offered.

And go where?

"Yeah," Jamie answered weakly, "whatever."

Richard scribbled something on a piece of paper, handed it to Teagan, then moved to stand beside Jamie. "I'm terribly sorry, love," he said sincerely, laying a sympathetic hand on her shoulder. "I do hope you're feeling better soon. I'll tell Preston you need a medical leave. It will do until you're ready to call him and explain everything yourself. In the meantime, I swear, if I think of anything that can help the police catch this bastard, I'll be all over it. Nobody messes with Richard's women!"

Jamie felt moisture welling up behind her eyes. She rose from the chair and—though she was fairly certain she'd never done so before—clasped her favorite sous chef in a hug. The look on his face when she released him confirmed his surprise.

"Poor baby," he said gently. "You have been through it, haven't you? You take care of yourself, all right? And by the way," he lifted her chin to meet his eyes. "Those new contacts are *totally* hot."

Teagan rapped her knuckles restlessly on the surface of the preset dining table at which she was seated. She was watching Jamie stare out the panoramic windows of *La Veduta*'s private banquet room. Jamie had insisted on walking around every corner of the empty restaurant, trying to get her bearings, while Richard went back to work. But for the last five minutes she'd done nothing but stand and stare, not saying a word.

At first, Teagan had welcomed the downtime. Her emotions were all over the place, in highly unprofessional ways, and she had to get a grip. She needed to stop thinking about Jamie's reactions to Eric in a personal way and move on with the rest of the equation. God knew Jamie could use the services of about ten social workers—not just one irritable, conflicted one. But Teagan had not yet succeeded in getting that grip. And five minutes of staring at a mute and emotionless Jamie hadn't improved the situation in the slightest.

If anything, Jamie's "woe is me" demeanor only irritated Teagan further.

"Coming up with anything?" Teagan asked shortly.

Jamie swung her head around listlessly. "Am I supposed to be?"

Teagan fought for patience. "Our goal here is to get you out of danger. We may have found out your workplace and your address, but you can't go back to that life until we figure out who attacked you and report him to the police. Do you remember him, or not?"

Jamie's expression was blank. "No. There's nothing helpful. I saw one flash... but that's it. I started work here over the summer. I can't remember anything past fall."

Teagan's exasperation erupted. "I don't believe you!" she barked, unable to stop herself. "Why did you freak out so much over what Richard said? We knew there had to be a man, we knew he was bad news... if you haven't remembered anything new, then what's going on with you?"

Jamie's pale cheeks flared with red. "I don't want to talk about it."

"Why not?" Teagan persisted. "You really think anything you say is going to shock me?"

"No! It's just that I'm... embarrassed," Jamie finished quietly.

Teagan's eyebrows rose. *Embarrassed?* That was a new one. "Embarrassed about what?"

Jamie's gaze returned to the window. Snowflakes the size of quarters engulfed the city skyline in an uneven veil of white. Her voice went deadpan. "Richard said he thought the guy was married."

Teagan blinked. "Yeah? And?"

Jamie spun around, her golden eyes flashing. "You really think I mess around with married men?"

Blood rushed into Teagan's head like lava. Her mouth dropped open, but no words came out.

"I would *never* sleep with a married man!" Jamie continued hotly. "How do you think I got here? Why do you think my mother got thrown out of her house? Because of some worthless, faithless, lowlife, *married* bastard who couldn't keep it zipped, that's why! My mother gave up everything to raise me. Everything! She had no life. She never looked at another man, never had any fun going out anywhere. She worked herself into an early grave, all for me, all so I would have the best life she could possibly give me, with no help from him, or from anyone! You really think I would fall into that same trap? Do I seem that pathetically stupid to you? Well, *do I?!*"

Teagan's mouth worked as mutely as a fish's.

"I've never claimed to be a saint!" Jamie continued bitterly. "But I do have my code, and I don't go around breaking it just to get a few *things*. I've never taken gifts from guys! Everything I have, I've earned on my own. No one buys Jamie Meadows, and no one owns her!"

"So maybe you changed!" Teagan spat out.

Jamie looked back at her, stunned. "Why would you say that?"

The blood in Teagan's head neared the boiling point. She shot up out of her chair, nearly knocking it over in the process. "Why do you think?!"

To Teagan's utter amazement, Jamie looked confused. "What are you so upset about?"

Teagan could only stammer. "What... I..."

"I thought you were trying to help me!" Jamie said accusingly. "You didn't trust Richard an inch when we walked in here—you thought he might have been the one who assaulted me. Now all of a sudden you take his word over mine? You think I'm some brainless slut who would sell her soul just to get some other woman's husband?"

The volcano erupted.

"Well, *why not?!*" Teagan thundered, accidentally banging her thighs against the table so hard the dishes rattled. "You sure as hell threw me under the bus to get mine!"

Jamie's face paled. It was not the reaction Teagan had expected. Her blood pressure began to drop; the sheen of sweat on her brow felt suddenly clammy.

For several interminable seconds, Jamie said nothing. She just blinked back at Teagan, uncomprehending. But the next words from her lips sent Teagan's blood pressure straight back up again.

"That was different."

Teagan closed her eyes. She breathed deeply. When her eyes opened again, she tried to focus on the cast — on the fact that the woman in front of her had been beaten nearly to death just four days ago. She steadied herself; tried to moderate her tone. "How do you figure?" she squeaked painfully.

Jamie had the decency to flush. "I told you, I wasn't making a play for Eric. Not really. It was just a moment of weakness — I needed somebody. And you have to understand... I did have him first."

Teagan felt her fingers tightening around a salad fork.

Jamie's pupils widened. "That's not what I mean!" she said quickly, daring to step closer. "I'm not laying claim to him, I'm just trying to explain how my stupid brain works! When my head's all fuzzy and my emotions are all haywire and I look at him, I don't see another woman's husband, least of all yours. I see the Eric *I* used to know. The available one. The one who was so sweet to me, who made me laugh, who *respected* me. I didn't get that too often. And when I think now about what some maniac tried to do to me, and I start to feel worthless..." Her voice trailed off.

Teagan's fingers relaxed around the fork. A little.

"Hell, Teag, I don't even know where I'm going with this," Jamie said roughly, turning back toward the window. "I don't know what to say to you. I told you I'd leave Eric alone from now on, and I will. I can't make you believe that, and I don't blame you for not trusting me. But please," she turned back again, her now-blotchy face imploring. "Can you just *try* to see the difference? There's a reason I didn't know what you were talking about." She paused a long moment, collecting her thoughts. "The Jamie you're seeing in action is a brain-damaged emotional wreck. She's screwed up, she's freaked out, and she's weak. But the Jamie that Richard knew... *that* woman was in her right mind. She was supposed to be strong."

Teagan watched in amazement as Jamie's lower lip trembled. "I don't understand what happened to her."

Teagan's pulse rate began to slow.

She did get it, actually. It was humiliating that Jamie had managed to assess herself more accurately than could Teagan, a professional. But that's what happened when objectivity was lost. And Teagan's was long, *long* gone.

"Jamie," she said finally. "I'm no saint, either. And I can't talk about Eric with you. I've tried. I can't. So can we just stay off the damn subject?"

Jamie's expression brightened. "Absolutely. But you brought it up. I didn't."

Teagan's fingers itched back toward the salad fork.

Jamie turned to the door and threw back her shoulders in a gesture of determination. "If you don't mind, Teag," she said with obviously false bravado. "I'm ready to go now. I think I've remembered all this restaurant has to tell me. And besides, my head is pounding."

Teagan said nothing, but replaced the chair she'd been sitting in and followed Jamie toward the exit. Unfortunately, the route Jamie chose required her to open a particularly heavy door that seemed stuck in its frame, and as she moved without thought to wrestle it open, she somehow jerked her broken arm. She cried out in pain and pulled the casted arm toward her side.

Teagan sidled around without a word, popped open the door, and held it.

Jamie began to move through, but stopped midway. "Teag?" she said softly, still looking ahead.

"Yeah?" Teagan responded.

Somewhere, far back in the recesses of her mind, Teagan heard again the lapping of canoe oars on lake water. The buzz of dragonflies. The honking of faraway ducks.

"Thanks," Jamie offered.

Teagan raised her brown eyes to Jamie's golden ones, and knew she heard them too.

"You're welcome," she answered.

Chapter Twenty-One

"The weatherman *said* one to two inches," Teagan groused as she popped open her car trunk, sending showers of icy flakes cascading off in all directions. "And that was supposed to be for all day. Look at this! Two inches on top of the car, at least, and that's just since we parked." She pulled out an ice scraper, slammed the trunk closed again, and used the brush side to begin clearing the windshield. "If I'd known we were in for this much I would have waited till afternoon."

"Sorry," Jamie apologized, wishing her very existence didn't seem to be such a burden. She knew she'd been demanding a lot of Teagan lately, but as much as she hated being needy, crap just kept happening to her. "It's probably just a squall," she said optimistically, shivering by the passenger door. "You have another scraper? I can help."

"No thanks," Teagan responded. She stopped scraping long enough to open the driver's door, lean in, and start the engine. "You might as well sit inside and get warm."

Jamie complied. She hated being cold. The bulky polyester coat she was wearing had been the only one of Teagan's that fit easily over her cast, but in terms of warmth, it left much to be desired. Furthermore, her borrowed bra was way too tight, and if she didn't get out of it soon, she'd have permanent furrows across her back and shoulders. They had planned to clothes shop today, but now her head throbbed painfully and she wanted nothing more than to return to Teagan's garage apartment, fire up the heater, strip down, crawl under about sixty blankets, and get unconscious. Maybe if she was lucky, she could stay that way. Then she wouldn't have to remember.

Teagan finished brushing off the car and got inside, her

hair and clothing dotted with melting crusts of white. She pulled the car out onto the unplowed street and its wheels slowly crunched over the new-fallen snow. The once scurrying flakes in the air had thickened to a shower, and visibility dimmed.

"You sure you're okay with driving back to the North Hills?" Jamie asked, hoping fervently the answer would be yes. "We could always just hang out somewhere until it lets up—or the plows get through."

"I've driven through plenty worse than this," Teagan replied confidently.

Jamie said no more. She should have known that Teagan would take conquering bad roads as a personal challenge.

They made their way down the side street back to Grandview Avenue, but found that corridor equally untouched by either plow or salt truck. Teagan slogged on, driving slowly and mingling cautiously with the sparse traffic. They neared the intersection with McArdle Roadway, the steep, narrow road that was the quickest way back down the mountain, and seeing that the road was open, Jamie's anxiety grew. McArdle was usually closed in bad weather, as it had no shoulders and was perched on the edge of a cliff. None of the roads had been treated yet. Already they'd passed one unfortunate SUV with its nose crinkled around a fire hydrant. She opened her mouth to suggest another route, but quickly reconsidered. This was Teagan she was dealing with. Any show of no confidence would only egg her on.

Teagan turned the nose of the car onto McArdle.

Jamie gritted her teeth and winced.

To her credit, Teagan did know how to drive on snow. She kept the car moving forward at a snail's pace, never fast enough to make slamming the brakes necessary. The powder was fresh and deep and not yet packed down to ice, so the tires did have some traction.

But *still*.

Jamie tried not to think—as she looked over Teagan's

shoulder at the otherwise pleasing view of downtown from across the icy water—about how far up the cliff they still were, or just how sturdy the concrete barrier was that prevented cars from tumbling down the side of it. She knew that the rocky, forested face of Mount Washington was even steeper and more forbidding than it looked. City crews were constantly rescuing idiots who thought they could climb up or down it, only to find themselves stuck midway and unable to move either direction.

So far, Teagan was doing fine.

No other car had passed them coming up the hill, which made sense, given the greater difficulty of traversing the road in that direction. When they passed the halfway point, Jamie began to breathe easier. Surely, when they reached the bottom of the hill and turned onto Liberty Bridge, the roads would be better. The busiest routes always got treated first. And any second now, this nasty squall was bound to start petering out—

The Hummer flew into view ahead like one of the monster dragonflies that used to accost their canoe. Armored, colorful, speedy... and erratic.

"Oh, hell," Teagan murmured, tightening her grip on the wheel. "Where does he think he is, Daytona?"

The women held their breath as the Hummer fought its way up the hill in a zigzag pattern, spitting snow out left and right behind its giant wheels. A certain amount of speed was necessary to move uphill on snow, true, but the driver of the Hummer was clearly on a power trip. Unfortunately, his method of tackling the road required at least two thirds of the breadth of it.

"Move over, you idiot!" Jamie ordered the other driver.

Teagan was already inching their car toward the right shoulder, but there was only so far she could go.

"He acts like he doesn't even see us!" Teagan exclaimed, and the two of them watched with disbelief as the Hummer continued coming toward them, its pattern unaltered. Only when it drew close enough for the women to make out the other driver's face were they certain that he had spotted them.

His expression of utter shock was less than comforting.

Instead of veering slightly to the right and continuing uphill straight, the man inexplicably slammed his brakes, resulting in an immediate, two-hundred-forty degree tailspin.

Jamie watched in horror as the Hummer slid over the snow-covered road like a bad ballerina, held back in its forward motion by sheer gravity, its weight and sudden loss of power combining to slow it quickly to a ungraceful, sideways halt less than ten feet in front of them.

Teagan did all she could. Her judicious use of the brakes reduced their own speed from fifteen miles per hour down to maybe ten. But there was nowhere for her to steer to, nowhere else to go. Their car certainly wasn't stopping. Even as Jamie felt her own feet reflexively stretch out and strike the front panel, she knew that slamming the brakes would only make the car go faster.

They were going to collide.

The scene unfolded in slow motion. Teagan's car drifted forward down the hill with all the grace the Hummer had lacked, moving slowly, easily, and perfectly straight to forge a direct hit broadside against the Hummer's front wheel. Jamie's body tensed and her eyes closed as the cab rocked with the impact. The sharp, sickening crunch of crumpling metal met her ears, and the world went white.

For one bizarre, fleeting moment, Teagan thought her body had been thrown out of the car and into the snow. Then she realized her face was in an airbag.

She pushed the rapidly deflating plastic pillow out of her way to find Jamie doing the same. "Are you okay?" she asked breathlessly, even as she assessed her own body for injury. Everything seemed fine.

"I'm good," Jamie answered. "But we'd better get out of

here. Another car could be coming behind us."

Teagan swore. She tried to open her door, but found it jammed.

"Come this way," Jamie urged, stepping through the passenger door.

Teagan scooted over and followed her out.

Her Corolla sat placidly on the road, quiet now except for the occasional creak or pop, fresh snow already beginning to cover its windows. Its entire front end was buckled.

The Hummer didn't have a scratch.

Its driver hopped down from the other side, walked around, and stood beside them. He was not some reckless teenager, or even a twenty-something. The man was fifty if he was a day, potbellied, sun weathered, and dressed upscale casual with pricey leather boots. He surveyed the damage to Teagan's vehicle with a frown, then whistled.

"Little car like that shouldn't be on the road in this weather, wouldn't you say, ladies?"

Teagan's head whipped up. A fire of fury blazed in her toes and spread up through the rest of her like lightning. Her mouth opened, her arms drew back—

All at once Jamie was standing in front of her, facing the man. "Now, don't go being an asshole," the sexy voice purred, smooth as butter. "She fights dirtier when she's angry—besides which, her husband's a lawyer. Now how about we all get off the road before the next car runs us over?"

Over Jamie's shoulder, Teagan watched the man blink. He looked up the hill, and his mouth twitched. He then hustled to the side of the road and over the guardrail, spewing profanity as he went.

Heavy breaths rocked Teagan's chest. The frigid air stung her lungs. "Let me kill him," she whispered hoarsely. "Please let me kill him."

"All in good time, Teag," Jamie answered, pushing her toward the far embankment. "I see another car."

Teagan hastened along with Jamie to the downhill side of

the road, where they scrambled over the concrete barrier but stopped short of the iron fence that marked the end of the level roadbed. One false step on the other side and they'd be tumbling through the treetops, but they could at least move lengthwise till the shoulder widened out. Teagan could appreciate Jamie's choice of safety zones. As the delivery van chugged toward them, the driver of the Hummer had cause to second guess his position in the three-foot trough that separated the opposite guard rail from a towering wall of rock. Screeching like a girl, he first hopped up and down in place, then turned and frantically tried to scramble up and out of the way by grabbing at snow-covered roots and spindly trees. But he made no progress. The cliff was too steep; the fresh snow too slippery, and as the heavy vehicle bore down upon them he lost his footing entirely and slipped to the ground out of view.

Teagan and Jamie stood poised for flight as the van careened uncertainly down the hill, attempting alternately to steer and pump out of an almost inevitable skid. But no movement on their part proved necessary. Despite all odds, the driver kept control, pulling the van to a gentle halt dead center in the roadway — a good six feet short of Teagan's rear bumper.

The women breathed out in unison. The van's driver jumped down onto the road and called to them. "Everybody all right?" She was a petite black woman, probably somewhere in her forties, and she wore an industrial looking uniform. Despite her size, everything about her manner bespoke authority.

"We're all fine," Teagan called back.

The woman stepped over and surveyed the stopped cars, then looked back at Teagan and Jamie. "Who all was in this one?" she asked, pointing to the Corolla.

"We were," Teagan answered.

The woman scowled over at the Hummer. "So where's the fool driving this?"

"Hiding over there," Jamie explained, pointing, just as

the man's beet red face popped up over the barrier.

"He better hide!" the woman fumed, heading toward the roadside where the women waited. "Blocking up the whole damn road; could have killed somebody. Still could!" She let loose a colorful string of curses, vaulted over the barrier, and began a determined march along the shoulder. "I'll go uphill and try to flag people before we get a pileup. You call the police yet?"

"Not yet," Teagan replied. "But we will right now."

The woman threw another glance over her shoulder to where the head of the Hummer driver had disappeared again. "Damn fool idiot! *Learn to drive!*" she bellowed.

"I think I love her," Teagan muttered, pulling her cell phone out of her pocket.

"Let's walk downhill a little," Jamie suggested, tugging at her elbow. "We can alert anybody coming the other way — and besides, it will be safer than here."

Teagan agreed.

The 911 dispatcher was blessedly efficient, and the city police arrived within minutes. The officer accepted Teagan's story without question; however, judging from the Hummer driver's outraged expression and wild gesticulations, he did not seem to be having similar luck. The van driver was lauded for having safely stopped traffic upstream; apparently no vehicle other than the police truck had even tried to make it up the hill, since it was necessary to skirt around two other stalled cars at the bottom to do so.

In the meantime, the snow, as if thumbing its nose at all concerned, had dried up to nearly nothing.

Teagan and Jamie stood huddled in the wind, waiting for the tow truck. The police had warned them it could be a while. An officer had moved the Hummer down the hill and out of the way, but the Corolla wasn't drivable, and until it was removed altogether the whole of McArdle Roadway would stay closed. Teagan had been able to pull her emergency blanket out of her trunk, and the women wrapped it around them both as they sought shelter in the closest thing to a windbreak—the area underneath the tracks of the Monongahela incline, which crossed over the road just downhill from the crash.

Teagan pulled out her cell phone, hesitated, then pocketed it again.

"Well?" Jamie asked, "Are you going to call Eric, or aren't you?"

"No, I'm not," Teagan answered, deciding as she spoke. "He's got lawyerball. I don't want to wreck his day, too."

Jamie's eyebrows rose. "Lawyerball?"

Teagan smiled. "A bunch of his attorney friends get together and play basketball on Sundays. He looks forward to it all week. I'm not going to make him miss it just so he can trudge down here in the snow and act like he's rescuing me."

"Oh, right," Jamie said wryly. "I forgot. Teagan Raye *never* needs to be rescued."

Teagan shot a look at her. "That's Teagan Raye *Hansen.* Don't forget it."

To her surprise, Jamie chuckled. "And how is Teagan Raye *Hansen* going to get herself out of this one?"

Good question.

Teagan thought a moment, then pulled her cell phone back out. "I'll call my mother," she answered. "She can't drive on snow worth crap, but by the time we get the car towed the roads will probably be fine again." Grimacing, she contacted Sheryl, gave the minimum necessary information, promised to let her know ASAP when and where they would be after the tow, and hung up.

When Teagan looked at Jamie again, she was disturbed to find her grinning. "And what exactly do you find so amusing about all this?"

Jamie's grin broadened to a smile, even as her teeth chattered. She gripped the blanket tighter around the two of them. "It's not this," she answered. "Although I admit, it has gotten my mind off my own problems. I'm smiling because I was remembering 'The Monsoon.' Do you?"

Teagan was about to say no when the wicked sparkle in Jamie's eyes took her back like a shot. They were huddled under a dock, and it was raining. No, not just raining. It was a torrential downpour of solid sheets of cold water, it had come out of nowhere, and it was threatening to last forever. The girls had gotten soaked in their canoe, paddled to the nearest point on shore, and scrambled for the closest cover. The "cover" was minimal, as water still leaked in through the slats of wood above, and they had to stand waist deep in the lake in order to get under it. But at least the weight of half the water in the world was no longer pounding straight down on their heads.

"Yeah," Teagan said with a smirk. "I remember it. It seemed like we were holed up under that dock for hours."

"It was probably more like forty-five minutes," Jamie commented. "But it stuck in both our minds, didn't it?"

"I even remember what we talked about," Teagan mused. "Do you?"

"Boys," Jamie answered confidently. "You always wanted to talk about boys."

Teagan's head whipped around. "I did not! *You* were the one the older guys at the lake used to watch all the time."

"Well, yeah," Jamie agreed. "But I wasn't the one who wanted to talk about it."

Teagan's teeth gritted. Jamie was right, dammit. Adolescent Teagan had been boy crazy that summer. And annoyed that the few prospects around had paid her so little attention...

"You would have gotten a lot more attention if you'd taken off that disgusting ball cap once in a while," Jamie added. "And it didn't help that you beat up a bully and were always strutting around pretending to be a lifeguard."

Teagan blinked. All this time, and distance, and anger... and Jamie's ability to peg her thoughts was still uncanny. Her lips drew into a smirk. "At least *I* didn't get caught in an elementary school bathroom kissing some guy named Marcus Slinkard."

Jamie frowned. "I would never kiss anybody named —" But then she smiled. "Oh yeah, I did, didn't I? Why would you remember a story like that? I could have been making it up."

"If you'd been making it up, you would have used a better name."

"Good point," Jamie agreed. "But for the record, *he* kissed *me*. I wasn't interested in guys until high school."

An icy wind blew in suddenly from off the river, whipping up the already fallen snow and swirling it around the two of them like a blizzard. But in Teagan's mind there was only rain, pounding hard on the wooden planks overhead, dripping through to pat her arms with steady drops of cool moisture. Her thoughts mellowed. "You wanted to cure cancer," she said quietly.

Jamie's smile faded. "Yeah, that would have been nice. But turns out I sucked at biology. Never could stand dissecting things. I was always good at math, though."

"You could have been anything you wanted," Teagan said, regretting the platitude as soon as the words were out of her mouth. The sad truth was that the odds had been stacked against Jamie academically the minute she entered the system. Foster homes were not always in good school districts, and moving frequently made sticking to any particular course plan difficult. Jamie's having graduated from high school and then worked her way through college entirely on her own, with no family safety net, was nothing short of miraculous. She didn't need to cure cancer to be proud of herself.

"We talked about what our tombstones would say, too," Jamie mused. "Do you remember that?"

Teagan considered. "I believe I was going to save the world."

Jamie chuckled again. "Well, you're off to a decent start, I guess." She let out a sigh. "You know, when I was a kid, I hated social workers. All of them. When I looked at my caseworkers, all I could see were people who were supposed to be doing all this stuff for me, but they were always so busy, and they were always saying *no*. No, you can't do this; no, the system doesn't work that way. The worst part was wanting to believe they really cared about what happened to me, when I knew they didn't—they were just in it for the money."

Teagan opened her mouth to say something, but Jamie quickly cut her off. "Don't bust a gut, Teag. I understand now. They're given impossible situations and ridiculous caseloads and expected to do miracles while working under dicey conditions getting paid virtually nothing... and they do it because, despite appearances, they really *do* care. Believe me, I get that now. I wouldn't take a job like that for any money. I think what you're doing is great."

Teagan looked into Jamie's warm golden eyes, then looked away again. She didn't do accepting praise well. But that didn't mean she didn't like it.

"I wanted my tombstone to say: 'cured cancer and traveled the world,'" Jamie continued. Her tone turned bitter. "Somehow I don't think that girl under the dock would be happy with: 'banged a married man to get to Europe.'"

The rain over Teagan's head transformed back to snow. She twisted in the blanket to face Jamie squarely. "Stop judging yourself. You don't have all the facts yet; Richard was only guessing. But even if what he suspected was true—" she struggled to find the right words, dismissing visions of Eric every time they intruded into her thoughts. "I understand now why the married-man thing bothers you so much. I do. In a way, you probably feel like you've failed your mother. But for God's sake, Jamie—you've got to let that go and concentrate on what matters *now*. Whether the guy was married or not, he's almost certainly the one who assaulted you!"

Jamie blinked back at her for a long moment, her face expressionless. "Wow, Teag. You really know how to brighten up a room."

Teagan's lips twitched reluctantly into a smile. Damn, it was cold. She adjusted the blanket, stamped her feet, and gazed hopefully down the road for signs of the tow truck.

One of us does, anyway.

Chapter Twenty-Two

With the heater in Sheryl's PT Cruiser blasting on full power, Jamie at last felt her fingers and toes beginning to thaw. It being Sunday, the tow truck driver was willing to haul the Corolla and its previous occupants out of the middle of McArdle Roadway and back to his own garage—and that was it. All the body shops were closed; he had other calls to make. Since the garage was also technically closed, the women could not have been happier to see Sheryl waiting for them in the parking lot when the truck pulled in. But despite the warmth blowing through the Cruiser's vents, Jamie felt a distinct chill emanating from the driver's seat. Teagan was still in the cab with the driver completing paperwork, which left Jamie alone with Sheryl.

"Teagan's a good driver," Sheryl commented, making a passable attempt at pleasantry. "But I do wish she'd let her husband ferry her around on days like this. He's wonderful behind the wheel. And they make *such* a good team, no matter what they're doing. So well suited to each other!"

Jamie fought a grin, but failed. Sheryl's efforts at subtlety were truly stunning. She had been nice enough during dinner on Friday, but that was before "the incident." Her resentment of her daughter's friend now was palpable. Which was unfortunate, because Jamie was rather fond of her.

"I think they're a great couple," she agreed. "Teagan deserves a guy like him."

Sheryl's eyes slid sideways. She appraised Jamie suspiciously.

Jamie almost choked trying not to chuckle. "Seriously, Sheryl," she assured. "I'm not after Eric. Not that he's not fabulous, but he's taken. And I know Teagan. And I value my eyesight. What else can I say?"

Sheryl studied her a bit more, then drew her carefully penciled-on lips into a reluctant, albeit relieved smile. "I'm delighted to hear that."

The women sat in silence for a long moment, both staring out the window at the relatively uninteresting figures of Teagan and the driver sitting motionless in the truck. The snow had stopped. As Teagan had predicted, by the time the truck arrived all the main roads had been salted, transforming the icy coating of white into a safer brownish-gray slush.

"I suppose one can hardly blame you for looking," Sheryl said charitably. "Eric is perfectly adorable, isn't he? If he wasn't married to my daughter—" Her face suddenly colored with embarrassment. She cleared her throat. "Well, anyway."

Jamie clenched her jaws tightly. She could *not* laugh. But she was pleased to note that Sheryl seemed to know nothing of Jamie's past with Eric. Teagan had been wise to keep that little gem to herself. Observing Sheryl—who had come to a garage to rescue two other women from a snowstorm wearing a low cut V-neck sweater, skinny jeans, and shiny leather dress boots—Jamie remembered how she had once viewed the older woman as exciting and worldly. In a way, she still did. Sheryl had traveled. Sheryl had dated scores of men, all types of men. Sheryl *knew* things.

The haze of ill feeling that Jamie had managed to hold at bay since the crash descended on her once again. She could not avoid this demon forever. Sooner or later, it would have to be dealt with.

"Sheryl," she said suddenly, before she could think better of it. "Can I ask you a question?"

Teagan's mother looked at her with a candid expression Jamie found oddly comforting. "Sure. Go ahead."

Jamie cleared her own throat. "I've been remembering more of my past all the time, and I'm almost up to the present now. But what's strange is that as I've been remembering different parts of my life, I've *felt* like I used to feel, too. When I was remembering my childhood, I didn't think about men, for example. So it hasn't been as simple as watching my life flash before my eyes—I've been reliving it. I remember what my goals were—how I felt when I changed them, what I was shooting for next. I remember my codes. You know what I mean by codes?"

Sheryl's thickly lashed eyelids blinked. Her forehead was creased in concentration. Jamie noted that Teagan's mother was, if nothing else, a good listener. "I think so," she answered. "Your own rules you live by, you mean."

"Exactly," Jamie said with relief. "I never cared about anybody else's idea of morality, but what I decided was right for myself, I stuck to. Except..." She bit her lip. She wasn't sure why she was telling Sheryl all this. But she was committed now. "Except I think I broke my own code. At the end. And I don't know why."

Sheryl emitted a sympathetic hum.

Jamie took a breath. She wasn't used to confiding in people; she'd never had any adult female friends worth confiding in. But the temptation was strong; her mother had always told her that talking things out was good for the soul. She would talk to Teagan if she could, but Teagan couldn't help her on this one—and that was Jamie's fault.

"I never had anything to do with married men," she blurted. "Ever. But I realize now that I did just recently—that I must have. And I don't understand how it could happen." She turned and faced Sheryl squarely. "I mean seriously, what the hell was I *thinking?* I'm not saying I was some pillar of virtue—I never worried whether a guy was dating somebody else or liked somebody else or even whether he was supposed to marry somebody else... I figured the choice was his to make. But I drew the line at guys who were already married because I had to be number one. Period. I would never let a guy use me like my mother got used. What could make me turn my back on everything I always cared about, everything I valued for myself?"

Sheryl's eyes studied Jamie's for a long moment. Then she turned her gaze to her lap, raised one perfectly manicured nail to her lips, and nibbled. After a long moment, she sighed and turned back to Jamie with a small, sad smile.

"I wish to hell I could say that I have no idea what you're talking about," she answered, speaking in an unfamiliar voice devoid of any affectation. "But it happens, Jamie. It happens to a lot of women."

"But why?" Jamie pressed. "I could have any single man I wanted!"

Sheryl's smile broadened. "Oh, I don't doubt that. I could have too, when I was your age. But sometimes the forbidden has its own appeal." Her expression turned wistful, then she caught Jamie's eyes. "Were you in love with him?"

"Absolutely not," Jamie answered immediately.

Sheryl's eyebrows arched. "You sure?"

Jamie nodded. "I would remember if I had those kind of feelings. I don't remember *him*, not really, but I can see flashes... and there's nothing warm and fuzzy anywhere in those pictures, believe me."

Sheryl's lips pursed. "Well, that's different, then."

"Different from what?" Jamie insisted. "I just want to understand... to figure out where my head was at."

Sheryl looked out the window toward the tow truck, as if confirming that her daughter remained out of earshot. "I understand, Jamie. Believe me. I've certainly done things I'm not proud of. Most of the time by accident—meaning that when I figured out the guy was married, I broke it off. But I wasn't always trying that hard to spot them, and when I was younger I saw what I wanted to see. The fact is, Jamie, if you weren't in love, and you knew he was married, he must have had something else you were after."

A silver strand, delicate, yet strong. Masculine hands over her shoulders, tiny stones twinkling in the light...

"But I never cared about *things* before," Jamie murmured. "I wanted to earn my own way."

"Wealth can be a very powerful lure," Sheryl said quietly. "It's more than just things. It's the freedom to do what you want. To make *other* people do what you want. It's travel around the world; it's exhilaration. For women like us, it can be a fantasy come true."

Jamie blew out a breath; ran a hand through her tangled, windblown hair. "I can't believe it," she protested. "Not me."

"There are other possibilities," Sheryl continued. "For some women, it's the excitement of having a man who... well, it's the thrill of living with a certain amount of danger."

Jamie frowned.

"I know, I know," Sheryl said apologetically, "the whole flying-bullets thing doesn't work for me, either. But I know women who are into it, and... I'm just saying."

Vibration. Darkness. The smell of exhaust; the rumble of an engine. Tightness all around... so tight... no way to move. No air. No way to breathe...

"Jamie? Are you okay?" Sheryl's voice brought Jamie up from the abyss into which her mind had fallen—but only just. "Teagan's coming back now."

A blast of frigid air shot through the Cruiser as Teagan quickly opened and slammed one of the rear doors. "Well, *that* took forever," she said with forced cheerfulness as she buckled herself into the back seat. "We're going to have to pay, again, to have it towed to a body shop in the North Hills tomorrow. But whatever. Nobody's injured, right?"

"That's all that matters, honey," Sheryl agreed. "Are we headed home, then?"

Home.

An L-shaped living room, the bed around the bend. A galley kitchen—what ghastly metal cabinets!—but functional enough. Windows that stuck. Hideous tan color on the walls. Nice new shower, never mind the cracked tiles around the sink...

"My apartment!" Jamie cried.

Sheryl stopped backing up the car and looked at her.

Teagan leaned forward between the front seats. "What

about it?"

"I remember it! I think I did before, actually, in my office. But I forgot again." Jamie reached into her coat pocket, felt the cold metal of her spare set of keys, and smiled. "I took these out of my desk," she said proudly, displaying them. "I barely thought about it—I just knew they were there, and I grabbed them." She turned to Teagan excitedly. "Do you realize what this means? I can go home!"

Teagan's smile disappeared. "Hold on, Jamie. I know you're anxious to get home, but the fact is, you're still in danger. Until the police have a name to follow up on, this guy is still out there. And he almost certainly knows where you live."

The window of sunshine that had warmed Jamie's nightmare slammed shut again.

"I didn't mean I could go home for good," she lied. "I only meant we could drop by. I could get some things. No offense, but I'd really, *really* like to wear my own clothes again." Even as she spoke, Jamie squiggled her shoulders to relieve the ache of the offending bra. "Please, Teag? If you don't mind, Sheryl? Five minutes is all I need, I swear. It's only a couple miles away from here, within walking distance of *La Veduta*. That's why I rented it. I never did get a car. Please?"

A shiny steel-gray Benz, gleaming chrome, heated leather seats...

Jamie squelched the vision with a fury.

"I know where it is," Teagan said uncertainly. "Richard looked up your address, and I've already left a voice message for the detective. I'm just not sure it's safe for you to be there."

"It's broad daylight on a Sunday afternoon!" Jamie protested. "And there are three of us!"

"She has a point, Teagan," Sheryl agreed. "Besides, seeing the place might help her remember the man's name, and that would make her safe sooner than anything, right?"

Collapsing on the bed... a queen mattress for once. Nice to have the space, since she wasn't alone...

STOP IT!

Teagan breathed out heavily. "All right. Five minutes. But I'm going to try the number the detective gave me again and see if I can talk to a real person this time. They should know where you live already, anyway. They've had your name since yesterday!"

While Teagan dialed—eventually hanging up again in disgust—Jamie hastened to direct Sheryl the short distance to the street she remembered, taking the back way up the mountain. When they reached the familiar building, an early twentieth century two-story wooden house now converted into three apartments, Jamie was surprised to find her emotions mixed. She had been so happy to recognize *La Veduta...* why was the sight of her apartment building not quite so positive? It wasn't the height of luxury, but she'd had her own place for once, hadn't she?

"Not this driveway," Jamie instructed Sheryl. "Go on around the block; you get to my carport from the alley around back."

The perfect place to hide the Benz.

Teagan's mother steered the cruiser onto the narrow gravel lane and parked under a makeshift but functional portico behind the house. "Well, this would at least keep off the snow and the bird poop!" Sheryl said cheerfully, sounding very much like a real estate agent.

Jamie had no response. All lightness in her heart had evaporated. The back door of the house, which was the only entrance to her downstairs studio apartment, looked suddenly foreboding. She hesitated.

"Still want to go in?" Teagan asked. "You don't have to. At least not right now."

"I need to," Jamie heard herself say as her hand moved toward the door handle. "I've got to get my stuff." She stepped out of the car and walked the few paces to the back steps. Her head felt suddenly muzzy. Her nerves were on edge. What was wrong with her?

The steps were slippery from the snow. She shivered from the cold, drew out her keys, and turned them in the lock.

Nothing happened. She turned the keys again. This time, the knob rotated.

It was open.

Jamie's muscles tensed. She always locked her door. Legend had it that some people lived in neighborhoods where you didn't have to. If such places existed, she'd never seen one.

Anger flared in her chest. She shoved open the door and stepped inside.

A tiny table with two chairs stood against the wall immediately beyond the door. To the right was her galley kitchen, narrow enough that she could grab a box out of the cabinet on one side while closing a drawer with her foot on the other. Her eyes scanned the counter for anything unusual. But there was nothing to see. All the doors and drawers were neatly closed. Two empty cups and a plate sat in the sink. Her bananas had gone brown. The trash can stank.

She noticed that both Sheryl and Teagan had shuffled into the small space she'd left behind her, trying to get out of the cold. She stepped out of their way and on into the narrow hall. On the right was the door to her bathroom. She glanced inside it only briefly, but then stopped and took a step back. Something was wrong.

"Does everything look okay?" Teagan asked, sounding dubious. "Jamie?"

Jamie continued to stare into the bathroom. "Not really," she heard herself say tonelessly. "I'm not in the habit of leaving the seat up."

Teagan stepped forward and looked over her shoulder. "Was the back door locked?" she asked pointedly.

Jamie didn't answer the question. She walked past the bathroom and on down the narrow hall. The only other room in the apartment, her combined living room and bedroom, was just around the bend. She could see her bookcase in the corner, as well as the beat-up desk which housed her dinosaur of a laptop. The computer was still there. Not that any robber with half a brain would look twice at it. She had never owned anything worth stealing.

Don't you have a safe to put it in?

Jamie halted at the memory.

It was his voice.

His.

Hell no, why would I? she had replied with a laugh. *I'll just hide it in the drawer.*

"Jamie?" Teagan asked again, pestering her like a gnat. "Are you remembering something else? What's going on with you?"

Jamie searched her brain frantically for a face to match the voice, but there was nothing else to see.

You are so beautiful, Jamie.

A shudder rocked her shoulders. She couldn't see him, but she could *feel* him. She could feel him all around this accursed place.

I'm going to give you the world, Jamie.

She heard herself laugh again. *And I'm going to let you!*

Teagan was still talking, but Jamie wasn't listening. She was back at *La Veduta*, in the kitchen after hours, chilling with Richard.

Did you see the rocks around that woman's neck? On a Tuesday night in Pittsburgh! Ordered three appetizers for two people, entrees, and desserts and barely touched any of it! They walked away and left a bottle of Verite La Joie Cab just sitting there... still two-thirds full!

What a coup for you! Richard had responded pleasantly. *Or did you let Tony snatch it up himself? Do NOT tell me that snotty little busboy made off with it!*

Tony took the wine, but that's not the point! Where do people get money like that? How can you ever have so much you can blow it on something that stupid and really not give a damn?

Richard had chuckled. *Never been around people like these before, have you, love? Well, you'll get used to it. Just smile and take advantage all you can...*

"Jamie!" Teagan's voice broke through. "If you feel like anything is out of place, like anyone else has been in here, then we should leave right now!"

Someone else *had* been here, Jamie thought grimly. That was why the place didn't feel like hers anymore. But he wasn't a burglar. She had let him in.

Many times.

"I'm just remembering some things," she said at last. "But I'm okay. I don't think I've been robbed or anything."

At least, not of her possessions.

Her self-respect... her very soul... maybe.

Let's drive to Cleveland for dinner tonight. We can go to Pier W, or the Lola Bistro — maybe Hyde Park? You can order anything on the menu. We'll call it "research."

Jamie's teeth gritted. That was how it had started, wasn't it? Expensive meals in other restaurants — assuaging her curiosity, whetting her desire to become more knowledgeable and competitive in the business. Just not other restaurants in Pittsburgh. He could be recognized here.

Richard again, down in the kitchens, mincing fresh garlic. *You're infected, Jamie.*

Infected with what?

Money lust, my dear. Sounds ugly, I know, but it happens to the best of us.

Her anger had erupted. *So what if I want more than I used to? Is that so wrong? I deserve more! I've got the brains. Half the people who drop hundreds a night here are idiots! They couldn't pass calculus if their frivolous little lives depended on it, but they have the money and I don't! You think that's right?*

She had moved into this apartment happy as a clam.

She had come to despise it.

Come on, princess. His voice again. *Why shouldn't you have something nice to wear out? You'll need it to blend in. And you know that you deserve it...*

Jamie shut her eyes tight, tried to see his face. His voice was everywhere, all around her, taunting her. She could see his waist, his hands, but not his face. Had she ever even *wanted* to look him in the eyes?

Teagan began to harass her further, and Jamie snapped. "I'm remembering something, okay? Can you just be quiet for a second!"

Things. They were like a drug to her. Things she'd never had, things she'd never dreamed of having. Never before had she encountered such profligate wealth, such careless privilege. *La Veduta* shoved it down her throat every damn day.

She'd never taken gifts from men before. She'd always just said no.

What he'd given her was worse than heroin.

"I don't know a name," she said brusquely, answering the question she was sure that Teagan had asked already. "I just remember his being here. Let me get some clothes and we'll leave."

She took a step forward into her living room and turned the corner toward her chest of drawers. She had not yet reached them when she heard Sheryl's scream.

Jamie whirled around. Sheryl and Teagan had moved behind her into the room. Sheryl was staring at the floor beside her TV table.

Jamie moved forward toward them, and her heart stopped.

Blood.

The stain spread across her once-cream carpet. Large, amorphous, threatening. One dark pool to the side of her television. Smaller pools, drips, smears, crisscrossing well out into the room. The largest pool was so thick that dried-up clots adhered to the carpet fibers.

"We have to get out of here," Teagan said calmly, laying a hand on Jamie's arm. "We have to leave right now."

Jamie's brain raced in frantic circles, searching for some connection. Some voice, some image within her brain that could explain the horror before her.

There was nothing.

"You could have slaughtered a pig in here," she heard

her voice say, nonsensically.

"Come on, Jamie," Teagan ordered, pulling on her arm.

"In a minute," Jamie resisted, staring at the blood that could only be hers. How much? How long had she lain here? Her chin lifted resolutely. She turned and looked at her bed.

Rumpled sheets. Brand new ones. A soft and fuzzy throw blanket to the side. Two wine glasses on the bedside table... one empty, one still half full.

One significant bedding omission.

"It happened here, Teag," she said, her voice a hoarse whisper. "He wrapped me up in my own damned bedspread."

Chapter Twenty-Three

Teagan had just thanked her mother for the ride home and shut the car door behind her when her cell phone rang. "Go on inside," she urged Jamie, handing her the keys. "This may be the detective."

Jamie wordlessly took the keys and began trudging up the snow-covered walk. Teagan looked after her worriedly. Jamie had said nothing the whole way home. Her last words had been to complain to Teagan, after Teagan hustled her into the car and Sheryl drove away, that she hadn't had the chance to get her clothes. She had seriously wanted to go back and get them.

Teagan had tried to explain, gently, about the importance of not disturbing evidence at a crime scene, but her explanation hadn't really mattered. Jamie wasn't listening, and from the look of Sheryl's pale face and glassy eyes, no amount of coercion would have made her turn the car around anyway.

Teagan took a breath and answered the call. "Hello?"

"Ms. Hansen? This is Detective Musser from Homicide. I've got two messages from you, here... you say there's bloodstains in Ms. Fukas' apartment?"

Teagan repeated everything they had seen, cursing the way her hands shook as she held the phone. It was probably just the cold. She walked up to her front door while she was talking, but didn't go inside. She didn't want Jamie to overhear.

"The unit was supposed to get out there this afternoon anyway—so we'll take a look," he assured. "We have her home and work addresses. You say there's no one at the restaurant who can give us this guy's name? Or a neighbor, maybe?"

Teagan released a frustrated breath. "You can try, but I doubt it. She was obviously keeping the relationship a secret. But I do think she's close to remembering it herself. Maybe if you talk to her again—"

"I'll be out to interview her as soon as I can," he confirmed. "But under no circumstances should she set foot in that apartment again until we've finished with the place. After that, it's up to her, but you understand she's taking a risk just by being there. This guy has every motivation to try and shut her up before she remembers enough to nail him."

Teagan's shoulders shivered. "Yes, I realize that. I'll talk to her."

"It says here that you're her caseworker and that she's been living with you since her hospital discharge?"

"Yes. We have a spare apartment."

"That's fine as long as this guy doesn't know where she is," the detective said heavily. "But you need to be wary. He could have been watching her apartment for her to come back."

Teagan stamped her feet on the porch. She didn't think her blood could get any colder. "I thought of that," she said grimly, wishing she had thought of it before letting Jamie go back there in the first place. She had always assumed that the assault happened elsewhere—it never occurred to her that it could have happened in Jamie's own home. But it should have. "I did think to keep an eye out as we drove home," she reported. "I'm certain no one followed us."

"Could someone have gotten your license number while you were inside the apartment?"

Teagan's stomach lurched. She hadn't thought of that, either. She was failing in her charge... on all counts. "My mother drove us," she answered. "Her number wouldn't lead him here, but—"

"I'm not trying to alarm you," the detective interrupted, "but it's something to be aware of. If he's having Ms. Fukas' place watched, and he's savvy, he could get your mother's address. No need to panic, just have her be on guard. Any suspicious characters, call 911, then us. Same for you at your own house, regardless of whether or not you think you were followed."

Teagan felt ill. It was one thing dealing with violence at work. Bringing it home to one's family was another. "We'll do that," she said weakly.

"Good. As far as next of kin goes, you should know that our background check came up empty. Ms. Fukas signed herself out of foster care at age eighteen. Mother deceased; father listed as unknown on her birth certificate. Maternal grandparents declined custody with request for no contact... no other relatives identified. Never married. Looks like she's on her own."

Not completely, Teagan amended silently. *She has me.*

"Just tell her to hold tight until I get there," the detective continued. "Under no circumstances should she attempt to contact this guy if she does remember him. She shouldn't do *anything,* period, until I talk to her. Understood?"

Teagan agreed, and she and the detective hung up. Her fingers were so stiff she could barely manage the buttons, but she stayed on the porch another minute anyway, shivering and cursing. She knew that the detective had only been so forthcoming because he assumed her to be Jamie's caseworker. But she wasn't Jamie's social worker anymore, not technically. Her responsibilities didn't extend outside the hospital. She was only doing what she was doing because Jamie was her friend.

Which meant that she could stop anytime.

Teagan cursed again. She would do everything she could to protect Jamie, there was no question of that, for any number of reasons. But she hated that harboring Jamie was putting her own family in danger—however theoretical that danger might be. She hated that her own stupid mistakes today had increased that threat. She hated the misogynist monster who had left a beautiful young woman bleeding and unconscious in the snow. But most of all, she hated that despite Jamie's seemingly genuine regret over crossing the line with Eric, she herself could not... *quite*... get past it.

She slept with him.

That was years ago!

She tried to kiss him in your own house just yesterday! Don't be naive...

She explained that. What kind of friend are you?

Teagan beat her frozen palms against her temples, then reached for the door. Her psychoanalysis of herself would accomplish nothing if she died of hypothermia in the process. She stepped inside and removed her wraps, then moved instinctively toward the kitchen.

Jamie stood in the dining room, her coat and mittens still on. She was staring at the wall of family pictures—one of way too many things in the house that remained unchanged since Eric's grandparents had lived here. Teagan and Eric did have other plans for the dining room—and in fact, the whole house—they just never seemed to get around to doing them.

Teagan stepped to Jamie's side and followed her eyes. She was looking at the portrait of four generations.

"I never asked Eric about his family," Jamie said softly. "And I wouldn't tell him about mine."

Teagan tried hard not to bristle. They were the first words Jamie had spoken in almost an hour; Teagan could hardly snap at her about the subject of Eric being off limits.

"He said he loved me," Jamie continued, clearly more to herself than to Teagan. "But I didn't answer back. I never did when guys told me that. Usually I didn't believe them; I figured they were just after sex. But even if they were telling the truth—and Eric's the only one I think might have been, looking back—I didn't feel the same way. I didn't try to. I didn't *want* to be in love."

Teagan was no longer cold. Her blood was increasing the ambient temperature of the room. She clenched her jaws tight, fighting the urge to speak... among other things.

"I don't know why I acted like that," Jamie continued, seemingly oblivious to Teagan's presence, much less her distress. "I always used to dream of being part of a big family. Not a makeshift family with kids who came and went along with support checks, but a real family, where everybody loved each other. Funny thing, though. Even after I grew up, I didn't picture myself as the mother of the family. I was always still one of the kids."

She turned and looked at Teagan. Her golden eyes brimmed with moisture. Her face contorted with pain even as she forced a smile. "I've been thinking... maybe I never really did grow up?"

Teagan opened her mouth to dispense the professional words of wisdom she was so terribly good at. But nothing came out.

"This thing you and Eric have," Jamie continued. "I don't understand how you get that. Until now, I didn't understand why you'd even want it. One guy, a bunch of strings, expectations... it never appealed. I used guys to get what I wanted, and they did the same. But this..." She raised her hand to the family portrait and loosely traced the outline of the baby with a fingertip. "This is a whole other ballgame, isn't it? This is being somebody *to* somebody. It's... real life." Her eyes narrowed in concentration. "And I want it."

Teagan drew a shuddering breath. She could see the wheels turning in Jamie's take-charge brain, and the sight wasn't pretty. The assault and all its ramifications had increased Jamie's self-awareness, obviously. But Teagan got the sinking feeling that, if Jamie was indeed considering a change in life goal, she was planning to approach it with the same methods she'd always used: attack and conquer. Fine for education and job hunting... less than optimal for marrying and having children.

Words failed her. "Jamie," she began uncertainly, "marriage and family are wonderful, but they're not something you can just decide to go out and make happen—"

She broke off as Jamie's face drew into a scowl, her gold eyes blazing. "You don't think I deserve it! Do you?"

Teagan was taken aback. "That's not what I said!" she

defended hotly. "I was just trying to explain that good relationships take—"

"Of course you have all the answers! You always did!" Jamie fired back. "Teagan knows *everything*. Teagan does everything *the right way*, all the time! And it's all because of her brains and her moxy, of course—not because her mother lived, or because her grandparents loved her, or because she's got a whole damned *second* family to bake her turkeys at Thanksgiving! Well, let me tell you, Little Miss Save the World, *I've* got brains, and *I've* got moxy, and I wound up left for dead with no one even missing me! Is that fair? And yet *you* think you deserve all this... and I don't!"

"I never said that!" Teagan shouted, even as warning bells went off in her head. Her rational brain told her that Jamie wasn't really angry at her—just at the entire lousy situation—but that didn't make the personal attack any less infuriating. If it was truth time, so be it. "You can be jealous of me if you want to, but the truth is, if you're alone now, it's your own damned fault! Love and friendship are two-way streets, and you just said you never even *tried* to care about anyone else! So if you're so damned smart, what did you *think* was going to happen?"

Teagan's cell phone rang. She would have ignored it, but she knew the ring. It was her supervisor at the hospital. She broke away from Jamie's livid stare, moved out into the hall, and answered it.

"Teagan, we have an emergency," the woman's voice stated calmly.

"I'm not on call."

"I know that. And I'm sorry. But Lisa had to leave twenty minutes ago. She's got a GI bug and was throwing up in the office. Rosalie is supposed to cover for her, and she's due to start her own shift in two hours anyway, but I haven't been able to reach her. Her phone is dead. And the hospital is desperate—they've got two rape victims in the ER, one's a domestic and needs shelter immediately, and the other's apparently in hysterics. I'd go in myself, but Ray and I are up in Altoona. There's nobody else I can call and the nursing staff's already short."

Teagan looked around for Jamie. She had apparently headed for the bathroom. Teagan closed her eyes and drew in a long, slow breath. Maybe the two of them could use some space.

"Fine, I'll go in."

The relief in the other woman's voice was palpable. "Thank you. I'm looking up an alternative number for Rosalie — if I reach her, I'll send her in to take over as soon as possible."

Teagan agreed and hung up the phone. She walked to the closed door of the half bath. "I have to go back in to work," she said flatly. "Just for a couple hours, maybe less." She briefly summarized the discussion she'd had with the detective, including his warnings. "Will you be all right?" There was no answer for several seconds. "Jamie?"

"I'll be fine!" the familiar voice said hotly.

Teagan bit back any retort. She grabbed her things and headed for the front door. As she shut it behind her, she thought she heard a noise coming from the bathroom: the sound of muffled crying.

She decided it was just the wind.

Not until she opened the door of her garage did she realize she had no car. Luckily, since Eric had caught a ride to lawyerball with a friend, his was available. She backed it out into the driveway, then let it idle a moment with the heater running. She hadn't talked to her husband all day. He was still asleep when she had left with Jamie; he had sent her a text later saying he was off to his game, but she had been too distracted to answer it. He still knew nothing about the car accident.

She drew out her phone and dialed.

He picked up almost immediately, sounding breathless. "Hey, good timing. You caught me on the bench. Where have you been?" In the background she heard the distinctive bounce of a basketball, along with the squeaking of shoes and the heavy pounding of feet. "Any progress with Jamie?"

The sound of his voice initially soothed her, as always, but the mention of his ex quickly ruined the effect. "She remembers where she worked and where she lived, and the detectives are going over there today," Teagan reported. The rest, she didn't feel like talking about. "Listen, my car got banged up—some idiot who didn't know how to drive in the snow. We're fine, but the Corolla is stuck at a garage, and I have to go back into work for a couple hours to cover an emergency. You mind if I take your car?"

She heard one of the other men shout his name. The phone was muffled for a moment as she heard him shout something back, then after a few seconds, the background noise diminished. "You were in an accident?" he said with concern. "Where? Are you sure you're okay? How did you get home?"

The edge of hurt in his last words made her feel worse, if possible, than she already did. Eric respected her independence, but he was also a man—which meant he enjoyed being leaned on once in a while. And once in a while, she was happy to indulge him. But not today. She gave the minimum necessary explanation of both the crash and the situation with Jamie, including the detective's warnings about the risk to the family. "I feel terrible about that," she admitted ruefully. Then she added without forethought, "I'm thinking maybe I should move her to a shelter after all."

There was a long silence, during which Teagan's insides churned uncomfortably. So, she had said it. Jamie's being in the house was a legitimate safety concern.

Wasn't it?

"Do whatever you think is best," Eric responded, his tone unreadable.

Unaccountably, Teagan's anger flared. "You don't think I should move her?"

"It doesn't matter to me either way," he insisted. "Why are you upset?"

"I'm not—" Teagan closed her mouth. She ran a hand through her tousled hair and realized she was heading to work in jeans and a fleece top. She swore silently. Never mind. She'd throw on somebody's lab coat. Just *let* them try and fire her over it.

"Teagan," Eric said more seriously. "Is everything okay?"

The sounds she'd heard from the bathroom reverberated in her ears. Jamie *had* been crying. She knew it, and she'd left anyway. Her own eyes burned with moist liquid, but she refused to give in to the urge. Everything was fine. Nothing had changed. What was she so upset about?

"Did you tell Jamie you loved her?"

The words shot out of her mouth involuntarily. She hadn't wanted to say them at all, but the accusation was like vomit. It was coming out whether she liked it or not.

"What?"

"Oh hell, Eric, I'm sorry," she said miserably. "Everything that's happened today—and yet, this is what gets me. You told me it was a physical thing, that you didn't have strong feelings for her. She says you told her you loved her. I know it's stupid, but... I just want to understand! Did you say that, or not?"

Teagan felt so pathetic, she wanted to crawl under the car seat. But dammit, she had to know. One of them was lying to her. It had to be Jamie. It just had to.

Eric exhaled roughly. "I thought we settled all this, Teagan. Did I imagine last night? Were you there?"

She closed her eyes with a wince. She had been there, all right. The most fabulous make up in the history of marriage. And now, this. "Please. Just answer me."

His voice lowered to a growl. "I told you the truth. It *was* primarily a physical thing. But at the time, I thought it was love. I didn't know any better because I didn't recognize the real thing until I met you. Satisfied?"

Tears escaped her eyes and started down her cheeks. In the background over the phone, she heard a man's voice calling. "I've got to go," Eric said gruffly.

"I—" she began. But the line went dead.

He had not even said goodbye.

She groped for a tissue, dried her face, blew her nose. She had to get a grip. She was needed in the ER. There were two women there in far worse shape than she.

She put away her phone and backed downhill out of the driveway.

Chapter Twenty-Four

Jamie emerged from the bathroom, wandered into the living room, and collapsed on the couch.

So, she insisted to herself, she had cried her eyes out. What of it? Other women did it regularly, and with far less provocation. Some philandering bastard had seduced her with his wealth and tried to murder her, she couldn't go back to her bloodstained apartment because he might try to kill her again, and she had just reamed out the only real friend she'd ever had for no particular reason that she could remember.

She could cry if she damn well felt like it.

If there was one good thing that had come out of her being assaulted and left for dead, it was her reunion with Teagan. Now their friendship was ruined. She had told Eric that if Teagan knew the truth, the women could never put it behind them—and she had been right. Teagan couldn't even talk about the subject without freaking. It had been the same all Jamie's life. Men always got in the way.

And it was always *her* fault that they did.

A small smile escaped her lips. There, now. Maybe nearly dying did have another upside—she had gained perspective. Teagan's assessment had been spot on, as usual. If there was no one out there who cared about her, it was her own damned fault. Who out there had she bothered to care about?

Richard?

Her smile broadened. Although they weren't terribly close, she did like Richard very much, and he seemed to like her. He would have reported her missing, might even have come to the hospital, if he had known. But she was under no illusions as to why their relationship worked as well as it did. Richard wasn't attracted to her, so there was no flirting, no tension. And since he wasn't interested in straight men, there was no competition, either.

Jamie had never taken the time or the effort to cultivate true friendships. She had always considered herself too busy; the effort too draining. Besides, she had always had Fantasy Teagan. Omnipresent and undemanding. The perfect, caring friend who was always out there, somewhere.

Until now.

Jamie's eyes strayed to the ceiling. It had water stains. The whole room, in fact, smelled a bit musty. And no wonder: this old part of the house had been built nearly a hundred years ago. She settled back into the couch cushions with a smile that was bittersweet. She would take this house in a heartbeat, must, dust, and all. It practically screamed "family."

If she'd never met Eric, she and Teagan would be as close as ever and she could have become a regular fixture here. If she'd been a better person when she met him, she might be living here herself.

Stop that.

She frowned. She *did* still think about Eric, and what might have been. In the suspended time of her fantasies, he wasn't connected with Teagan, or with anyone else. But in the real world he was a married man, which ruled him out no matter who he was married to. The fact that was he with Teagan ruled him out all over again, regardless of whether they were married. So why could she not stop thinking about him?

Perhaps, she thought dispiritedly, because he was the most tender, the most affectionate, the most genuinely *nice* guy she had ever dated.

And on a day like today, he was exactly the kind of man whose arms she would like to fall into.

The doorbell rang. Jamie started and sprang to her feet, but her vision began to black out. She sat back down a moment. Realizing she hadn't eaten since breakfast, she rose again, slowly, and walked to the door. Her hand was on the knob and starting to turn when she remembered Teagan's warnings. She stopped and looked through the peephole. A tall, thin man with wild black eyebrows glared back at her while holding up a badge from the Allegheny County Police Department. "Detective Musser," he said brusquely. "I need to talk to Jamie Fukas."

She opened the door and admitted him into the living room. "I'm Jamie," she said shortly, bristling at his mispronunciation of her surname. Though relatively few people ever had the occasion to pronounce it, it had not escaped Jamie's notice that she heard the short u sound more often from men. The probable Freudian slip never failed to set her teeth on edge.

"I'll keep this brief," he said, not bothering to sit down. "We've got a unit at your apartment now. Looks like there's no question you were assaulted at that location and then moved to the park. The place is also crawling with prints. We got yours at the hospital, so we should be able to run the others pretty quick. What I need is a list of other people who've been in your apartment recently. Particularly the men."

Jamie's jaws clenched. She didn't think the detective meant to be insulting. But she was in no mood. Her legs were tired, and she wanted to sit down. Who interviewed a crime victim standing up? Teagan would never treat a client like that.

She stepped away from him and dropped into a recliner. He could sit if he wanted to; she didn't care. "I don't completely remember the last month or so," she said stiffly. "But I can't remember anyone else being in my apartment except the man I was—" she broke off. Her face had reddened, which made her even angrier. "Except for the man I was unfortunately dating. I liked to keep my place private."

"Surely you had women friends over?" he said skeptically.

Jamie's heart pounded. Was he trying to torment her? "No. Not that I remember."

"What can you tell me about the man himself? The one you were... uh... dating?"

Jamie blew out a breath. *The man himself* was the last thing she wanted to talk about. The pounding headache that had begun to plague her at the restaurant was back in full force, and all she wanted was to close her eyes and shut out the world. But she described what she could remember in a dull monotone. Brief glimpses of his appearance, the car he drove, his marriage to somebody else, his wealth. The detective asked her repeatedly for a name, but her brain seemed no closer to an answer than before she had remembered the man at all.

The detective's questions kept coming, and her increasing vagueness seemed only to irritate him. The other detective had been nicer.

"If you'll excuse me," she said finally, "I have a horrendous headache, and I'm sure I've told you absolutely everything I can tell you. But when I remember more, I'll let you know."

The detective scowled at her, his bushy eyebrows arching comically. "See that you do. The sooner we get this guy, the safer you'll be. I hate to see these people who've taken you in being put at risk, too. Maybe you should consider a women's shelter? They have excellent security and the staff are trained to handle these situations."

Jamie's pulse rate quickened. Was he right? Was her very presence here putting Teagan's whole family in danger?

Her stomach soured.

She showed the detective to the door. She shut and locked it after him, then turned and began to shrug off the coat she was still wearing. She had yet to get warm, but the too-tight bra had become insufferable—she could swear it had worn inch-deep gouges along her ribs—and it was coming off. *Now.* She struggled one-armed to remove her coat, unzipped and removed the hoodie beneath it, then unhooked the offending bra and sent it sailing across the living room like a slingshot. Shivering, she threw the hoodie back over her arms, clutched it tightly around herself, and collapsed back onto the couch again.

She knew that she should go back to the garage apartment, now that the detective was gone. Her painkillers were there, and it was a hell of a lot warmer. But getting there meant going back out in the cold, and the steps would be snow-covered again. She couldn't stand the thought of it. Instead, she pulled the coat over her like a blanket and closed her eyes.

Her body was desperate for rest, but her mind refused. Between throbs of pain, her brain threw up random, taunting images. A thick pool of blood, dried into her carpet. A faded hospital gown. Bottles of fine wine and tempting aromas wafting up from the restaurant's kitchen. Eric's strong arms catching her as she nearly fainted in front of his old apartment. Teagan, chewing gum, bragging about her prowess at the butterfly stroke. The warm heater and unprecedented quiet of the garage apartment at night. Annoyance at a persistent man... his eyes... dark as pitch and blatantly dishonest, but burning with desire... Diet Mountain Dew in a cooler, floating in lake water at the bottom of a canoe. A giant box of SweeTarts she had spent her allowance buying for Teagan, just because. Had she really? Yes, she had! *He* sent her flowers... but she gave them away to one of the cooks. She had spurned him, teased him. Not interested. No way.

Jamie groggily adjusted the coat and squirmed into another position on the couch. She was still freezing. Why was it always so cold?

Her apartment had steam heat. The pipes banged all night long. Once, she'd heard a gunshot. *I'll park the Benz in your carport; no one will see.* She had told him to give up. But had she really wanted him to? Jerry playing his guitar, dreaming of moving out West to be a cowboy. What had become of him? Teagan at the hospital, clipboard in hand, looking so professional, so efficient. Dark, sated eyes gleaming at Jamie from her own pillow — she was using him, it was her decision... Darkness and a blanket, stifling, suffocating. She was all alone, now. There was no one. *No one.* Two hands in the air, splattered with mud. *We'll be just like real sisters... You can't break that bond... It's for life.*

Jamie's limbs grew heavier; the images, less distinct. *Danger.* Teagan was in danger again, but Jamie would save her. She would take herself to the damn shelter and let Teagan live her life in peace. There. That would do it.

Alone... so alone. Always alone. A pretty, blond child that called her Mommy. Roasting turkey in the oven. Her picture on the walls. Strong male arms coming around her, comforting her.

She drifted off to sleep.

"We'll be sending you to the women's shelter in a cab as soon as you've been discharged," Teagan explained to the patient in the hospital bed before her. The woman was in her mid forties, she had cigarette burns on her face and arms and bruises everywhere else, and she looked as terrified as a hunted doe.

"He'll... he'll see me leave," she stammered. "He'll be watching outside; I know he will."

"We're prepared for that," Teagan answered firmly. "You'll leave by an unmarked staff entrance, and a policeman will stay with you until you're checked into the shelter. You'll be safe there. You heard what the officer said — this man is going to be arrested and he's going to be prosecuted. In the meantime, the staff at the shelter are all trained to help you get back on your feet."

The woman swallowed, wincing painfully as she did so. "I guess that's what I have to do, then. 'Cause he'll kill me next time. I know he will. Or I'll kill him."

A nurse returned with some paperwork, and Teagan wrapped up her interview and quietly left the room.

Her other patient had been discharged already; still in bad shape emotionally, but not quite as hysterical as before Teagan had arrived. At least the woman had accepted a referral for further counseling.

Teagan walked down the hall and opened the door to her office, which still smelled like a sick room, despite the best efforts of the housecleaning staff. The space had virtually no ventilation and the door couldn't be propped open because of confidentiality concerns. Teagan took a deep breath out in the hall, then entered and sat down. She checked her cell phone for messages, but there were none. Her brow creased with worry. She had left her mother a voice mail explaining the hypothetical risk of a trace on her license number, but Sheryl had yet to respond, and Teagan was growing worried.

She started to dial again when Rosalie burst into the room. "I am *so* sorry, Teagan," the pleasant looking, dark-skinned woman gushed, dumping her keys and purse on the desk and shrugging quickly out of her coat. "Damn cell phone went completely dead. Not the battery, either. I don't know what happened. But I'm here now, so you go on home to that gorgeous husband of yours, okay? Thanks so much for covering for me — I owe you one."

Teagan quickly filled in the other social worker on the duties at hand, grabbed her own bag, and headed back to Eric's car. She always exercised caution in the parking garage, keeping an eye on her surroundings, appearing aware. But today her vigilance was heightened by a new anxiety. An anxiety with more than one source.

She had called Eric twice, but he hadn't picked up. He must have been out on the court playing; it was sheer luck that she'd caught him on the bench before. By now he was probably catching a ride home, waiting until he was alone again to call her back.

They were fine.

As for her mother not responding to her message — well, that was commonplace. Sheryl got lots of calls and was easily distracted. She probably wasn't even home.

I'm not trying to alarm you... but if he's savvy, he could get your mother's address...

Teagan picked up her phone and tried Sheryl's number again. It went straight to voice mail.

She started up the car and pulled out. She was anxious to get home, but her mind wouldn't rest until she'd made sure her mother was okay. Light snow was falling again, but traffic was sparse, and Teagan made good time out of the city. She pulled into the drive of Sheryl's condo complex with her heart pounding against her ribs. She parked in front of her mother's door, but rather than climbing the steps and ringing the bell, she peeked in the window of the garage. Then, at long last, she exhaled. The PT Cruiser was gone. She wasn't home.

Teagan's cell phone rang just as she was settling back into Eric's car again. It was Sheryl. "Mom!" she began in a rush. "Did you get my voice mail? Are you okay?"

The background was noisy with conversation and the drone of a distant television. It sounded like a bar. "What? Oh, yes, I got it. Don't worry about me, honey... the DMV still thinks I live in Ross."

Teagan blinked. "You haven't updated your address yet? But you moved—"

"Last April," Sheryl finished. "I'm getting to it! Listen, that's not why I called. It's about Jamie."

Isn't everything?

"What about her?" Teagan asked gruffly.

"I know I told you I thought she was a home wrecker. But I was wrong about that. I really don't think she would intentionally sabotage your marriage."

"I already told you—"

"*But,*" Sheryl continued heavily, "she's a very vulnerable woman right now. And sweetheart, as much as the two of you have in common, I'm telling you—in this area, Jamie is a whole lot more like me."

Teagan tensed. "Meaning?"

"Meaning that even though she's independent and spirited and all that good stuff, she's still the kind of woman who *needs* a man. You know what I'm saying?"

"No."

"I'm saying that if she's feeling lonely, and Eric's there, even though she might not *intend* for anything inappropriate to happen, she could still wind up putting him in a situation that—"

"I get it, Mom," Teagan interrupted, her pulse racing. "I'm going home, now. I just wanted to make sure you were all right. Where are you, anyway?"

"Après-Open-House Happy Hour, of course!" Sheryl chirped. "I didn't have a showing today myself, but someone always does. And Lorraine promised me she would bring along her ex brother-in-law. Just divorced last month!"

"I have to go, Mom," Teagan insisted. "Be safe."

"You too, honey. And don't you dare go back to Jamie's place again, either one of you!"

Teagan had no trouble agreeing to that.

The snow fell heavier as she turned toward home, and Teagan realized she was gripping the wheel so tightly her fingers were tingling. What was wrong with her?

"The kind of woman who needs a man..."

"Eric said he loved me..."

"Shut up with that!" Teagan snapped at herself, squinting through the swirling flakes. Only a few blocks to go, now. Why was she so uptight?

Lunch. Of course! She had forgotten about lunch entirely; no wonder she was losing her mind. Her paranoia was nothing more than glucose deprivation.

He didn't even say goodbye.

Teagan turned into her driveway and hit the remote button on the garage door. She wondered if Eric was home yet. She wondered if Jamie had returned to the garage apartment. What would she be doing now if she had?

Teagan got out of the car, closed the garage door behind

her, and headed for the house. Yes, Eric was home already. She could see his tracks in the fresh snow leading up the front walk. There were some older ones too, partly covered now. The detective?

Her pace quickened.

She reached the porch, opened the unlocked front door, and stepped inside. Her heart stopped.

Jamie was lying on the couch. Eric was sitting on its edge and his arms were reaching out toward her. As the door closed behind Teagan, Jamie startled and sat up with a jerk, the loose fabric of her unzipped hoodie flapping to either side, exposing bare skin to her waist.

Chapter Twenty-Five

Eric stood up.

For a moment, time stood still.

Jamie threw an anguished look at Teagan, pulled the hoodie tight around herself, and curled up into a ball.

With an effort, Teagan raised her eyes to her husband.

He looked horrified.

Teagan's heart began to beat again. Her brain seemed to be working in slow motion. It was her nightmare all right—playing out before her eyes. All the evidence was there. In all its 34D glory. For everyone to see.

But this couldn't be right.

It could *not*.

No one said a word. In Eric's eyes she read a curious mixture of two distinct things. Distress... and defiance. Both of which, oddly enough, could be read either way.

Teagan drew in a breath. There was what she saw; and there was what she knew. She would not be a fool. She'd played the idiot enough already.

She walked across the living room to where Eric stood, still as a stone, looking like a magazine cover in his basketball tank top, the well-formed muscles of his arms still shining with sweat.

Without hesitation, she threw her arms around his neck and hugged him.

His own arms tightened around her immediately, and moisture sprang to her eyes. After a long moment, she drew back just enough to speak. "Why don't you go ahead and take a shower?" she suggested, her voice only slightly unsteady. "I'll order some pizza for the two of us."

Eric drew back and looked at her, his blue-gray eyes brimming with emotion. He said nothing. He kissed her instead.

This time, it was no peck on the cheek.

After some time, during which Teagan could honestly say she gave no thought whatsoever to the woman huddled on the couch a few feet away, Eric released her and stepped back. Without so much as a glance in Jamie's direction, he turned and walked away up the stairs.

So there.

Teagan steeled herself. She cleared her throat and pivoted toward Jamie. "I'm going to the apartment to pack up some stuff for you. They have a clothing pantry at the women's shelter, so you'll be able to get more there. If we hurry, you'll be settled by dinnertime."

Jamie stood up. Her hoodie was miraculously zipped now. "Teagan, I—"

"*Shut up!*" Teagan screeched in a voice barely her own. "*Just. Shut. Up!*" She stomped into the kitchen, grabbed an empty garbage bag from under the sink, and headed for the back door. "I'll be back in three minutes," she threw over her shoulder as she passed the living room. "Get your coat and meet me at the garage."

"This will be your room," the shelter supervisor instructed Jamie, opening the door to a sparse cubicle that housed two twin beds, a sink, two chests of drawers, and a desk. "Your roommate will be LaShanda—she's at dinner now."

Jamie's tired eyes took in the happy yellow paint, the attempt at stenciled daisies along the ceiling, and the frilly lace curtains that inexpertly concealed thick security bars outside an opaque window. "There's meatloaf tonight. It's pretty good, I hear," the woman continued. "Why don't you just set your bag down now, and I'll introduce you to everyone and you can get something to eat?"

Jamie complied without comment. Teagan had stuffed a trash bag full of something—of what, she still wasn't sure.

Most likely her dirty laundry. Perhaps a living reptile.

"Snake!"

Giggles of girlish laughter. Sun, ripples on the lake...

Jamie swiped at her watering eyes with her broken arm and banged her cast on her cheek again. It hurt.

She didn't care. She didn't much care about anything anymore.

***

Teagan was stuffing the empty pizza box into the recycling bin when Eric's arms came unexpectedly around her waist. "Have I told you lately that I love you?" he murmured into her ear.

Teagan leaned back and put her own arms around his. "Yes, and in very creative ways, too," she said with a smile.

But it was a smile she didn't feel.

Eric held her a moment more, then turned her to face him. "I know you're making a point of not asking," he said softly. "And I appreciate that. But I'm going to tell you anyway."

Teagan stiffened. It was over and done with. She had done what she had to do. It wasn't even about Eric, not really. Jamie needed to be at a shelter for her own safety. They couldn't guarantee her security in an old farmhouse, not if this lunatic managed to trace her. And they couldn't be sure that he wouldn't. As long as Jamie was in the house, none of them would be safe.

"Maybe you shouldn't," she replied.

"No, I definitely should," he said firmly. "Because it isn't just our relationship it matters to."

"It doesn't—"

He interrupted her with a kiss. "Just listen. I got home maybe five minutes before you did, and I headed straight to the kitchen for a drink. I didn't even know Jamie was in the house until I heard something—like a muttering sound. When I walked into the living room I saw her lying there with a coat thrown over her, taking a nap. I decided to let her sleep, but then a minute later she started crying out and thrashing around like she was having a nightmare, so I went over and shook her shoulders to wake her up."

Teagan stared up at him, incredulous. She had trusted that his part in whatever had transpired was innocent; she hadn't imagined it could be *that* innocent. How close had she come to—

It didn't bear thinking about.

"Until you opened the door and Jamie sat up," he continued earnestly, "I had no idea what she wearing under that coat. Or not wearing."

Teagan blinked. A scene as damning as she had witnessed couldn't possibly have come about without calculation. Tempting as it was to believe, it was ludicrous. "You can't know for sure that Jamie was asleep," she replied stonily. "She must have set the whole thing up."

"That's possible," Eric admitted, still holding her close. "But honestly, I don't think so."

The voices echoed in Teagan's tortured brain. *From now on,* she had warned, *if you so much as look at Eric sideways—*

A waste of my valuable time, Jamie had agreed. *He's in love with you.*

Teagan closed her eyes against the memory and sagged into her husband's embrace. Jamie had not said one word the entire ride to the shelter. No protestations of innocence. No resistance. No complaints.

What better evidence of guilt could she give?

"It doesn't matter," Teagan proclaimed. She let out a heavy breath and burrowed her head deeper into the warmth of her husband's shoulder. "It really just doesn't matter."

Chapter Twenty-Six

Teagan wrapped her bathrobe tighter around herself and dropped into an armchair. She put her feet up on the ottoman and surveyed her fluffy slippers. They needed a wash.

She grabbed the remote to turn on the TV, but then set it down again. She was not in the mood for morning news. Working in an ER had blunted her ability to ignore the endless reports of gun violence, house fires, and child abuse that composed the local newscasts. They were all too real now. And today, believe it or not, she had an actual whole day off from work. She intended to make the most of it.

Unfortunately, Eric could not enjoy the occasion with her. To the rest of the world, it was a Monday.

She took a sip of coffee and glanced around the room. Perhaps today would be a good day to get rid of the wallpaper with the hunting dogs carrying bleeding pheasants in their mouths? Eric's grandfather had been an avid sportsman, but she was pretty sure his grandmother had hated this wallpaper as much as Teagan did. Thank God that Grandpa Dietz had at least taken his mounted antlers to Arizona with him.

She stood up, walked to a corner of the room, and pulled back a bit of the paper where it was already peeling. There was more paper under it. She excavated a small section, then sighed out loud. Marching Revolutionary War soldiers. Complete with cannons.

Teagan sat back down with a plop. She did not have that much energy.

Then she smiled to herself, remembering how she and Eric had redone the master bedroom before they moved in. She could still see herself laughing at the paint dripping down both his arms, and his threatening her with a wet roller brush. It had been the only room they really cared about. Still was, actually.

Life was good.

For you, maybe.

Teagan frowned. She was not going to do this. She was not going to feel guilty about Jamie, worry about Jamie. That chapter of her life was done. The girl from Indian Lake was gone; the adult replacement had been given more than enough chances. Teagan could not, and would not, risk her family's safety, her husband's peace of mind, and her own flippin' sanity for some sentimental fantasy. She had no need for Jamie in her life. She had plenty of other women friends.

The frown deepened to a scowl. The last part wasn't true, and she knew it. Before she married, Teagan's closest friends had always been guys. She was every boy's favorite gal pal: adventurous, direct, uncomplicated, and unaffected. Eric was the first one who even seemed to notice that she was female. Yet once the two of them became a couple, her other guy friends had drifted away. And although Teagan had countless female acquaintances whom she liked very much, there were none that she felt close to. She didn't understand other women, and they didn't understand her — perhaps because their predominate interests bored Teagan to tears. She didn't like to shop; had no interest in fashion, decorating, or cooking; and could not for the life of her fathom why any woman would pay someone else to fuss with her toenails. She didn't get it and never would. She simply didn't fit in.

But somehow, Jamie had understood. She *got* Teagan way back then, and when they were reunited — after more than a decade's worth of separation and growth — Jamie still got her. They were not completely alike in their interests, nor had they always gotten along. But through myriad spats and disagreements, there was always an underlying understanding. They were sisters. They had each other's backs. They knew each other's worst faults and accepted each other anyway. And even now, if Teagan was alone and had a hankering to do something bizarre on the spur of the moment—take a kayak down the Clarion River, eat chocolate donuts for dinner, check out every store and kiosk in the city looking for a pink pop-top water bottle with the Pittsburgh Pirates' logo on it... if she were looking for the company of a friend, it was Jamie she would call.

If she could.

But she couldn't. Not anymore.

Teagan stood up with her coffee and moved to the dining room. Her cell phone lay on the table where she had left it. Eric had texted her earlier; but there were no messages now.

She picked up the phone.

Her fingers found the relevant number in her work folder, and the line began to ring.

"Women's Services, this is Darla."

"Hi, Darla. It's Teagan."

The woman on the other end of the line let out a good-natured groan. "You're not sending me another one now, are you? Girl, I'm going to have to start blocking your number!"

Teagan grinned. Darla had an extremely tough job, but always managed to keep her spirits up. Teagan endeavored to follow her example. "No new ones," she answered. "In fact, I'm off work today. I just thought I'd check up on—" She hesitated. "The two women I referred to you yesterday."

"Hmm," Darla replied. "Well, Madge is settling in just fine. Told me this morning she got the first good night's sleep she's had in years. Which was a miracle, considering we've got a toddler with an ear ache and a colicky baby that screamed till three. The other one I can't help you with."

Teagan's breath caught. "Why not? You mean... Jamie Fukas?"

"Yeah, her. Hell of a name, isn't that? I'd have it changed if it were me. Anyway, she signed herself out first thing this morning. Very polite about it and all, but no convincing her otherwise."

Teagan's heart pounded. Why was she even surprised? Hadn't she suspected this would happen? "Where did she go?"

"We asked her if she had someplace safe, and she insisted she did," Darla continued. "But she wouldn't give details. I don't know whether she was telling the truth or not, but I will say she didn't seem afraid to me. Just determined."

That's Jamie, all right.

Teagan thanked Darla for her assistance and hung up the phone. Her face paled as she remembered the twenty dollar bill she had, in a moment of compassionate weakness, thrown into the garbage bag along with Jamie's borrowed laundry and medication. She had intended it for snacks or drinks in the facility.

Jamie had used it for bus fare.

And Teagan knew to where.

***

Jamie paused in her one-handed scrubbing and sat back on her knees with a grimace. It wasn't working. She could have four hands scouring simultaneously and still never get all the stain out. She'd emptied two buckets full of reddish-brown water already, but the original cream color was nowhere to be seen. A little bleach, perhaps? No, that would only turn it yellow. Or cause what few fibers remained in the already threadbare area to fall off altogether. Which would also be no help, because the backing was stained, too.

She blew out a breath. The whole carpet would have to go. Which meant her security deposit was toast.

She rose and carried the bucket and sponge back to the kitchen. She had a lot of cleaning to do today. She couldn't remember exactly what shape she'd left the apartment in, but the troupe of police technicians who had swarmed it yesterday had clearly not had neatness in mind. She emptied the dirty water in the sink, rinsed out the sponge, and put both away under the cabinet. What next?

She moved back out into the main room and glanced toward her rumpled bed.

Hot anger swelled within her as the image appeared.

There's something I have to tell you, gorgeous. And I'm afraid you're not going to like it.

Jamie stared at the bed as if it were on fire. He was in it. She was in it. She had been so excited, so happy. She was going... somewhere...

The memory ended. Jamie continued staring, tried to concentrate. But all she could see were the rumpled sheets. His eyes were brown; she remembered that. She could almost see his face. A flash of teeth, a sense of hair that was dark — except where it was gray. But there was no face.

And no name.

Jamie swore out loud. She descended on the bed and ripped everything off it, including the mattress pad. She would take the bus to the laundromat this afternoon. She would wash every piece of fabric in the apartment if she had to. She wanted nothing —

She paused with the bundled sheets in her arms. She lifted them to her face.

His scent. She recognized it without question. It was the smell of dry-cleaned suits, expensive wines, and the occasional cigar. It was the smell of... *money.*

I want you so much, Jamie. I've never wanted any woman like this. You're driving me out of my mind. I'll give you anything. I'll do anything. Just name it, beautiful. It's yours.

"Shut up!" Jamie cried out loud, throwing the sheets onto the floor and putting her hands to her head. "If you can't remember anything useful, just *stop!*"

She pulled her hands away and looked around at the silent, empty apartment. She breathed in deeply. She could do this. She *would* do this. She was going to get this accursed apartment in the best shape possible, and she was going to turn in her notice. Today. She would not live here one minute longer than was strictly necessary.

She was going to start all over again.

More alone than ever before.

The taunting voice in Jamie's head was hard to bear. It wasn't enough that she had sold her soul to the devil—a devil with even white teeth and a big fat wallet. It wasn't enough that she had nearly been murdered. Oh, no. She had to go and find—and then promptly lose forever—the only real friend she'd ever had.

But there was no use crying about it now.

She picked up the sheets again and stuffed them into her laundry bag. She collected all the bathroom towels, added them to the load, and laid the bag ready by the door. Then she returned to stare at the stain again. The carpet would have to be replaced, and her landlord would have to be the one to do it. But no way was she putting up with that stain until he did.

She strode purposefully to the kitchen, then returned with a retractable blade. She dropped to her knees on the carpet, pulled the stained portion up off the floor, and started cutting.

Everything would be all right. She would make it so. And she would not hide in some shelter like a scared rabbit waiting for it to happen. LaShanda had called her crazy for leaving—told her any man who would try to kill a woman once would absolutely try to do it again. Jamie was certain her roommate was right. She just didn't care.

If Mr. Moneybags wanted another crack at her, he was welcome to give it a try. She knew that she should be afraid of him, that she should be quivering in her shoes to be back in the same apartment where he'd assaulted her—but she was beyond feeling afraid. The only emotion she could feel for him was pure, unadulterated rage.

Why had he done it? Had he not gotten what he wanted from her? At least eventually?

She drove the knife through the carpet backing with long, vicious, strokes. She had not submitted to temptation easily, she remembered that much. She had resisted a long time. She had teased, he had wheedled and prodded, and eventually she had succumbed. But when, *when*, had everything changed?

You're so beautiful, Jamie.

You're so married, Br —

Jamie's heart skipped a beat, then pounded. It was there... his name... so close. It had been on the tip of her tongue... Dammit! If only she hadn't *tried* to remember! Now it was gone again. B something. Br something. Brent? Brandon?

Her neighbors were banging around outside. She closed her eyes tightly and attempted to refocus.

That was amazing, Jamie. YOU were amazing, he had gasped.

Wish I could say the same, she had thought, but kept to herself.

Still she saw him only in flashes... why never the whole? Had she despised him so much, or been so ashamed of herself, that even then she couldn't bear to look him in the face?

She had nearly cut the stain out, now. At least the biggest one. There were plenty of smaller spots as well. They were scattered all over the carpet, even the furniture. What had he done with her?

Jamie tugged harder on the carpet to pull more of it up, but it suddenly seemed less slack. She tugged again, but found it anchored by two perfectly polished, black leather shoes.

Chapter Twenty-Seven

She looked up, and the face her mind sought came into perfect, crystal-clear focus.

Her fingers tightened around the knife. "Hello, Brad," she said calmly. "Imagine meeting you here."

He was wearing his idea of business casual. Dark slacks, a silk button-down shirt, and knee-length leather coat. His hands were empty. His face was pale.

Jamie stealthily moved back a pace and stood up. "Damn. You're even uglier than I remembered." Even now she could hardly stand to look at him. He was only a couple inches taller than she, but solid, with square shoulders and a strong upper body. His face, although not objectively unattractive, had always struck her as weak chinned and languid. His dark eyes were wide set and unexpressive — disturbingly difficult for her to read.

His jaw muscles tightened. "I'm very glad to see you, Jamie. I'm relieved that you're all right."

She smirked. "I'll bet. Attempted murder is a lighter sentence."

His shoulders slumped, and he made a slight movement forward. But Jamie moved back quickly, her carpet knife prominently displayed.

He exhaled and made a show of stepping back. "I didn't come here to hurt you!" he declared. "I only want to talk to you. To explain what happened."

Jamie extended her blade an extra notch. "How charming of you. By all means. Go right ahead."

His eyes were anxious, but his chest puffed. "I tried to tell you in a card. I told you to call me. Did you get the message?"

"After the police finished with it, yes," Jamie offered. "Go on."

His face paled further. He moved his lower jaw back and forth in a sawing motion. Jamie remembered the mannerism well. It meant that he was nervous.

"I told you, it was an accident!" he insisted, his voice verging on a plea. "We struggled, right here" — he pointed to the floor near his feet — "and you hit your head on the corner of the TV stand. You dropped like a rock, and there was blood everywhere. It was horrible... I didn't know what to do!"

Jamie's heart thudded so loudly she was certain he could hear it, but the hand that held her knife was steady; her mind, eerily calm. "Struggled?" she repeated. "Over what?"

He swallowed. "We were... planning a trip together. You'd been looking forward to it, but at the last minute, I had to cancel."

Pictures of castles. Snowy mountains. Misty forests.

"Austria," Jamie breathed. "You were taking me to Austria."

"I hated to disappoint you," he continued insincerely, "but you understood the risks. My life isn't my own. I tried to get away, but I couldn't. I explained all of that to you, but you didn't understand. You went ballistic!"

Jamie's mind flashed another picture. *Rumpled sheets. Two glasses of wine. One still half full.* She didn't remember, but she was pretty sure she understood. "And did you tell me that the trip was off *before*," she tilted her head in the direction of her now bare mattress, "or *after*?"

His cheeks colored slightly.

"I see," Jamie said dryly.

"I never meant to hurt you!" he insisted again. He took a half step forward, but a renewed flourish of Jamie's knife halted him. "I didn't *do* anything to you! When I told you the trip was off you came after *me* like an animal! I had to protect myself!"

Jamie gave a scornful laugh. "Clearly."

"All I tried to do was get you off me! I don't know how

you fell the way you did. But when you hit the floor, and with all that blood... I *swear*, Jamie, I thought you were dead!"

"How traumatic for you. Ever think of taking a pulse?"

"I did!" he sputtered. "You didn't have one! There was nothing, I'm telling you! Nothing!"

"Didn't realize I had such an in with the Almighty."

"Okay, so obviously I missed it!" he defended. "But my intentions were good. I never meant you any harm!"

Jamie's teeth gritted. "So, when you called 911 to have a professional check me out, they... what? Told you they didn't make house calls?"

Brad's mouth opened and closed again. His jaw jerked back and forth. "You *know* that no one can know about... about us. It would ruin me!"

"Of course," Jamie replied, her voice like ice. "Terribly inconsiderate of me, wasn't it? Dying at your hands like that. What a predicament for you. I don't suppose you could have called for help, and then left?"

His face broke out in a sweat. Jamie felt a wave of nausea. She could never stand his fleshy cheeks. Spoiled brat had never generated an honest sweat in his life. Lifting weights at a pricey gym didn't count. He was soft, inside and out.

"I was afraid they could trace me here," he responded weakly, his voice imploring. "My prints must be everywhere... one of your neighbors could have seen me... I don't know." He ran a hand through his thinning hair. "I wasn't thinking straight. I figured if I took you somewhere else, it would look... you know... random. Then I could come back and clean the place up... and no one would know I was involved."

Jamie's own eyes widened. "How fiendishly clever of you," she drawled, relishing the apt cliché. How good it felt to make him squirm. "You even lifted my keys for the purpose, I see. And my wallet and cell phone?"

He made no response.

"Uh huh," she continued. "Bottom of the Ohio River?"

"Jamie, please," he pleaded, the beads of sweat on his forehead coalescing into droplets. "I told you—I thought you were dead. What happened to me afterwards couldn't make any difference to you! I came right back to clean everything up, but some of your neighbors were outside, and... I was going to try again the next night, but then I heard on the news that you were alive, and—"

"And you rushed to my side to hold my hand and explain everything?"

His lower jaw worked like a paint mixer.

"I *couldn't!*" he wailed. "I heard from... a source of mine that you had amnesia, but I couldn't come back here in case the police were watching—I knew they would identify you sooner or later. I've been absolutely frantic, not knowing what you would remember, or when, and whether or not you would remember that it was an accident! It's been hell!"

Jamie made no response. She hadn't thought that anything Bradley George Oswald the umpteenth did or said could possibly surprise her. But she was wrong. He seriously expected her to feel sorry for him.

"We can still make this right, you and I," he said more gently, attempting a crocodile smile. "All you have to do is tell the police that I left your apartment before all this happened—that I had nothing to do with it and you don't want my name involved. Make up somebody else—another lover, some homeless bum who broke in... anything!"

Jamie's blood was near to boiling, but she was determined not to show it. She cocked her head to one side. "And I would do this... why?"

He faltered. "Because... because I can take care of you! You know that. We can still take that trip to Austria. I can take you anywhere in the world! You know I want you more than I've ever wanted any woman. You're perfect! You're—" his voice broke off. "What's happened with your eyes?"

Jamie's lips curled slowly into a smile. "These eyes belong to the real Jamie. She's been in hiding for a very long time, but she's back now." Her shoulders straightened.

"And FYI, Bradley dear... I wouldn't let you touch me again if you were the last lazy, shiftless, gutless, overweight, self-important, stuffed shirt, incompetent *momma's boy* on the face of the whole freakin' planet!"

His cheeks colored. The quavering jaw clenched tight. His dark eyes narrowed.

Jamie's hand on the knife began to sweat. Personally running the bastard through with a dull blade would be poetic justice, but she had made a tactical error. Spineless slug or no, he was still stronger than she was—and furthermore, he was desperate. Although she could easily picture herself striking out at him on the night in question, premeditated physical confrontation was not her style. Brawling with larger males was Teagan's bag; Jamie was more of a manipulator.

She drew in a slow breath. "Satisfying as it is to watch you sweat, Brad," she said steadily, "your attempts to win my cooperation are too little, too late. I remembered your name at exactly 6:34 AM this morning. I was afraid the detective wouldn't appreciate a call at that hour, but as it turns out, he was delighted. I'm rather surprised you haven't heard from him yet, actually."

The ruddy color that suffused his cheeks drained away. "You didn't."

"I did. Perhaps you should check the messages on your home phone. Or does your wife answer that one?"

His breath came in rapid, heaving gasps. "You traitorous little bitch! How dare you!"

Jamie tensed as his fists balled up at his sides. She had removed his motive for murder, but now he was furious with her, and if he felt he had nothing else to lose...

"Jamie?"

Startled, she looked up toward her open doorway as Brad whirled around in his tracks.

"The detective said he would be here any minute," Teagan said calmly. "A squad car is on the way as well."

Jamie's heart leapt up into her throat. The social worker

looked like something out of an ad for morning coffee — or mental health services. She was wearing faded sweats, bright green rubber snow boots, and what looked like a flannel pajama top poking out the neckline of her coat. Her hair was wild and she had on no makeup whatsoever, but despite all appearances to the contrary, she held herself like a Supreme Court justice.

"You might want to leave now," she said to Brad, stepping purposefully out of the way of the door. "Or you can stay and turn yourself in when they get here. It's up to you."

Streams of sweat now rolled freely down Brad's pallid face, dampening his carefully starched collar. His jaw worked furiously as his gaze swept from Teagan to Jamie, then back. After a few ragged breaths, he straightened, throwing his shoulders back with dignity. "I think it would be best, under the circumstances, if I spoke with my attorney first," he said rigidly. He stepped toward the door, came abreast of Teagan, and offered a respectful nod. "I'm sure we can work this out peaceably. I've done what I can to make amends, but since Ms. Meadows has chosen to threaten me with a deadly weapon, there's only so much I can do to reason with her. Sadly, it seems she has a penchant for violent assault."

Teagan threw a glance at Jamie. Then her eyes drew level with his. "That's funny. I don't see any weapon."

Brad's face turned into a tomato. He threw one more caustic, furious look at Jamie, stomped out the door, and slammed it behind him.

Teagan locked the door and turned around.

Jamie slowly unbent her near-frozen elbow, retracted the knife blade, and dropped it onto the floor.

"You know," she said to Teagan, her voice suddenly shaky. "You really do have the most uncanny timing."

Teagan's face remained expressionless. She shrugged. "It's a gift."

Their eyes met. For a long moment, neither woman

moved. "You shouldn't have come back here," Teagan said finally, her voice chastising.

Jamie's eyes moistened. "Neither should you."

Teagan's mouth twitched. "Touché."

"Why did you?" Jamie asked, her voice barely above a whisper. "I didn't think you'd ever talk to me again."

Teagan exhaled slowly. "Shouldn't I?"

Jamie swallowed. "I wouldn't blame you if you didn't. You think I'm trying to steal your husband."

"Am I wrong?"

Jamie held Teagan's gaze. "Yes... and no. What you saw last night was nothing. That damned training bra of yours was killing me, and I took it off so I could sleep. I didn't wake up until you came in."

Teagan let out a groan. "Then why didn't—"

"But that didn't mean I didn't think about it," Jamie interrupted. "Because I did." She inhaled deeply. "But it wasn't really Eric I wanted. I don't even know him that well; I never did. What I wanted—" she faltered. "What I *still* want, is what he represents. Real love. Not just sex, not even just the romantic stuff. But something deeper, something that lasts. Your house, your family... it's like everything I ever wanted, all wrapped up in one warm, welcoming, TV-perfect package. The pictures, the sappy figurines, ten decades of grease on the kitchen walls... hell, Teag, I even love that awful avocado-green toilet!"

A stray tear escaped one eye. "What's pathetic is, I didn't even *know* that's what I wanted. Not until I had nothing else. I'm grateful to have my old life back, minus the last two months, anyway—but I'm not going back to the way I was. I want to make a fresh start."

Teagan's own eyes were glistening, but her jaw was set firmly. "Well, I'm glad to hear that. I'm sure you can make it happen. I... I do want you to be happy."

Jamie smiled ruefully. "And I'm glad you already are. Without me around to screw everything up, anyway."

A door slammed outside the front window. Jamie looked

over her shoulder to see a police car parked on the curb. "You really did call them, didn't you?"

"Of course I did," Teagan answered. "I saw him through the window. The detective was right—he must have been having your apartment watched."

Jamie nodded. "I guess so." Teagan made a move as if to head for the door, and Jamie's gut twisted painfully. "Teagan?" she began, not knowing what she would say. All she knew was that aside from a potential court date, she might never see her friend again. "Before you go, I just— I just wanted to say I'm sorry. For all the grief I've caused you. And Eric. And I'll never forget everything you did for me. Not just the social worker stuff, but... everything else. Including coming after me this morning. I don't know what would have happened if you hadn't come in when you did. Thank you."

Teagan's chin trembled slightly. But her return gaze was steely. "Well then, I guess this makes us even."

Jamie's brow furrowed. "Even?"

Teagan harrumphed. "You did save my life once. I would have drowned without you—or have you forgotten? Seems to me like rescuing you from a homicidal maniac should strike out that debt once and for all."

Jamie's face fell. A sense of obligation. That explained it.

"And if anyone takes a picture of me in this getup," Teagan continued, "your debt's going back up again. When I found out you'd left the shelter I was so flustered I only got half dressed and totally forgot I had no car. I had to run around and borrow one from a neighbor; he thinks I'm a lunatic now."

Jamie allowed herself a grin. "There's a Cocoa Puff stuck over your ear."

"Shut up!" Teagan made a fruitless attempt to smooth the rat's nest on her head, then stopped and turned her back on Jamie.

Jamie stiffened. *Don't go, Teag.*

The images now were torment. Clear as day, bittersweet.

Two girls, two fistfuls of mud. *We'll be just like real sisters. Just like if we had the same parents and everything. You can't break that bond, no matter how far apart you wind up living. It's for life.*

Jamie's jaws clenched tight.

Goodbye, Teag.

"And by the way," Teagan continued, swinging back around. "If I ever catch you within a one-mile radius of my husband—not excluding any form of communication including calls, emails, texts, photos, smoke signals, or detectable thought waves, I will personally and repeatedly stab you through the heart with a sanded canoe paddle. Am I making myself clear?"

Jamie stared back, confused. "I don't—"

"I'm not having you over at my house unless I know he's gone, and you can't drop by uninvited *ever*. You run into him accidentally and you immediately turn and run—not walk—the other way. Maybe someday when you're married to some other guy and are six months pregnant and bloated up like a whale I'll lighten the restrictions, but until then, they're sacrosanct. You got it?"

A sister's always a sister...

Jamie's heart swelled. It wasn't over.

Teagan did still care.

She *did*.

"I promise," Jamie whispered softly.

An officer rapped on the door. "Police! Everything okay in there? Open up, please!"

Teagan started to turn around. "Oh, and Jamie," she said offhandedly, her brown eyes twinkling with mischief. "You can have the damned toilet."

Two palms slapping together; mud raining down like a shower.

Jamie's face broke into a smile.

...No matter what.

About the Author

USA-Today bestselling novelist and playwright Edie Claire was first published in mystery in 1999 by the New American Library division of Penguin Putnam. In 2002 she began publishing award-winning contemporary romances with Warner Books, and in 2008 two of her comedies for the stage were published by Baker's Plays (now Samuel French). In 2009 she began publishing independently, continuing her original Leigh Koslow Mystery series and adding new works of romantic women's fiction, young adult fiction, and humor.

Under the banner of Stackhouse Press, Edie has now published over 25 titles including digital, print, audio, and foreign translations. Her works are distributed worldwide, with her first contemporary romance, *Long Time Coming*, exceeding two million downloads. She has received multiple "Top Pick" designations from *Romantic Times Magazine* and received both the "Reader's Choice Award" from *Road To Romance* and the "Perfect 10 Award" from *Romance Reviews Today*.

A former veterinarian and childbirth educator, Edie is a happily married mother of three who currently resides in Pennsylvania. She enjoys gardening and wildlife-watching and dreams of becoming a snowbird.

Books & Plays by Edie Claire

Romantic Fiction

Pacific Horizons

Alaskan Dawn
Leaving Lana'i
Maui Winds
Glacier Blooming
Tofino Storm

Fated Loves

Long Time Coming
Meant To Be
Borrowed Time

Hawaiian Shadows

Wraith
Empath
Lokahi
The Warning

Leigh Koslow Mysteries

Never Buried
Never Sorry
Never Preach Past Noon
Never Kissed Goodnight
Never Tease a Siamese
Never Con a Corgi

Never Haunt a Historian
Never Thwart a Thespian
Never Steal a Cockatiel
Never Mess With Mistletoe
Never Murder a Birder
Never Nag Your Neighbor

Women's Fiction

The Mud Sisters
Soccer Mom in Galilee (as Rachel Stackhouse)

Humor

Corporately Blonde

Comedic Stage Plays

Scary Drama I
See You in Bells

www.ingramcontent.com/pod-product-compliance
Lightning Source LLC
Chambersburg PA
CBHW050609190726
48283CB00007B/2343